Among the Fallen

MAKENA SONG

ACKNOWLEDGMENTS

First and foremost, I would like to thank my mother, Tina Song, who spent countless hours not only listening to my endless brainstorming sessions but also editing my fantasy novel from start to finish. Without her loving support, I wouldn't have been able to pursue the path of a full-time writer or publish my first novel!

Second, I would like to acknowledge my incredible friends, who have supported me from my first draft on Wattpad to my final publication on Amazon. Because of their heartwarming comments, I was able to push through to the end of the novel! During every instance of writer's block, they served as a major motivation to continue writing.

Third, I would like to thank a wonderful woman, Ivy Gilbert, who formatted this book! Not only is she an amazing adviser who has answered any and all of my questions, but she also is an inspirational author who has published many of her own books! Without her expert insight and patient soul, I wouldn't have been able to navigate this process so smoothly.

TABLE OF CONTENTS

BOOK I – AMONG THE FALLEN

Among the Fallen

BOOK I
The Fallen Realms Series

Bluewater ✪

Kingdom of
Avrith

Acton

Talis Mountains

Twyndale

✪ Faeran

Shimmering Glades

Portacle
Sea

Forest

Dark Lands

I

THE FATE OF
THE FALLEN

 *Caelum*

resh blood stained the floorboards. Lucian lay on his side, coughing up chunks of blood. Warm drool drizzled down his lips, the bitter taste of metal sticking to the back of his throat. His vision wavered; his heart raced; his throat burned.

He wanted the madness to end.

His wish wasn't granted.

Remus, his father, loomed over Lucian's battered body, kicking Lucian until he couldn't breathe anymore. His father cursed his name, spit flying in his direction.

A hefty kick to Lucian's side sent him rolling across the wooden floorboards.

Each kick, each punch, reminded him of one undeniable fact.

This was his reality.

"Lucian!" Remus yelled with a bloody cry, wiping the drops of alcohol off his hickory-colored beard. "You good for nothing!"

Lucian braced for another kick, but it didn't connect.

Remus paused mid-kick. His father groaned, the effects of the alcohol starting to take its toll. With one leg hovering in the air, he quickly lost his balance, knocking several empty bottles off the nearest table. The bottles shattered on the floor, shards flying everywhere.

A few shards flew Lucian's way, so he reflexively shielded his head.

"Oh, my poor darling, my poor Lucille..." Remus lamented as he propped himself up against the table.

"Argh..." Lucian whimpered, "Please make it stop."

The hoarse, slurred speech of his father continued.

Lucian dared to peek at him after hearing his father's rambling taper slightly off.

Is it over? he wondered.

Tears flooded down his face.

"It's all your fault, you *murderer*..." Remus rambled. "If only you weren't born, she'd still be alive! If only you weren't Morpheus's Reincarnate, I would've still lived in the upper districts!"

Lucian's body started shaking uncontrollably. *When is this going to end?* He spat out more saliva mixed with thicker, darker blood.

A knock drew his father's attention to the door.

Is it over? Lucian repeated.

Remus refused to budge, but the knocking ceased to quit.

Clicking his tongue, Remus steadied himself and stumbled over to the door.

Thank the gods.

Lucian drank in the air, ravenously gulping it down like a dehydrated animal. In between breaths, he let out a course, wet cough, with blood and mucus trickling out of his nose and his mouth onto the hardwood floor. Drool continued to ooze down his chin. His lips were swollen from his father's right hook to the face, while his throat felt raw from the times when his father choked him in the heat of his rage.

Lucian kept his eyes trained on the door, watching Remus receive a parcel. With a flick of his wrist, Remus shooed someone away. Lucian didn't know who the parcel was for, and he honestly didn't care.

Remus appeared busy inspecting the parcel, letting out a disgruntled sigh as he read the address. His face grew red, and he hurled it at the wall.

Staggering toward Lucian, a ravenous look filled his

father's monstrous green eyes. Lucian covered his head, bracing for another assault. Much to his surprise, his father went straight past him, huffing and puffing off to the master bedroom.

Not having to brace himself anymore, Lucian relaxed his battered body. He stared at the ceiling, trying as hard as he could to catch his breath.

It's finally over...

He let out another small whimper.

Turning to his side, he saw his reflection in the broken bottles: A weak and pathetic boy peered back.

His eyelids were nearly swollen shut, so he could only see a sliver of his blue irises. His blond hair had been smeared with blood stains. Even in this miserable state, he could still see a surviving trace of his mother. And that made it worse.

Hours seemed to pass by when the front door creaked open. Melinda, his stepmother, and Rosalie, his half sister, stepped inside, returning from their daily errands.

Melinda appeared the same as always, donning a dull gray dress that swayed along her knees and covered her tall and lanky form. She wore a stone-cold look on her face that didn't change even as they made eye contact.

Then, there was Rosalie, his lovely and precious younger sister, who wore a lighter-colored garb that complimented her shiny silver hair. She lifted her lips to form a forced smile and approached him to survey his wounds. Thick puddle-like tears filled her eyes.

After assessing the severity of his wounds, she hurried over to the kitchen, grabbing a clean, gray towel lying flat on the counter.

She then moved to the water basin, slowly turning on the faucet. Placing the towel under the faucet, she let the water seep into the fabric. After ringing it out, she returned to where he was helplessly lying on the floor.

This process was nothing new, and after a few years of seeing him in this state, she seemed to have grown accustomed to it.

She's all grown up now, he thought, a warmth filling his chest.

And then there's me...still trapped in the past.

However hard he tried, Lucian couldn't shake off the fear of his father. He was so pitiful that every time he looked into his sister's eyes, all Lucian could think of was Remus's monstrous green eyes. But the gentle gaze reflecting in her eyes made her different from his father. Her kindness and sympathy were two traits that his father had long since abandoned, allowing them to collect dust in the man's calloused heart.

She's a sweet soul, he repeated in his head. *She's nothing like him.*

How she slumped her shoulders and glanced nervously

to the side every few seconds like an anxious squirrel reminded Lucian of another cruel fact.

Rosalie, unfortunately, was no stranger to Remus's rampages.

There were times Remus tried to lay hands on her, and Lucian, as often as he could, would intervene and take the beating for her. He looked to where Remus, in one of his fits of rage, had scarred her face.

After that incident, Lucian vowed to protect his sister with his life, even if death was the result. He vowed never to become like his father, no matter how much he hated and wanted him dead. After all, if Lucian had retaliated and killed his father, not only would he become a true murderer, but he also would prove his father and the villagers right.

"Lucian," she sobbed, tears streaming down her cheeks. She softly ran her fingers through his hair, the blood staining her fingernails. "I'm so sorry, Lucian."

Mustering a smile and coughing out the words, he said, "It's not your fault, Rosalie. None of this is your fault. It's my fault... I'm the cursed one."

While Rosalie tended to his wounds, he glanced at Melinda, who quietly cleaned up Remus's mess.

"I think you should try to wash up," she suggested in a soft yet distant tone. "Remember, the boy from the black-smithing family has his Succession Ceremony this afternoon, and you're expected to attend and look presentable."

"I know," he curtly said, as his eyes roamed to the place where the parcel had been thrown. "Also, seeing how angry Father was, I'm pretty sure that parcel over there is yours." He pointed toward it, assuring she saw the smashed box before he left.

And to think my life was saved by a random box...

Lucian clicked his tongue, as he left the house.

TO AVOID UNNECESSARY CONTACT WITH THE other villagers, Lucian headed on his normal route, a long-forgotten dirt path only used by him and his mother. The two of them walking hand in hand and embracing nature's beauty was a memory he held dear to his heart.

Along the path sprouted flowers with petals shaped like snowflakes. He remembered her telling him a story about it: The flowers represented the eternal promise between the goddess of love to the god of spring many eons ago. His mother loved those flowers because she said they reminded her of her childhood home. He also remembered how sad she looked when she recounted old memories.

The promise that he made to her was also vivid in his memory.

After her death, Lucian used this path when he wanted some time to think. This dirty path was the only place where he felt safe to let his mind wander, dreaming about the better days: a time when his mother lived and when his father loved.

The sun reached its pinnacle in the sky. Lucian felt it was a perfect time to wash in the spring, as the warm sun rays would surely combat the cold water. While Lucian could've bathed at home, the spring was a better alternative, as it was a beautiful, hidden paradise amid a dull, wretched village. And, either way, the water would've been unheated.

Walking toward the spring, he glanced back at the tiny dwellings that formed his village. Caelum was littered with two-story, walnut-colored, wooden buildings that all looked identical to each other. And, in those houses, there were also people, who were all identical to each other, at least in their communal hatred of him.

Contrary to the dreaded feeling he had when he looked at the village, the spring was his special blessing with its clear blue waters and its refreshing atmosphere.

Much to his benefit, most of the village children who loved to torment him were studying in class, working in the fields, or helping their parents at home. So, on the off chance any children accidentally discovered his secret spot, they would never cross paths.

When he had free time to think, he wondered what his life would've been like if he was *normal*. However, as soon as that thought emerged, he was sorely reminded of what The Var would always say to him growing up, "*You are not like the other children, Lucian. There is a reason you are forbidden from interacting with them. You wouldn't want them to be influenced by you, the Reincarnate of a Fallen god, now, would you?*"

It's not like I wanted to be cursed, he thought, anger welling within him.

The Var's words, once they infiltrated his headspace, felt impossible to ignore: "*Do not curse your fate, child. It is not as if the village wants anyone to be born this way. They just are. The ancient gods have given us this hierarchy for the good of the entire village. Some people, Lucian, are just born lesser. That is all.*"

He couldn't shake those words out of his mind, no matter how hard he tried. And, according to the village's hierarchy and standards, Lucian was the worst of the worst.

Before he could fully collect his thoughts, Lucian reached the spring. His spirits lifted at the sight of the glistening waters. Located between The Sage's Forest and the town's outskirts, the spring represented a respite for him, where he could daydream as much as he liked.

The only drawback to the spring, however, was its proximity to The Sage's Forest, an area that was strictly forbidden by The Var.

Why can't we enter? There's not even a gate around it. They wouldn't even know if I just—No! I can't do that... Lucian snapped himself back to reality, remembering the punishment that he would face if he rebelled against The Var.

Distracting himself from the temptations of the forest, Lucian stripped off his faded, mud-stained clothes and eased into the pure, crystal-clear water. He winced while entering, the water stinging his open wounds. No matter how painful they were, he knew that this would be his only chance to get cleaned, so he took a deep breath and submerged himself in the water.

He attempted to scrub all of the blood off, but sadly, he couldn't wash away the bruise marks. After his skin was cleansed from the film of grime, dirt, and blood, he climbed out of the spring.

While reaching for his clothes, he heard the faint sound of rustling from the direction of the forest. He knew he shouldn't, but he couldn't help his curiosity. He kept staring at the edge of the forest, distracted, as he rushed to put his clothes on. He almost tripped over his pant legs, hastily slipping them on.

He walked to the very edge of the forest.

Warm waves of wind flowed out from the depths of the forest, caressing the side of his face as they passed through. Hundreds of oak trees followed a straight line that seemed to stretch out to the ends of Gaia. He took in a deep breath, letting his nostrils fill with the scent of a heavy, smoky aroma —a scent that reminded him of the days when he and his mother used to sit by the fireplace reading bedtime stories.

So, this is The Sage's Forest, he thought, marveling at its magnificence.

He almost crossed the line between the open field and the forest floor, but then he stopped. Images of The Var, his father, and the village flashed in his mind. If he were to cross the boundary line, then a fate worse than death surely would await him.

He turned around, trying to force his feet back onto the pathway headed home. But *something* stirred within him not letting him leave.

This is my only chance, he recited. *My only chance at freedom.*

With a burst of energy, he cast away his hesitations and sprinted headfirst into the forest.

Through the thickets, thorn bushes, and whatever else

snagged his clothes and scraped his skin, he raced at full speed deeper and deeper into the forest. The further he went in, the colder and stronger the wind became, slicing against his face like a knife and crashing into his eyes, causing them to water profusely. Even as his wounds ached, he couldn't—no, he wouldn't stop. He ran like this for many minutes until his breathing became labored.

As soon as he stopped, something rustled nearby.

Where's it coming from? he thought, frantically flitting his eyes every which way.

Although he listened intently, the rustling sound didn't return. What replaced the rustling was something indescribable... Something akin to a sizzling, buzzing, high-pitched noise pierced his ears and lured him further and further into the forest. He followed it almost in a trance, eventually reaching an area where no trees or grass grew and where no insects or creatures chattered. The only noises that could be heard were endless *hums* and *buzzes.*

The closer he walked toward the noise, the more it intensified. He turned his head to both sides, trying to figure out why the dead, brownish-gray grass extended into a straight line from one end to the other.

Something within him beckoned him to continue. Against his better judgment, he walked forward, inching toward the noise. After taking only a few steps, his chest collided with an invisible structure. He reached out his hand to touch it, and his fingertips felt a weird texture that was solid yet flexible and slippery yet firm.

A paradoxical experience.

What in Gaia's name, he thought, perplexed at what he had discovered.

Tapping the invisible structure with his right index finger, ripples started to form. Rays of sunlight glistened off it, revealing a ginormous barrier. It stretched as far as the eye could see.

Reflexively, he forced his hand backward and retreated, observing the barrier with unbridled attention.

After fully grasping what he had uncovered, he tried to approach it again. He almost touched it a second time, when he heard a familiar voice calling out to him in the distance—the voice carried by the wind.

"Lucian!" a female's voice echoed through the trees, coming from the direction of the spring. "Come on, this isn't funny! We're going to be late for the ceremony!"

"Okay, Rosalie!" he shouted, hearing his voice bounce off the surrounding trees.

Lucian didn't want to leave. That weird feeling inside him that guided him to the barrier rooted his feet to the ground. His eyes lingered on the slight shimmer of the barrier, and his body was in a trance-like state. However, his sister's voice returned him to his senses, and he tore his eyes away from it. Something unusual was occurring, but he didn't have time to investigate.

Another day, he thought, transitioning from a steady jog into a full sprint. *I'll come back another day.*

He raced faster toward his sister's voice.

Each stride toward the unforgiving village of Caelum reminded him of *who* he was and *what* he was. The chains of a lifetime couldn't disappear that easily.

He returned to a reality that he couldn't afford to forget.

After running for what felt like forever, Rosalie's figure came into view. The tension in his body started to ease up just by looking at her. As soon as he could see the worried expression on her face, he skidded to a stop.

"What's wrong?" he asked.

In tears, Rosalie answered, "Father hit her... He thinks she's 'seeing' someone else behind his back. He was so scary. What's going to happen to us, Lucian?"

"It's okay, Rosalie," Lucian said, gently taking her hand in his own. "Nothing's going to change. I'll protect her, too, from now on..."

"Then, who's going to protect *you*?" Rosalie asked, gripping his hand tighter.

Lucian looked into her eyes, and he comforted her by saying, "Don't worry about me... Father knows he can't get rid of me until my Succession Ceremony, so nothing will happen to me..."

For now... He finished the statement in his head.

Rosalie suddenly hugged him from the side, solemnly proclaiming, "Don't say that! We're all going to live happily ever after just like the family in Momma's bedtime story!"

She smiled brightly at him, wholly believing that they would end up like the children in her bedtime story. Her innocence comforted him. She was the only good thing to happen to him since his mother died. He stroked her silver head, combing his fingers lightly through the strands. That same silver hair served as a reminder that he wasn't the only one struggling. A foreigner's blood ran through Rosalie just as the blood of the ancient god of destruction ran through his.

Off in the distance, he heard The Chapel bells chiming.

"Come on, Rosalie. That's our cue."

Tightening his grip on her hand, he tried to run toward the village. However, Rosalie stopped him, pulling him backward with a powerful tug.

"What's wrong, Rosalie?" he asked, turning to look at her.

A look of fear crossed her face, as she asked, "What do you think will happen *this* time, Lucian? Do you think that perhaps—"

Shaking his head, he reassured her by saying, "No, Rosalie, the ceremony will end the same as always. After all, the entire thing is just a—"

"—show," she said, finishing his sentence.

Patting her head with his other hand, he said, "Yes, Rosalie, it's only a *show*."

Tolling and tolling and tolling, the bells called until all the citizens of Caelum heard its beckoning and assembled at The Holy Chapel.

It was finally time—time for the *next* Succession Ceremony.

2

THE MENTOR

 *Caelum*

The entire Roux Family congregated at The Holy Chapel, a sacred venue where the Succession Ceremony was held. Separate from their guardians, Lucian and Rosalie entered The Chapel along with the other children expected to attend the ceremony.

With Rosalie in tow, Lucian chose one of the front-row pews on the right side for them to sit, so they could easily see the ceremony. Normally, Lucian would've hidden in the very back pew away from all the prying eyes, but this time, he had a mission to complete.

As the adults filed in behind the legions of children, Lucian felt their eyes burning on his back. However, their stares were nothing like the intensity of his father's murderous glares, so they were more tolerable. Rosalie, on the other hand, was visibly uncomfortable. He tried the best he could to distract her with stupid jokes about the adults and the Elders, trying to help her feel less anxious and overwhelmed. Even so, the atmosphere was still tense.

Lucian felt a moment of relief, as The Var's entrance to the stage peeled the adults' eyes away from them. At least during the actual ceremony, the adults' attention was diverted.

With the appearance of the stars of the show, the ceremony had finally begun.

The Var, the Grand Elder of Caelum, appeared with a boy only a few years older than Lucian himself. The two of them walked out onto the medium-rise platform, The Var's pointed shoes clacking with each step that he took and the boy's feet dragging as he walked.

The boy's name was Silas Elwood. His defining features were his copper-colored hair and forest-green eyes. He was the second son of the village blacksmith and the next sacrifice for this ridiculous farce. Anyone could tell that the excited eyes of the adults frightened him senseless. His knees trembled, his limbs shook, and his lips quivered.

Teardrops started to form in his eyes.

To the right of The Var and Silas stood the central piece of the ceremony, The Aegis. Lucian examined the relic, inspecting the fire within the furnace as per Master

Felix's request. The relic's bright azure flames nearly blinded him. As if the relic was alive, it exuded a mystical aura that captivated all of the children's gaze.

What broke this hypnotic trance was The Var's commanding voice, which instinctively drew everyone's eyes to him.

The Var's dried lips creaked open, as he announced, "Welcome, my dear children of Caelum. Thank you for attending this momentous occasion, and I pray that the gods will hold Silas Elwood in their favor. Oh, glorious and gracious gods and goddesses of Gaia, lead this young man to whatever placement you have in store for him! We shall honor your decision."

The Var waved his bejeweled scepter around like a king, exhibiting his absolute control over his audience. He wore a white robe lined with golden stripes and tassels. Although he showed signs of aging with his wrinkled face and salt-colored hair, The Var had complete control over the procession...even if The Var was old enough to be Lucian's great-great-grandfather.

The Var placed his spotted hand on the boy's shoulder and urged him to move forward and toward the relic. Silas's legs shook like a newborn deer, and his face was frozen in fear.

The Var, however, remained emotionless. As per custom, the Grand Elder handed the boy the ceremonial knife. Silas hesitated but ultimately took it. Both of his hands shook erratically, and his breathing became labored. Forced to follow the ceremonial procedures, Silas slit his palm, letting the blood ooze from the fresh cut into the engulfing flames.

Lucian watched with bated breath.

The Aegis devoured the sacrificial blood, its flames growing stronger and rising several lengths higher toward the ceiling.

It's almost time, Lucian thought, anxiously waiting to see the results.

Lucian recalled the ceremonial outcomes that he memorized from one of Master Felix's ancient textbooks. The relevant text flashed in his memory: "White meant *Chosen*. Black meant *Fallen*. Any color that followed white would mean the gods gifted a special ability to the Reincarnate. For example, blue meant the Reincarnate possessed *Sense*: the gift of locating other Reincarnates; Green meant *Connection*: the gift of knowledge to know one's past life or another's; Purple meant *Manipulation*: the gift of using an ancient god's power; Red meant *Interpretation*: the gift of speaking to or understanding the language of the ancient gods."

The suspense was a killer. Silas looked as if he would pass out at any second. The Aegis went through a myriad of colors until it flashed...white...and only white. Even after a minute or two passed, no color followed the first.

After The Var confirmed The Aegis's will, Silas returned to his family, who appeared content with the outcome of the Succession Ceremony. Unlike families who vied for power and looked to move up in the village's ranks, the Elwood family had long established their roles as master blacksmiths. Their position would remain stable so long as their son ended up Chosen, which wasn't even a question in their minds.

What was I expecting? Lucian asked himself, disappointment firmly taking hold of him. *Of course, he's a Chosen One. Aren't they all? Everyone but me...*

For Lucian, this ceremony only reaffirmed his fears about his fate. Momentarily, his mind traveled back to his Placement Ceremony when he was a child, where the broken stone sealed his cursed fate *forever*.

No matter how many times he brooded over his bleak fate, the results of his Succession Ceremony were set in stone: As black as night, the flames would be.

From the mouth of his mentor, Master Felix, Lucian had only learned of one instance where The Aegis produced black flames many, many years ago. The failed ceremony was that of a boy named Damian Marlais. Lucian tried to remember the details of the ceremony, but something blocked him from recalling it.

"Lucian, you're lost in thought again." Rosalie poked him several times, trying to get his attention. "It's time to leave. Momma's been calling for us."

Returning from his thoughts, he replied, "Sorry, Rosalie. I was just thinking about something Master Felix said."

"I wouldn't say his name in front of our father if I were you," she warned.

"Why is that?" he whispered. "Did Father say something to Master Felix?"

"No, it's the other way around," she said. "I peeked at the package before Momma threw it into the trash... The sender was Master Felix."

Melinda called to them, disrupting their conversation. Fearing a violent punishment for their lateness, the two scurried through The Chapel's elaborate, multi-story doorway.

As they left, Lucian took one last glance at The Holy Chapel. Even though most other places in the village were outdated, The Chapel stood out with its pure whiteness and its ornate furnishings.

On the way back home, Melinda and Remus separated from Lucian and Rosalie, saying they needed to purchase something from the marketplace.

Right after they left, Lucian told Rosalie that he needed to run an errand for Master Felix, so she should return home by herself. Although eccentric by nature, Master Felix was the only Elder in the village who didn't detest him. Master Felix was like an older brother, acting as Lucian's only safeguard on days when his father became too destructive to bear.

In order to reach Master Felix's observatory, Lucian had to pass through at least several district gates to arrive at the last district, The Fallen District.

Contrary to its name, The Fallen District didn't have any Fallen Ones living inside it...not yet at least. Instead, this area housed non-Reincarnates who committed crimes and unlucky souls who displeased The Var, for one reason or another.

Entering through the front gates of The Fallen District, the pungent odor of the area assaulted Lucian's senses. The putrid stench of human excrement and rotting corpses and a ghastly, green mist hung in the air.

After passing through the gate, Lucian retrieved the purifying talisman Master Felix gave him to combat the looming sickness. The talisman was a thin piece of paper—the paper was so worn out that it was practically falling apart.

I had better ask for another one. He tightly pinched his nose. *It reeks!*

Even though Lucian had his share of horrors, it was far better than the hell the inhabitants of this district experienced. On top of being closed off from the other districts, the residents were forced to wear a restrictive device attached to their necks, preventing them from escaping. Abandoned by the gods and by their families, the only purpose of their lives was to waste away.

A few feet from the observatory, a strong force gripped his right ankle. He jerked his leg, finding himself unable to escape the entity's grasp. He looked downward, seeing a wrinkled hand with curled, yellowish nails tightening its hold on him.

"Let go!" Lucian wailed, blindly kicking the stranger.

Finally, the stranger's grasp loosened, and Lucian managed to pull away. Right as he escaped, the owner of the weathered hand started to speak.

"Youngster," an old man with a raspy voice asked, "could you spare a Mon?"

At the bottom of his pocket sat two disk-shaped, metal Mons which he held on to in case of an emergency. He shoved his hands in his pockets, debating whether he should part with a single Mon or not. His fingertips smoothed over the familiar engravings: the sacred Tree of Life with its ancient name carved beneath it, "*Lignum Vitae.*"

"I don't have any Mons!" Lucian lied, a feeling of guilt sticking to the back of his throat. "You can't even use Mons, so what does it matter? Use your Credit Slips."

The old man, on a closer look, had a scraggly salt-and-pepper-stained beard. His ribs were visible through his tattered shirt, and his teeth were chipped and crooked. With every passing second, the nightmares Lucian suffered from while asleep spiraled to the forefront of his mind. Lucian's legs locked, and he couldn't move. A moment's hesitation allowed the old man an opportunity to stand and wildly grab at Lucian's pocket.

Out of disgust, Lucian tried to push him away.

The old man almost reached into his pocket, when...

To his surprise, a guardian angel came in between them.

It's Master Felix!

Holding the old man at bay with a single outstretched

arm, his mentor gave him a warm smile and mouthed the words, "It's alright."

With the click of his tongue, the old man hurriedly limped away.

"Didn't I *specifically* teach you self-defense skills for this very *situation*?" Master Felix stressed each syllable of his scolding.

Lucian lowered his head, cheeks burning red from embarrassment.

With a quick wink, Master Felix then ruffled Lucian's hair and said, "You know I was only teasing you."

Before Lucian could respond to Master Felix, the man was already on the move.

With slumped shoulders and quickened steps, Lucian followed Master Felix toward the observatory located in the depths of The Fallen District. The observatory was an imposing tower that cast a sinister shadow over the entire district. With sturdy bricks forming its foundation and a well-constructed metal gate surrounding it, not a single soul could enter without its Master's permission. No matter how many times Lucian looked at the observatory, he was still mesmerized by its grandiosity.

Lucian's eyes and feet followed Master Felix into the tower. His mentor wore his usual black robe with red and blue linings. His hand was decorated with a Mage's favorite accessory: a magic ring. Each of his rings had a magical attribute: one to boost attack magic, one to boost defense magic, and one to enhance summoning magic.

Lucian marveled at his teacher.

Unlike the rest of Caelum, Master Felix possessed a mystical aura. He was exceptionally youthful-looking with vermilion-colored hair and striking green eyes. He was also a master Mage, who was the youngest Elder in history.

Lucian imagined that Master Felix would've been the next Var if he hadn't defied The Council of Elders by taking Lucian as his protégé.

Reaching the inside of the tower, a nostalgic scenery greeted him. Floating pots filled with peculiar flowers and sweeping brooms without a handler floated around the observatory. They passed by the animate objects and headed toward the spiraled staircase. Numerous books lined the shelves at the top of the observatory.

"On the History of the Ancient Worlds," "On the History of the Phoenix," and "On the History of the Ancient Scrolls" were only a few of the various history books lining the shelves.

Master Felix, transcending the stairs with ease, selected several books without so much as a side glance. He momentarily looked backward while asking, "What did you think of the ceremony?"

"Same old. Same old," Lucian reported. "Silas Elwood was deemed a Chosen One."

"Any specific attributes?"

"None," Lucian replied, snatching a paperweight off the shelf. "His family looked more relieved than disappointed, so I suppose that's a positive."

"I see..." Master Felix muttered. "Anything different about the relic itself?"

"Nothing out of the ordinary," Lucian said, as he was distracted with his new toy. "It was the same procession as always... The Aegis burned the blood and changed colors."

When they reached the apex of the staircase, Master Felix directed the books, with the flick of his fingers, to fly toward a stack of books on his desk. Lucian looked at the study, hoping to find another magical tool.

"Since you always provide feedback about The Aegis," Master Felix started by saying, "I'll let you pick out today's study topic."

"I want to learn about the barrier!" Lucian exclaimed.

After seeing Master Felix's startled look, Lucian rephrased, "I mean... I think it would be good for me to learn the background behind the creation of the barrier and its significance."

Good job, Lucian... You put your foot in your mouth again.

Master Felix's eyebrows knitted together like a ball of yarn, signaling to Lucian that the topic was extremely sensitive.

"I'm sorry," Lucian said with a lowered gaze. "I didn't mean to..."

"No, it's fine. Since you have such a curious mind, I might as well tell you about the barrier but only the basics, alright?"

With a brightened smile, Lucian exclaimed, "Thanks, Master Felix!"

"Of course, Lucian. A curious mind is always welcome here! On that note, I suppose we should start with the barrier's history. The first Var, Magus Satori, the one who created the barrier, possessed two abilities: the gift of Manipulation and the gift of Connection. With those attributes, he configured a great barrier to protect the Reincarnates of the ancient gods and the location of The Heavenly Pillars. He knew mankind would covet the powers of the Reincarnates, so that's why he chose the monster-infested Sage's Forest. And that's enough for now."

"More, more!" Lucian pleaded, imitating puppy dog eyes. "Please!"

"Perhaps another day," Master Felix said, wagging his finger. "If I tell you too much, then I'll run out of things to teach you. On the topic of teaching, I think it's time that we continue your studies on the principles of sorcery."

"Fine," Lucian said, openly dissatisfied, "whatever you say, O Great Magus Felix."

His mentor pointed at the crystal paperweight in Lucian's hands.

"This is your next lesson in practical sorcery," Master Felix said. "I want you to channel your energy into this crystal. Don't worry, even if you aren't gifted with any attribute, anyone can use this device with enough practice."

Sitting in Lucian's palm, a sparkling crystal with a deep crimson hue rested. He closed his eyes, remembering Master Felix's prior lectures and lessons about manipulating energy. He synchronized his breaths, clutched the crystal tightly, and envisioned the emotions that he wanted to convey. His mother's face, her embrace, and her smile appeared in his mind. He felt the flow of energy transfer to the crystal.

He opened one of his eyes and witnessed the rays of light flooding out from the object. It astonished him so much that he lost focus for a few seconds. And when he lost focus, bad things tended to happen...

The crystal lost control and shattered, shooting its shards haphazardly in all directions and almost harming Master Felix and Lucian in the process.

One loose shard was heading straight toward Lucian, and he instinctively winced. Without so much as a frantic motion or a spoken curse, Master Felix chanted, "*Congelo,*" and all of the shards froze in midair.

Lucian held his breath, as the shard stopped in front of his face.

With a flick of the wrist, Master Felix summoned the brooms that had been sweeping downstairs. They flew to the top and cleaned up the glass shards littered on the floor.

Master Felix calmly said, "Don't worry, Lucian, mistakes are bound to happen as you learn more lessons and apply more spells. But you must remember to be extremely careful when infusing energy into any magical device. Remember what I always say about letting your mind wander while using sorcery." Master Felix lectured, letting out a prolonged sigh, "Although, I suppose it *is* too much to ask of you on your first try."

"I understand, and I'm sorry," Lucian sheepishly said. "I'll remember your warning for next time."

Forming a small smile on his face, Master Felix said, "You don't need to apologize, Lucian." His mentor playfully flicked his forehead. "After all, these things take time."

After spending the next few hours practicing more basic spells and infusing his energy into smaller, less dangerous devices, Lucian slowly but surely improved his sorcery skills. If only a baby step toward mastery, at the very least.

From downstairs, the old grandfather clock chimed five, and the sound reverberated throughout the whole observatory.

"May I have permission to leave!?" Lucian exclaimed, wide-eyed and clumsily bowing. "Thank you for the lessons, Master Felix!"

Master Felix nodded his head.

Before Lucian raced down the stairs, he remembered what his sister had told him.

"Master Felix, I have one more question!"

"And what would that be?"

"Rosalie told me that you sent a package to Melinda," Lucian explained. "I'm sorry to tell you that she threw it away. Was it something important?"

Master Felix's eyes wavered for a moment, but he then responded with a lower tone, "No, nothing important, Lucian. Just something that Melinda and I had spoken about in the past."

The last chime of the clock sent a clear warning of Lucian's curfew. He sprinted down the stairs. Out of the corner of his eye, he saw a flash of Master Felix waving him farewell.

Lucian's mind was consumed with the information he had obtained about the barrier. But there was one thing that was completely clear to him: Something deep within his core was beckoning him to return to it. So much so that he fought with himself along the route back home.

Even though trespassing into the forest was forbidden and could lead to dire consequences in the future, Lucian couldn't contain his insatiable curiosity...

3

THE ELECTOR

 *Caelum*

acing along the winding dirt paths, The Sage's Forest came into view. Adrenaline pumped through Lucian's veins. After going back and forth between whether he wanted to be beaten now or later for disobeying his curfew, he chose the latter.

When he reached the forest's edge, he lessened his pace and peered within. A chill ran down his spine, and he hadn't even crossed the boundary. Whether it was from the howling wind or the fear of disobeying his father, he didn't know.

Once in the forest, he attempted to retrace his prior tracks. Through the bushes, past some trees, and listening for the same buzzing noise, he followed his intuition.

Before he fully retraced his past route, he heard an awful *thud* nearby.

Carefully and silently, he tiptoed toward the strange sound. He first heard garbles, whispers, and then audible, intelligible words.

Peeking around an oak tree, Lucian noticed three familiar faces: James and Peter Parsley—a.k.a. the Parsley Twins—and Elias. While the Twins were known for their mischievous and rebellious natures, Elias was known for his status as the village's angel. If only the villagers knew the truth about their sweet and innocent idol, Elias Daye.

Huh. Lucian grimaced. *It must've been one of those dunces who made that terrible thud.*

"Hey, James, what was that for, you dimwit!?" Peter shouted, spit spewing out. "Elias told us we're not 'ere to be foolin' around, and 'ere ya are hittin' me! We're supposed to be kickin' the cursed boy's tail into submission."

"Just be glad I didn't stuff your face with that fine-looking mud over there," James replied, swiping his loose, carrot-colored hairs to the side.

"That's dung, you imbecile."

"Exactly."

"Enough, you two." Elias intervened, glaring at them. "Remember what I told you to do."

"Kick 'em," James said.

"Beat 'em," Peter continued.

"And make him cry for his momma!" the Twins simultaneously said, snickering.

Lucian rolled his eyes.

"But wait." Peter looked stumped. "What if Lucian don't come 'ere today?"

James slapped his brother on the back of his head, making another loud *thud*.

"Hey, why'da hit me!"

"Boys," Elias warned, with a venomous tone. "It's only a matter of time before Lucian returns. I know because I'm *special*. I don't suppose you've forgotten who I am, have you?"

"No, siree!" Peter piped up. "You're our future Var, the next Elector!"

Here we go again... Lucian rubbed his temples. *He hasn't even had his ceremony, and he's already spouting this nonsense.*

He drew out a long sigh and turned to leave, stepping straight into a pile of dead leaves.

Crunch!

Elias's head whipped around.

At that very moment, Lucian felt his heart drop into the pit of his stomach.

Elias pointed his finger at Lucian's general location. Lucian tried to run, but he was overtaken, dragged, and tied to the oak tree by the burly and brusque Parsley Twins. James and Peter stuck their faces right in front of Lucian's face and contorted them into hideous expressions. Their breaths stunk like rotting fish, and their eyes glowed a menacing black hue.

James and Peter were identical twins, so he couldn't tell which one spat while the other one sang. If it was necessary to describe them in a few words, then Lucian would have to say that they were a pair of brutish and plain-looking pigs.

Elias, on the other hand, was a different story. He was intelligent, resourceful, and handsome. With mesmerizing azure hair and eyes, even the old hags swooned. Instead of the external beauty that deceived others, Lucian knew the raw nastiness of his enemy's character: a twisted and cruel snake.

Like commanding a pair of wild dogs, Elias let them loose with a whistle and three words, "Sick 'em, boys."

The Parsley Twins tore into Lucian. Left and right, punches rained down, the taste of iron filling Lucian's mouth and the nerves in his face painfully pulsating with each consecutive hit.

As he was beaten senseless, time seemed to pass by so slowly.

Even when their hands were soaked in blood, the Twins

continued their cruelties. Left and right, up and down, Lucian was treated like a filthy monster: one to be scorned and beaten. A kick to the shin sent prickles through his leg. His body lurched forward, but he didn't fall. The restraints held him up. In between assaults, he cursed his abusers.

"You're the real monsters!" Lucian tried to yell in between wheezes.

Elias with a sadistic smile ordered, "Give 'em hell."

Lucian's resolve to escape or to rebel dissipated. His body hung over the restraints like a lifeless doll. His face burned a bright array of red, blue, and purple. His teeth were painted with his blood. His eyes were even more sore and swollen, now.

While Lucian knew he couldn't beat their brute strength, it didn't stop him from challenging them in his head. *Is that all?* he wondered, as his vision blurred. *But it's not enough. Not enough to kill a Reincarnate. Not enough to kill me...*

That internal defiance eventually died out too. Once the fire left Lucian's eyes, the Twins plopped to the ground, taking a short break. Their bloodied hands clutched the fallen leaves, playing with them in between their fingers. Like children, they became bored of him.

Elias sent a sharp glare at them. James and Peter sprung back up and chose to continue with verbal attacks over physical attacks, which were certainly not their expertise. Not at all.

James spat out the words, "You should be grateful. The only reason you're still alive is because Elias don't want you dead yet. If you weren't a Reincarnate, then we woulda drowned you in the 'ol river near the ruins, you hear?"

Lucian knew his fate very well. Even with all the trouble that his Reincarnate status caused, he still clung to it to restore his confidence: *Reincarnates are strong, stronger than any soldier. Reincarnates are smart, smarter than any scholar. Reincarnates are cruel, crueler than any criminal. Reincarnates are...*

"You're too weak," Lucian taunted, spitting out a slush of blood. "Weaker than my old man and even weaker than a little girl. Even if I wasn't a Reincarnate, you'd still be weak."

The Parsley Twins growled, clenching their fists, ready to punch Lucian's face.

Elias looked dissatisfied, his face dropping to a frown. Waving off his goons, who begrudgingly receded to the background, Elias approached the still-restrained Lucian.

With a twisted smirk and a hand gripping onto Lucian's hair, Elias tugged on it, pain shooting through his scalp. After a bit of teasing, Elias slammed Lucian's head into the bark.

"Argh!" Lucian's scream filled the air.

"Listen well, Lucian," Elias sneered, pushing Lucian's head further into the bark, "as long as you mind your own business and stick to the soil, I'll spare you. If you try pulling one of your tricks with Emilia like during last year's Summer Solstice, then I'll thoroughly remind you how cursed you truly are. Understand?"

Lucian, though on the verge of passing out, replied with wheezing laughter and restoring defiance in his eyes. As the saying goes, "An animal backed into a corner is the scariest." Elias retracted faster than a wounded deer.

"Y-Your eyes are..."

"My eyes are *what*?" Lucian snickered, trickles of blood sliding down his face. He could only imagine a look of pure insanity had surfaced on his profile since even the great Elias retreated. Lucian's eyes widened, playing the role of a madman perfectly, having seen time and time again his father acting that very role.

"Come on, boys!" Elias ordered, slightly faltering in his domineering tone.

As Elias left, he tripped over a branch, twisting his ankle. He cursed profusely under his breath and used the Twins like crutches on either side.

Even if it was a dumb stroke of luck, Lucian wasn't going to question the situation.

Serves him right, that bloodthirsty hound.

When the Twins looked back at Lucian, they produced

a cringe-worthy expression: one of uneasiness and fear. Afterward, they returned their focus to Elias, who they helped pitifully limp away.

"Cowards," Lucian cursed under his breath.

Once they were out of sight, Lucian took the next few minutes to recover. He was a mess of sweat and blood. He struggled out of the restraints, knowing from former experiences the trick to loosen them.

Even if he had managed to untie the restraints earlier, he could've never outrun the Twins, who exceeded him in both physical strength and sheer stupidity. Traits that seemed to work hand in hand in their case.

After catching his breath, Lucian headed toward the barrier, his body leading him through muscle memory. Instead of joy or curiosity, he felt fatigued. His whole body protested every step that he took.

However, his obsession with adventure pushed him past his limits, as the only thing hindering him was his battered body. Even with the severity of his wounds, this experience was neither the first nor the last time he had been beaten without respite.

Ah, I'm going to feel so sore tomorrow, he thought, as he rubbed his stomach.

Lucian perked up when he heard the barrier's unique sound. He approached it with as big of strides as he could manage and as excited as he could be. He noticed that the barrier was slightly more visible than last time. At first, he thought that his mind was playing tricks on him, so he rubbed his eyes several times.

After reopening them, he realized that with every passing moment, the barrier's clarity grew sharper and sharper. Master Felix had been wary and dismissive of Lucian's interest in the barrier, but he needed definitive answers—answers that neither Master Felix nor the villagers were willing to provide him.

It was time to figure out the truth behind the barrier. He recalled one of Master Felix's books that mentioned ceremonial rituals. Containing a wide variety of ceremonies, they all shared one common theme: blood, bowing, and ancestral recitations. So, he attempted to mimic the motions of the ceremonies to glean something, anything out of the mystical force.

"Oh, Great and Mighty Barrier," Lucian recited, closing his eyes and raising his hands. "Impart your wealth of wisdom to your humble servant, one of the children of the Seventy-Sixth Generation of Reincarnates, Lucian Roux."

Upon reciting the respectful words, he knelt on the ground and bowed his head, lightly touching the dirt with his forehead. Since he hadn't washed yet, the first requirement of the ceremony was easy to fulfill, as his bloody forehead smeared the soil.

Following several seconds of silence, he lifted his head to find the barrier still the same. Disappointed and disillusioned, he staggered to his feet and pretended to leave, hoping that something would stir in the barrier.

And it did.

A crackle like lightning stopped him in his tracks.

He swiftly turned around and gasped at the sight of the barrier's irregular movements. It looked like it was struggling to keep something from passing through—a small object. The object's exit from the barrier turned out to be the source of the crackling sound.

Once the object successfully pushed through the barrier, it crashed onto the forest floor. Lucian squinted, trying to ascertain what it was. Upon an even closer look, the object appeared to be a stone of sorts, letting out streams of steam and sizzling loudly.

Despite the clear suspicious nature of this object, Lucian was too excited about his discovery to care. He experienced a rush of happiness and apprehension, pacing around the area. Several times, he tried to touch the stone, but it burned his fingers with even the slightest contact. So, he unfortunately had to wait for the stone to cool down.

After confirming the steam had fully dissipated, Lucian cautiously picked up the clear stone and held it to the sky, the sun rays radiating through its core.

He stood there, gazing at it in awe and wonder.

He was so focused on the stone that a few seconds turned into fifteen minutes.

The grumble of his hungry stomach, however, brought him back to reality.

Looking up at the sky, he noticed the sun had dipped too deep into the nightly abyss.

Fear gripped him.

And so, he raced home.

For he knew his fate...that of a starving, dead boy.

ARRIVING HOME, LUCIAN GRATEFULLY DEEMED HE was safe from his father's fury. Only the kitchen and front porch were lit with illumination crystals, meaning the entire family was either asleep or they went out to some nightly gathering.

He thanked his lucky stars.

Rushing into the house, he went straight for the cabinet where the third-grade healing crystals were located. Even though his father banned him from using healing crystals, Lucian knew his father wasn't the type to count them. And while these crystals paled in comparison to their first-grade and second-grade variants, they were able to address the surface wounds: They tended to the fresh and old blood, stitched together the cuts on his skin, and removed the black and blue bruises on his battered body.

Other than using the off-limits crystals, Lucian was worried about a more pressing problem. If his father knew he had a run-in with Elias and injured him, then all hell would break loose. However, Lucian reasoned that Elias's words would also incriminate his crime: Trespassing into The Sage's Forest, after all, violated The Var's laws.

Ascending the stairs, Lucian still felt the prickles in his legs. After a rough climb, he threw himself into his room, crawled into his bed, and fell into a sore yet desired sleep.

MORNING CAME, AND LUCIAN WAS AWAKENED BY the sounds of glass shattering and wooden chairs splintering. Looking up at the ceiling, he knew who was making all the ruckus, but he didn't know why his father was making such a fuss so early in the morning.

Rubbing the crust from his eyes and still in a half-asleep state, Lucian left his bed and cautiously reached the staircase. He tiptoed down the steps, hoping that the victim of his father's tantrum was only the furniture.

However, that wasn't the case.

Upon reaching the bottom of the stairs, Lucian stood frozen, staring at the scene.

Remus was on his usual rampage. Melinda was on the floor weeping. Rosalie was cowered in the corner.

"You ungrateful wench!" Remus shouted, sending another chair flying with the kick of his boot. "Who do you think you are? He's *my* son, and he'll do whatever *I* say. You have no right to stick your nose into our affairs."

Melinda didn't reply.

Remus slammed his fist on the table.

"Papa, spare mother!" Rosalie pleaded, her entire body shuddering uncontrollably. "Please stop hurting her! It wasn't her fault!"

Raising his hand, Remus tottered toward her and swung. Lucian reflexively ran toward them. He jumped in between father and daughter, swiftly pushing Rosalie out of harm's way. His father's hand smacked Lucian across the face, causing Lucian to stumble.

"It's your fault!" his father screamed, pointing at Lucian. "I wish you were never born!"

Calloused by these words, Lucian replied to him while wincing from the recent hit, "I don't care what happens to me, but don't you ever hit my sister. Or else I'll make you pay."

The same defiance that sprung up when Lucian faced the bullies resurfaced.

Remus paused, his eyes squinting at Lucian, as he cackled and said, "My boy, you only have one future...as a Fallen One!"

While his father was busy rambling to himself and trying to retrieve another bottle from the cooler, Lucian asked his stepmother, "What happened last night?"

Melinda said, "The village Elders have decided to combine your ceremony with Elias's."

Lucian grew angry at the mention of that demon's name, and he exclaimed, "Hah! Now, that's a joke, alright. Pairing me, an outcast, with the village's idol. What a show indeed!"

"That's not the point. The last time the Elders held a combined ceremony like this..." Melinda paused and then whispered, "...one of the Reincarnates died."

Pausing at her words, Lucian asked, "D-Died? W-What do you mean...died?"

"It's ancient history," Melinda explained, hesitation laced in her words, "and it might've been an accident, but it doesn't bode well. I just didn't want you to get hurt."

Lucian didn't understand her actions. If anything, he thought she would've been glad for him to be out of their lives for good. Remus's main trigger was Lucian, after all.

He didn't have the time to fully process Melinda's

words, as his focus was still on his drunk father. Gleaning from his father's slumped-over figure, Lucian confirmed that his father had moved onto the next stage in his daily routine: a pity party with endless drinks. At least, during this time, Remus was too wasted to rise from his stupor.

He motioned Melinda and Rosalie to retreat upstairs, while he cleaned up the mess of broken shards and splinters. Remus wasn't exactly in a state to think straight, so if the place wasn't sparkling clean by the time he sobered up, Lucian would pay a hefty price.

Better ignored for an hour than beaten for one, Lucian rationalized, as he retrieved the cleaning supplies and started to tidy up.

After scrubbing the dirt off the floor and throwing the glass shards into the waste pail, Lucian threw away what was left of the destroyed chairs into the outside garbage bin. Returning inside, Lucian removed any weapons that Remus could reach within a certain radius, which were usually empty bottles or random kitchen utensils.

For what seemed to be the hundredth time, Lucian overheard his father's incessant ramblings, "Lucille...my love, I'm sorry... I'll see you soon."

Before heading upstairs, Lucian noticed something clutched tightly within Remus's fist: a crumpled letter. Lucian hadn't noticed it on the table before. And upon closer look, the letter had the official seal of The Var engraved on the top of the parchment. He managed to pry it away from his father's grasp without waking him. Unfortunately, he couldn't translate the entirety of the message, as it was in the ancient language, but he could decipher pieces of it thanks to Master Felix's lessons.

"Risen. Fallen. Two boys. Prophecy fulfilled," the letter translated.

Lucian's face contorted in confusion. He carefully folded the paper and tucked it into his father's empty fist. Shaking his head, he retreated upstairs.

Those words continued to haunt him. Even as the morning passed, his attention latched onto that one decipherable phrase.

Although Lucian didn't have lessons with Master Felix today, his homework was to practice what he had learned in the previous session. As he continued to learn and apply Master Felix's teachings, his powers were steadily growing stronger. However, there was the feeling that *something* was reacting inside him, growing stronger with him.

Instead of the normal training crystal, Lucian tried to harness his energy into the stone that he retrieved from the barrier. He firmly held it in his right palm, slowly infusing his energy into the stone until a steady stream flowed.

Everything was going well, and the stone even reacted positively to his efforts...until it couldn't contain the mass of energy entering anymore. When it reached its breaking point, the stone dulled. What was once a sparkling stone turned into a charred gray color.

He sighed, defeated by the day.

Today had already been too stressful, and he didn't want to be more depressed than he already was. He slunk back into bed early, trying to sleep, despite the recent events.

Unlike the daily nightmares that haunted him, he dreamed of something different.

Tonight, Lucian's dream was of his mother. She approached him with her hands held out to him. A crown lined with the most magnificent jewels that he had ever seen was cradled within her palms. She smiled sweetly, urging him to take it. However, when he tried to grasp the crown, it cracked and shattered into thousands of shards.

With an apologetic look on her face, she said, "I'm so sorry that I broke my promise to you, Lucian... I really tried to protect you... Never forget who you are."

Before she finished, her voice became muffled and indecipherable. He tried to talk to her, but it was too late. Everything faded to darkness.

4

REBIRTH FESTIVAL

 *Caelum*

t the advent of spring, The Rebirth Festival commenced. As a brief respite for the hard-working villagers, the festival goers participated in the bustling market shops, joyous festivities, and cheerful music. And like any other major festivity, the only "absentees" were the residents of The Fallen District.

Although an unspoken tradition, every festivity served as a celebration of the Reincarnates: the pride and joy of the village. With the sheer number of children running around and the various activities for the adults to relax and enjoy, Lucian could blend into the background at least for a day.

Reincarnates were expected to wear extravagant ceremonial robes provided by their families to set them apart from the normal villagers. Purples, blues, reds, and other shades represented the different power levels of each family.

Although his father was once a respected and powerful figure, Lucian's robes were a mixture of muted grays and browns: a sign of disgrace due to falling out with the highest rungs of society. His attire barely met the minimal requirement of a "ceremonial" robe, but he didn't mind the negative social undertones that it represented.

After all, this festival was one of the only times Lucian could run free, and Remus would remain sober. Other than when his father had to meet with The Council of Elders.

Inside the Roux abode, Melinda helped Rosalie get dressed. She tied the sashes on Rosalie's pink dress and the pink bows in her hair. Not saying a word or changing her expression, she also fitted Lucian in his ceremonial robe. He refrained from speaking to her, even though she half-heartedly tried to protect him the other day.

A feeling of awkwardness filled him.

When the church bells tolled, he and his sister were herded off. In terms of the procession, the village's custom was to send the Reincarnate children first, the non-Reincarnate children second, the Reincarnate adults third, and the non-Reincarnate adults last. Rosalie was in the second group, as for whatever strange reason, the girls were less likely to be born Reincarnates than the boys.

Files of Reincarnates clogged the narrow streets. Like machines, they followed the leader until they reached the most prestigious district, The Central District, where the Elders and Mages resided.

Turning and looking backward, his eyes searched the crowd for Rosalie. She was several feet behind the first group and surrounded by a group of girls adorned with the finest fabrics and accessories. He worried that she was treated as an outcast because of her lesser-quality clothes or her status as an outsider, but that didn't seem to be the case.

Instead, she smiled brightly and carried herself with dignity and grace.

An attitude he was grateful for.

His only solace was her happiness.

After a fifteen-minute march across several residential districts through the gates, the hordes of children arrived at the core of The Central District.

As soon as the crowd ceased moving, the children dispersed in all directions. Several sprinted toward the food stalls. Others went to the game stalls. And a few decided to leisurely roam and scrutinize the festival's offerings.

Everyone but Lucian.

Lucian was drawn to the Stage of the Songstress, where

The Var's daughter, Emilia, was about to start her performance for the pompous Elders and the arrogant adults. Although he remembered Elias's threats, Lucian was never the type to follow the rules.

Emilia, with a silk sash in her hand, majestically danced across the platform and sang like a songbird. She wore an elegant dress and entranced anyone who watched. Her blonde hair shimmered like golden sunlight, and her eyes were as soothing as his mother's. She reminded him of the sunny days in his life.

He suddenly regained his senses.

Stuffing his hands into his pockets, he ferreted around for the charred stone. He clutched it in his right fist and started to walk away, leaving the performance. With the freedom granted to him during the festival, he decided to search for his mentor, Master Felix. While he had openly disobeyed his mentor by returning to the barrier, Master Felix was the only one that he could confide in with his secrets.

Weaving through the crowd, Lucian spotted a familiar muted-brown cloak with its weathered phoenix insignia on the back. The old, rugged thing had always hung unused in Master Felix's observatory, so it was strange to see the garment outside The Fallen District.

He strained his hand to reach the cloaked figure.

The crowd thickened, so he resorted to hurdling over

obstacles and pushing people out of the way. He accidentally knocked over several items, including a vendor's barrel of booze and a truth-seer's table.

As he clumsily raced through the stalls, yells and curses followed him. In the hustle and bustle of the masses and drones of tedious conversations, the sounds dissipated. He lost the figure for a few seconds but then spotted him again. But this time, the figure was standing unmoving and gazing in the direction of The Holy Chapel. Finally, the cloaked figure was within Lucian's reach, the person whom he assumed to be his teacher.

Without thinking, he grabbed the figure's shoulder with his right hand.

"Mast—"

The mysterious stone slipped out of his hand and fell to the ground. It rolled away, dancing along the stone street.

Lucian crouched and hastily retrieved the stone, stuffing it back into his pocket. The figure made a complete one-eighty turn, looming over him. His face was fully visible to Lucian.

Under the hood, Lucian saw a boy around the same age as himself. The boy had unkempt, pitch-black strands and dark purple eyes. These characteristics were uncommon in Caelum, whose citizens possessed lighter features.

An outsider... Lucian gulped down his shock. *That's impossible!*

The sacred barrier surrounding his village repelled all living beings, so no one could simply wander into the village by mistake.

The moment their eyes met, a peculiar pang of recognition washed over Lucian, and he felt a strange pressure in his heart. They had never met before; he was sure of it.

Then, why does he feel so familiar? Lucian wondered.

By the time that Lucian regained his bearings, the figure had already slipped between the stalls and mingled into the crowd. Desperate to catch up, Lucian tried to run but physically couldn't follow him. Someone's nails dug deep into his shoulder, preventing him. And Lucian knew exactly who it was...

Neither his father nor the Elders paid attention to him during these public events. This was the worst-case scenario. It was the little demon himself.

"Well, well, well, aren't you a conniving little skunk," a disgustingly familiar voice said. "You ignored my warnings and even wrecked my favorite festival stalls. How are you going to pay for this? Huh, Lucian?"

Lucian turned and was met with the huffing-and-puffing wolf, Elias, and his porky minions.

"I don't know what you're talking about," Lucian

replied, irked by Elias's intervention. "Can't you scum ever take a day off?"

Elias's expression remained the same: calm and collected. If any fight started, the devilish boy would simply blame Lucian for the disturbance. Although Lucian dared not swing, he wasn't about to bow down to Elias's sadistic ego. Feeling around in his pocket, Lucian confirmed that the stone was there. Thankfully, for now, his secret was safe.

"I told you never to look at Emilia ever again," Elias spat. "Are you deaf like you are dumb? She's mine! Why don't you understand that!?"

To not cause a huge commotion, the dictator and his goons issued a final threat to Lucian: He needed to either disappear from their sight or suffer the consequences. Whatever punishment he would receive for disobeying, Lucian chose the latter. Freedom was like a flighty bird, and he never knew when he would see it next.

"Not as dumb as you are," Lucian cheekily said, racing away as quickly as he could.

Like a thread weaving through a needle's eye, Lucian escaped into the crowd, completely losing his tormentors.

Once they faded into the distance, Lucian caught a glimpse of the real Master Felix, who was wearing his distinctive black robe. His mentor seemed to recognize his gaze and approached him. A giddy expression lit up Master

Felix's unblemished face. A peculiar expression to Lucian in their time together.

Lucian bit his tongue. He knew he was supposed to report the cloaked figure from before, but there was something about the stranger and the situation itself that kept nagging him.

If someone from the inside had invited him, then... Lucian conjectured.

He shook his head. It was absurd to even humor the thought.

"You're so quiet today," Master Felix said. "It's very unlike you not to say anything the moment we meet. You're usually so talkative."

"Actually!" Lucian blurted out, affirming Master Felix's statement. "Look what I found!"

He thrust the stone into Master Felix's hands. His mentor's expression, upon seeing the charred stone, was that of shock, like the outsider's reaction. However, his shock quickly turned into a beet-red fury and then deep wrinkles formed on his forehead.

Lucian watched as Master Felix struggled to find the words to say. For a while, his mentor stayed silent, occasionally glancing around as if he was wary of something, or someone.

In a voice as soft as a whisper, Master Felix said, "Lucian, I know where you found this stone. Since you've already broken the village's rules, you need to be extra careful to not let anyone else see it, understand?"

Lucian nodded and started to say, "I'm sorry."

"What's done is done," his mentor said, bluntly.

With a generic spell, his mentor configured a leather-bound necklace with an insert for the stone. He wedged the stone into its holder and singed it with a small flame into place. He hung it around Lucian's neck, ordering him to tuck it under his shirt, so it wouldn't be noticeable.

"I need to tell you something," Master Felix said. "There's no reason for you to go to the barrier again. What you'll encounter is nothing like before. You'll only run into danger, so don't go near the barrier again unless I tell you to, okay?"

Lucian nodded.

"Good, now, go and enjoy the festival."

Although Lucian wanted to avoid another lecture, the outsider's presence weighed like a boulder in his mind. So, before Master Felix could leave, Lucian whispered into his mentor's ear, "I saw someone wearing your cloak or a cloak that's like yours. He doesn't look like someone from our village. I think he's an outsider. He also seemed interested in the stone. What should I do?"

His mentor's forehead further creased with concern.

"Nothing," Master Felix said. "You will do nothing. If the Elders know what you've done, then your punishment will be far worse than simply sitting in the underground cells for a week or two."

With that final exchange, they headed their separate ways. Master Felix still had his ceremonial duties to fulfill, and Lucian had enough mystery and suspense for one day. For the remainder of the festival, Lucian's only objective was to make sure that his father never caught sight or wind of him.

The Rebirth Festival ended with the chime of The Holy Chapel's bells. Before dismissal, it was customary to announce the upcoming Succession Ceremonies as well as any other pressing issues in the village, which, for the past several years, were close to nil.

Everyone gathered at the Stage of the Songtress. The Var and a few of the Elders were perched on the platform with a voice amplifier in their hands. One by one, the Elders thanked the villagers for their attendance and continued loyalty.

Then, they listed the names of the Reincarnates who would have their ceremonies in the coming months. All the names were promptly addressed, except for two in particular: Lucian Roux and Elias Daye.

The villagers lingered on the absence of those two names from the list, until The Var, who was the final person to speak, brought clarity to their confusion.

"I am pleased that this Rebirth Festival has come to a successful close as those in the past have. I am aware that we have passed over two names for the upcoming Succession Ceremony," The Var said. "The Council of Elders has decided to combine the ceremony of Elias Daye and Lucian Roux, who are the Reincarnates of the twin gods of creation and destruction, Adonis and Morpheus. In the history of Caelum, we rarely hold a dual ceremony. However, it is also true that the twin gods being reincarnated in the same generation and on the exact same day is a rarity in and of itself. Our decision is final as determined and solidified by The Aegis's will."

The instance of shocked silence was followed by an enraged uproar. Prior to The Var's announcement, Lucian hid in the nearest alleyway. He was keenly aware of the break in tradition and the hatred of the villagers toward him. He was a fair distance from the stage itself, but the shouts and cries filled his ears regardless. The Var was quick to silence the noisy crowd. With the raise of his hand, silence ensued.

"As this is such a rare and unprecedented occurrence,

and to ensure tranquility and purity, only the guardians and direct family members of the Reincarnates and the Elders themselves are permitted to witness the ceremony," The Var stated. "There will be no exceptions. However, parts of the ceremony will be broadcasted through the All-Seeing Portals stationed throughout the districts."

After The Var finished, the crowd was forced to disperse. No one noticed Lucian in the alleyway, but he saw the twisted expressions of the Reincarnates, non-Reincarnates, and Elders, who listened to The Var's proclamation.

Not for a single moment did he want them to witness his ceremony firsthand. The Var's decision was welcomed, but at what cost?

When the Festival finally concluded, and there wasn't a soul in sight, Lucian ventured home. He took a different path, weaving in and out of side alleyways and abandoned streets.

As the sun dipped into the sky, he could barely see the ruins of The Heavenly Pillars, which were located past the furthest district. They had always piqued his insatiable curiosity, but he chose not to cause any more *incidents* brought about by his curious nature.

Nearing a familiar pathway to his house, he walked along the forest's edge. A rustle in the bushes caused him to jump, but he continued onward. From the corner of his eye, he swore that he saw the cloaked figure, but he ignored the illusions playing with his mind. He trusted and respected Master Felix, his one-and-only ally, so he wouldn't press the matter further. Lucian earnestly wanted to avoid disappointing him again.

When he reached home, the door was misaligned and cracked in several spots. The inside of his house looked ransacked. The illumination crystals were shattered and scattered on the wooden floorboards.

His eyes widened and his mouth opened slightly ajar as the full image settled into his vision. His father lay deathly still. He was stuffed like a lifeless doll against the collapsed wall. His stepmother was also unconscious but had fared better than his father.

More horrifying was that Rosalie was nowhere to be found. No matter how long that Lucian waited, she didn't return to the house.

Another huge shock to Lucian's system was neither the state of his house nor his injured guardian...

It was the bejeweled dagger that his father always carried with him.

Wedged into the floorboard, blood stains and a familiar brown piece of cloth were trapped beneath its silvery blade. He clutched his palms into a fist until they turned white.

He came to a harrowing resolution.

The culprit could only be one person...the *outsider*.

5

COUNCIL OF ELDERS

 *Caelum*

Early the next morning, an envoy came to escort the Roux Family to The Central District. Since this assault held grave implications for the Council's seemingly stainless reputation and the village's carefully constructed peace, The Var ordered the victims to travel at discretion. They were disguised in thick garments and transported in a special caravan.

To prevent news of the attack from spreading like wildfire to the other districts, the Roux Family's house was quickly searched, scanned, and restored. Any evidence was retrieved and locked in a storehouse.

Within his district, the Elders released an official statement reporting an explosion due to faulty mechanics. It eased the villagers who strove more for peace of mind than for the unadulterated truth. The incident was so contained that the other districts weren't even aware of it.

The transport caravan had a bulky beige fabric surrounding Lucian and his family with thinner flaps covering the rear exit. A few bumps in the road caused the thin coverings to loosen. Lucian took advantage of the coincidence and peered out the back.

He caught Melinda anxiously glancing a few times at him and then at Remus. Too busy sightseeing, he ignored her strange stares and looked back outside. More than ever, Lucian needed a distraction.

However, Lucian grew increasingly uncomfortable with his guardians' injuries. Melinda had a black-and-blue bruise on her forehead, while Remus had a black eye and bloodied scrapes crawling up his arms. Even though karma seemed to finally have struck his father, Lucian wasn't all that comfortable seeing Melinda's.

His guardians needed second-grade healing crystals, which were exclusively owned by residents of The Central District. These second-grade healing crystals restored not only external but also internal injuries. When the Roux Family arrived, Remus and Melinda were set to meet with the village's primary Healing Mage and treated with the crystals.

To avoid suspicion or recognition, the caravan rode on

a restricted pathway used only by the Grand Elders and Head Mages. This passage sat next to where the forest and the river met. On the bright side, this path was a perfect place for Lucian to view all the various districts and their unique architecture, including their massive security gates.

In a low but anguished tone, Remus muttered, "That's where *we* used to live."

Lucian followed his father's gaze to Caelum's most distinguished and valued district, apart from The Central District, of course. This district housed the first-grade officials and the most celebrated Reincarnates, including Elias Daye himself. It also was the district where his family lived before his disastrous Placement Ceremony.

Districts held no official titles or "names," but they were delegated certain tasks, and their inhabitants were endowed with ranks and rewards. Only the gates had specifications. Gate I, Gate II, Gate III...all the way to Gate VIII.

Eight Districts in total with perfectly impenetrable gates.

Aside from The Fallen District, most villagers were afforded mobility between districts until curfew. Each Gate had active guards constantly monitoring them. Promotion to another district was gained through occupational tests or significant contributions to the village. Marriage served as a rare exception. The details of

Caelum's marriage laws slipped his mind, as he saw no interest in things like love.

Not that anyone would have any romantic interest in him anyway.

Lucian's District, while not as prestigious, was surprisingly normal. His family lived between Gates IV and V. While the Roux Family wasn't assigned a special duty in an occupational-based community, the state of his district wasn't that lacking in comparison to the upper districts. Every district had the same fundamental services for a sustainable and comfortable life: water, food, and shelter. The disparity lay in the fact that the upper districts had greater value to The Var. Thus, they were bestowed extra privileges, including the finest educations, amenities, and medicines.

Even the lowest districts were treated with a base level of resources beyond survivability alone. These districts consisted of family units and individuals living between Gates VII to VIII. They were either manual laborers or families without Reincarnates. Although rare, male children could be born without a godly connection.

Ironically, Lucian's status placed him above the lowest districts, even though he was socially treated worse than them. Although openly condemned, he was technically still a Reincarnate—a status that couldn't be ignored within his strictly hierarchal village.

In one cautious but swift motion, Melinda leaned over and retied the loosened fabric. His vision was obstructed. He looked at her confused and frustrated. Before he could voice his feelings, Lucian watched as she flicked her eyes to the front, revealing the envoy was monitoring his movements.

He sighed and then relaxed.

He closed his eyes.

The caravan abruptly stopped. The envoy left the front seat and rounded the caravan to unfasten the ties. One by one, they exited. A grandiose yet disturbing building stood before them: The Sanctuary of Gaia.

Out of all the establishments in Caelum, The Sanctuary of Gaia was the most ornately decorated. Marble pillars, freestanding sculptures, and myriads of murals were a few of its awe-inspiring features. But this place held a deeper meaning for Lucian, as it was where he was condemned to an unwanted present and a desolate destiny.

"Mr. Remus and Mrs. Melinda Roux," the escort said, "an Apprentice Mage will arrive shortly to escort you to the Head Healing Mage."

The escort turned to Lucian and emotionlessly said, "Follow me. The Elders are expecting you in The Grand Hall."

Since Lucian was unscathed, he was obligated to report to the Elders first. From Lucian's prior experiences, these *reports* tended to be more like an interrogation than an investigation.

He followed the escort through long hallways adorned by blood-red carpets and portraits of the living and deceased Elders. However, even the living members featured in the portraits were as good as dead. Their eyes were soulless, and their deflated faces were downright disgusting. His focus momentarily flashed to Master Felix's portrait, who was the only good fruit among the rotten bunch. The portraits of the previous Vars were even more atrocious. All of them had pointy noses with bushy eyebrows and hollow eyes.

After minutes of walking down straight hallways, Lucian and the escort rounded the corner and reached their destination: The Grand Trial Room. Stationed in the center of The Sanctuary as well as isolated within multi-layered barriers, this meeting room even had its very own fancy, dome-shaped rooftop.

The escort approached the enormous wooden doorway and placed his hand onto an empty circle. He infused energy into the magic circle, causing the right door to unlock and automatically open inward. Lucian approached the entrance but was stopped.

"Take off the garb," the escort said.

Lucian ripped off the cloth and shoved it at the guard. Now that Lucian stood before the entrance, he hesitated.

A tight ball of nervousness entangled in his stomach. He suppressed it and headed inside, expecting nothing less than a harsh, unfair sentence.

All of this for a single stupid room? He clicked his tongue. *What a waste of Mons.*

Lucian took his place in the center of The Council of Elders. His eyes adjusted to the brightness of the illumination crystals and the faces of his condemners: a pack of ancient ghouls with their ghastly-white features and wrinkles.

All but one.

Master Felix sat on the east wing of the first row.

His mentor's presence alone relaxed him.

After mentally steeling himself, Lucian's eyes followed the line of Elders until he reached The Var. Even as their eyes met, The Var remained silent. Instead, Elder Pershing, the Elder who represented the District of Rituals, was the first to speak, no, to mock Lucian.

"You haven't been here since your Placement Ceremony, have you?" Elder Pershing scoffed. "You should be grateful we haven't summoned you before this incident. Your record of defiling sacred rituals precedes you."

This was the very man, no, the monster who conducted Lucian's Placement Ceremony: the ritual that determined the godly soul residing in him. Elder Pershing was the judge who condemned Lucian to a life of eternal discrimination and suffering. In order not to prove the Elder right with his response, Lucian outright ignored the distasteful comment.

"You're a failure and a despicable rat!" Elder Crane shouted, another one of The Var's cronies. "How dare you ignore Elder Pershing."

Other Elders felt pressured to act, adding to Elder Crane's berates. Their voices rose like a wave, flooding him with vile insults and baseless rumors. It was easy to block out the garbage that the Elders dumped on him, but there was one thing Lucian couldn't stomach: The Var, who idly watched as it all happened, smiled.

After a few more minutes of being subjected to these insults and threats, The Var raised his hand. The multitude of voices ceased. His authority was absolute. It was time for the true test.

"Young Lucian," The Var said, "it's time for you to tell the truth about the recent incident."

Even though his words were to fall on deaf ears, Lucian explained, "I believe the attacker to be an outsider. He ransacked my house and hurt my family. When I returned home, he was nowhere in sight, but the damage had already been done."

Expressions of disbelief appeared on the Elders' faces. The barrier guarding the village was believed to be impenetrable.

"Your words are blasphemy," Elder Crane accused. "You should be executed for your lies!"

"I'm not lying," Lucian said. "Why would I lie? Also, why would I report to The Council if I was the culprit? If I were guilty, I would've fled or hidden the evidence."

"There were no other witnesses," she said, "and your sister is still missing."

"What about the evidence?" Master Felix interjected.

"There was none," she argued, lying like a viper. "Everything was burned in the fire."

"There was no fire," Master Felix stated. "Elder Maroon went to restore the house's condition, and he reported there were no signs of burn marks or ashes. Broken glass and blood stains were the primary evidence, suggesting an armed struggle took place more akin to an assault than an arson."

She sneered and said, "Why are you protecting an inevitable Fallen One? Oh, right, you're that monster's teacher. Hah! Looks like the apple doesn't fall far from the tree, does it?"

"Silence," The Var ordered. "Even if it was an intruder, how did you know about his existence if you didn't see him during the attack?"

Lucian had two equally unfavorable choices: expose his disobedience for not reporting the outsider or live as a liar.

Suddenly, a stroke of luck graced him. The guard who

escorted him from earlier entered the room and hastily approached The Var.

He whispered something into The Var's ear and then departed. The Var's expression darkened, and he concluded the interrogation.

"You are all dismissed," The Var announced. "I will decide on Lucian Roux's punishment at a later date."

Every Elder, besides Master Felix, looked dissatisfied with the results of the trial. During the interrogation, they acted like ravenous wolves ready for the kill. Anything less than Lucian's decapitated head was a failure in their books.

With a sense of relief, Lucian exited The Grand Trial Room after The Var. Since all of the Elders were caught up with other affairs, he managed to slip away and decided to meander while waiting for his father and Melinda to be treated and released.

While wandering, Lucian avoided several patrolling guards, as he scurried in and out of abandoned rooms, hid behind stone statues, and ducked behind doorways. Coincidentally, he managed to return to The Grand Hall. Passing through, he sighted some apprentices and Master Mages, but he avoided them all the same.

After mindlessly roaming, a man with a familiar cloak caught his attention on his way down the straight and endless hallway. He cautiously approached what looked like an office.

He poked his head slightly past the door frame to look inside, and he found Master Felix. His office was rather plain but had an elegant air to the room. It was lined with shelves of books that were different from the ones displayed in the observatory.

Lucian then turned his attention to Master Felix himself. His mentor was mumbling under his breath, and he seemed rather distracted and distraught.

A sudden chiming filled the air, and Master Felix immediately responded. It originated from a metal device sitting on his wooden desk. Lucian watched as a holographic image materialized. The image was too tiny for him to see in his position, so he leaned forward to see more clearly.

With a firmer and slightly louder tone, Master Felix said, "I know what you're going to say, so please spare me the lectures."

"Humph," a raspy female voice responded. "Report. How's the boy? This is a crucial time for him and us. You know what will happen if we don't make a move before The Harvesting begins..."

"He's on the right track," Master Felix confirmed. "Everything is falling into place. Now, we just have to..."

Lucian was so engrossed in the conversation that his hand pushed a little too hard on the door. *Creak!* His mentor's attention went straight in his direction. Lucian instantly retreated and rushed to the nearest turn in the hallway.

Oh, no! Oh, no! Oh, no! If he finds out it was me, I'll be dead meat!

His back was against the wall directly around the corner. He frantically scanned for a place to hide. His heart pounded furiously and sweat trickled down his forehead.

A pair of footsteps echoed down the hallway, but they weren't approaching him. After checking and re-checking that the footsteps were off in the distance, he relaxed his tense muscles and wiped the sweat off his brow.

Too close. He sighed, allowing himself to breathe. *That was way too close.*

With the crisis averted, Lucian tried to make sense of what he had just witnessed... Since Master Felix's back was partially blocking his view, he couldn't identify who the person was, but he determined that it was someone Master Felix didn't want anyone to know about. His mentor's tone was too serious and too jittery.

He was acting like a different person.

Lucian was so preoccupied with his thoughts that he forgot about his surroundings. Out of nowhere, a hand rested itself on his shoulder and slightly squeezed it. His mouth dropped, his eyes widened, and his heart quickened, as he turned to look at the figure.

Please not him! Please not him! He pleaded, bracing himself. *I'm so dead!*

Expecting to see Master Felix, a sense of relief washed over him, as he realized who it *actually* was. Upon identifying the figure, Lucian spoke words that he never thought he would in his entire lifetime.

"Thank the gods," he mumbled, staring into a familiar pair of cold, silver eyes.

6

THE FALLEN

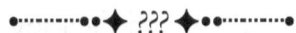

Without warning, Lucian was engulfed by the Darkness. It slithered and wrapped around him like a snake. It overwhelmed him, forcing itself down his throat, chattering in his ears, and pouring out of his eyes like tears.

He couldn't scream. He couldn't cry. He couldn't blink. His fears choked him. As soon as he was released from its deathly grasp, he closed his eyes, shut his mouth, and interlocked his hands together. He did the only thing he could think of: He prayed to *them*. To the wicked and depraved gods who endlessly tortured him. What did he pray about?—About his cursed fate, his miserable existence, and his tortured soul.

A child's laughter broke through the eerie silence. White light vanquished the Darkness.

He found himself standing in a blank space.

The color suddenly splattered on the pure-white scenery and whisked him away to a nostalgic scene.

Three figures danced in a field of flowers. Their faces were blurred, but their voices were clear. The thinnest figure had a soft, soothing voice: his mother. The bulkier figure was his father, whose rough voice was gentler. The small, fragile figure was himself, foolishly happy.

The three figures turned to him. Each smiled. His heart broke at the sight of them and their joy. Then, they disappeared. He closed his eyes, tears threatening to fall. He was thrust into another more serious and haunting memory.

He was back in that *room*.

Reopening his eyes, his view was obstructed. He could only see what was right before him. Everything seemed foreign and frightening. His hands were smaller. His words were caught in his throat. Gripped tightly in his hands was his lucky marble: his one-and-only treasure.

He soon realized that he was reliving The Placement Ceremony: the ritual that had cursed him as the Reincarnate of the god of destruction, Morpheus.

His attention turned to Elder Pershing, who spoke unintelligible phrases.

Lucian was four years old again, and he obediently

followed instructions. Elder Pershing's gaze and tone were soft as he instructed Lucian. The Elder's words were stale but not cruel. Not yet at least. Lucian was told to place his right palm on The Selection Stone.

So pretty, his four-year-old self thought.

The Selection Stone was marvelous. It was as tall as fourteen-year-old Lucian. Its markings were entrancing. Like streams of tears, a gold-and-blue light spilled out of its core. He was lifted off his feet and placed onto a set of stairs to reach the stone. It had a crevice that fit his child-sized hand perfectly. He climbed the stairs and placed his palm in the space.

The stone shook, sending shockwaves throughout the entire room. Its colors changed into an ominous red and black, summoning uncontrollable flames. The flames seared the sides of the stone as well as the surrounding area. It even burned him. And ultimately, it scared him.

He was on the verge of tears.

He looked at Elder Pershing, whose expression frightened him even more than the stone's meltdown. The Elder ripped Lucian's hand off the circle and threw him to the ground. The flames and shaking stopped, but upon falling, his favorite marble fell out of his pocket and split into two pieces upon impact.

He couldn't understand. He hadn't done anything

wrong. No, how could he have? He was only four years old. Only four years old...

Then, Lucian's perspective changed. Now, he was viewing his four-year-old self as an observer. He watched as his former self cowered and shook on the floor. His past self's cries were coldly ignored. At that time in his life, there was no way he could've comprehended the repercussions of the stone's results. But now, he knew—now, he fully understood the ramifications of what he was to become: a monster of irreconcilable destruction.

From that moment on, Lucian was looked at differently. He was a cursed child, a future Fallen One, and a disturbance. Being Fallen ultimately had nothing to do with his current life but rather had everything to do with the ancient god residing within him.

He had just been born unlucky.

"I can't believe this!" Lucian heard Elder Pershing exclaim, continuing the traumatic memory. "I thought we successfully sealed Morpheus's soul away. What is this *abomination*?"

Lucian's child self was dragged out of the room. He was treated worse than an animal. Even when Lucian wailed and begged for comfort, he only received an intense glare from the Elder and violent motions herding him out of the testing area.

Watching this exchange made his current self ignite with anger. The true monsters were the ones who would curse an innocent child to fulfill their ridiculous customs. Nonetheless, this was reality—the reality of a village still shackled to a worthless religious system and countless inhumane traditions.

Fallen or not Fallen, no child—no human deserved this type of treatment.

The name of his predecessor rang in his ears repeatedly. Out of all the gods, Lucian was the Reincarnate of Morpheus: the god who destroyed The Heavenly Pillars, which was the direct link from The Heavenly Realm to The Earthly Realm. *That* evil god.

THE SLAM OF A DOOR AWOKE LUCIAN WITH A startle. His body hurled forward. He had been trapped in a nightmare. His pajama shirt was drenched with sweat. He was slightly feverish and a bit drowsy. Rubbing the crust from his eyes, he slowly prepared for the day.

After changing his clothes, he went down for a late breakfast. He was surprised that his father hadn't come in and burst down the door since he overslept, but he deduced his father was still too shaken from what had happened several days prior.

The results of The Council's investigation were delivered to Remus by a messenger: The Var had ordered Lucian to be placed under house confinement. Until the culprit was found, Lucian was to remain the prime suspect. His house confinement would remain in effect only until the dual Succession Ceremony. Regardless, to Lucian, this punishment was nothing less than a prison sentence.

Reaching the bottom of the stairway, Lucian saw two papers on the table: an informal note and an official letter addressed to him.

The note was from Melinda, who reported that she and Remus had to meet with the Council to discuss Rosalie's disappearance and provide their testimonies.

Paired with the note was a Credit Slip worth 10,000 units. Credit Slips were only distributed to and used by members of The Fallen District, so he wouldn't have been familiar with them if not for Master Felix showing him one in the past.

Unlike the Mon, which was a coin, the Credit Slip was paper, a mixture of purple and dark blue coloring its surface. It felt smooth but somewhat slippery. The "10,000" number was painted boldly in the center of the slip. Etched into each of the corners was a unique symbol: In the upper right corner, there was a black sword; in the upper left corner, there was a treasure chest; in the bottom right corner, there was a ship; and in the bottom left corner, there was a white pillar like the ones at The Sanctuary of Gaia.

What a cruel joke, Lucian thought to himself. *It's like she's already condemning me to The Fallen District.*

After disposing of the written note, he opened the letter next. Based on his *unique* handwriting, Lucian deduced that Master Felix was the sender. He wondered why his mentor sent a letter, instead of waiting to talk to him in person. But even more curiously, the letter was blank. Completely devoid of words.

Oh, wait! Let's try this!

Taking in a deep breath and recalling a happy memory, he infused a sliver of his energy into the paper. Slowly, words started to form. There were only two sentences, but the message appeared urgent:

"Come to the observatory immediately after you receive this letter. Time is of the essence."

For a moment, Lucian was conflicted about whether to stay or to leave. However, his loyalty to Master Felix outweighed his fear of The Var. He quickly took his father's beaten, ragged green cloak off the coat hanger on the first floor and put it on. When he finally decided to leave the house, he checked what the outside situation looked like through the kitchen window.

Although the punishment was supposedly house arrest, The Var didn't seem all that worried about Lucian disobeying his order. Perhaps because it would draw too much attention or because The Var knew Lucian wasn't as much of a threat as The Var claimed him to be, there were *no* guards posted outside the house.

After making an uneventful escape, Lucian headed for the observatory. Just to be safe, he chose a series of seemingly "random" trails. However, these trails had been carefully selected by Lucian and ultimately led to his intended destination.

While weaving in and out of alleys and through bushes, Master Felix's strange words and actions during the festival and in his office consumed Lucian's mind with doubt and confusion. Even so, years of knowing and trusting his mentor trumped his suspicions.

Before Lucian reached the observatory's entrance, Master Felix flung the door open. His mentor displayed an anxious expression and yanked him inside. Master Felix locked the door behind them and checked to see if anyone had followed Lucian. Master Felix seemed too cautious. No one wanted to enter The Fallen District, except the two of them, so what was with all of the urgency and the secrecy?

"I believe you," Master Felix said. "There *is* an outsider

in the village. I need you to rescue him. I don't have time to explain. Here, take this!"

Lucian was handed a rusty key and a leather-bound notebook. Everything happened so fast. From the nightmare to this odd turn of events, he couldn't fathom why his mentor was so keen on helping an outsider who attacked Lucian's family and threatened the village. This request was contradictory to Master Felix's previous warnings.

"But—"

"If you trust me, please do me this favor," Master Felix pleaded. "Once all of this is over, I'll tell you everything. Any questions you have, I promise I'll answer them. Can you do it?"

"Where is he...?" Lucian asked, hesitantly. "I trust you, Master Felix, but it's all too confusing. Why me? Why not you? If you give me a reason, I'll go, but I can't just ignore the outsider's hostile actions."

"We don't have time, but the outsider isn't who you think he is. As for his location, he's confined within the deepest part of the underground prison cells beneath the ruins of The Heavenly Pillars," his mentor hastily explained. "I'm an Elder. If I'm found anywhere near the cells, I'll be suspected of treason and lose my leverage. You're the only one who can save him. You know what it's like to feel trapped, right? I beg of you."

Lucian tightly clutched the key, stuffing it into his pants pocket and the larger notebook into his cloak's inner pocket. Stifling any emotional response, he reminded himself that he was already fourteen—a responsible adult who knew what was right and wrong.

The *right* option, in this case, was to save the outsider from suffering what he lived through daily, even if the outsider was someone who shouldn't exist within the village. Lucian also needed to ascertain for himself whether the outsider was truly worth saving after hearing his reason for attacking his family. Something Lucian would have to decide after he confronted the outsider in person.

"The ruins of The Heavenly Pillars are too exposed. I'll be easily discovered," Lucian said. "How can I sneak past the guards?"

After hearing those words, Master Felix seemed to have an epiphany, running up the spirals of stairs and rummaging through a storage bin on the top floor.

One by one, items fell from the sky. After the shower of items ceased, his mentor reappeared before Lucian, holding a thin scepter with a pointy purple jewel stuck to the end of it.

"A Mage's best friend is his scepter," Master Felix said, excitedly. "If you chant a spell, then the scepter will translate it and respond with a reaction. Got it?"

"Master Felix, I don't know that many spells!" Lucian

protested. "I don't even know the spell for hypnosis or petrification."

A knock interrupted Master Felix's indecipherable explanation, and a look of fright crossed his face.

"It's time to go," Master Felix urged.

Lucian was quickly ushered to the back entrance and told to cross the river to the ruins.

"Be careful, Lucian. Not everything you see in the ruins is what it appears to be," Master Felix warned. "If you don't know a spell, then call on the gods. They will protect you."

Lucian scoffed at the thought of the gods, but he hesitated to fully denounce them, as he remembered the way he desperately pleaded to them during his recent nightmare. Lucian barely had time to formulate his next thought, as Master Felix was already approaching the front door to greet his unexpected guest.

Without a moment's delay, Lucian fled from the observatory to where the river met the forest. This crossing was the most desolate as well as the safest place—this being the place where the river's water level was lowest. However, no one dared to approach the area because it too was deemed forbidden by The Var. A common theme amongst the village laws and taboos.

Lucian had spent the last several hours hiding in a nearby bush and concocting a plan to sneak past the guard. The guard in question was one of The Sanctuary's Apprentice Mages, and he had an intimidating mien. After a while, the guard suddenly grabbed onto his stomach and headed for a different, thicker patch of bushes to relieve himself.

This is my chance!

Lucian took out the scepter for reassurance and sprinted toward the entrance, where the underground prison cells were located. The entrance was covered in a disgusting array of fungus, moss, and other slimy substances.

By pure luck, Lucian managed to enter before the guard returned to his post. As soon as he ran inside, he was met with darkness. His eyes had yet to adjust properly, so he had to traverse stealthily, taking one step at a time.

After a few minutes of walking, Lucian arrived at a staircase. Using the wall for support, he descended the stairs as quickly and quietly as possible. Not able to see where he was stepping, he argued with himself about whether he should cast an illumination spell or not.

Thankfully, random illumination crystals were hung on the damp and dirty walls when he reached the bottom of the staircase. He expected to encounter a few guards, but there were none. Aside from the guard who stood outside, there was no one else. It seemed irregular and strange. But he soon realized why...

The first cell that he passed by emanated a black mist and a godsawful stench.

Getting back on track, Lucian kept walking while gagging. He didn't know exactly where the outsider was confined, but Lucian knew he would eventually run into him. However, the more cells he passed, the more uncertain he became. One consistent theme that he came across in all of the cells was faded murals. Each cell had a mural etched into its walls about the history of a specific Fallen god or goddess.

The murals were chilling.

Some of the gods and goddesses, who descended into The Fallen Realm and turned into wretched Fallen Ones, were depicted as vile creatures. They devoured humans, tortured animals, destroyed worlds, and roamed endlessly.

He gulped down a squeal. Now, he *really* didn't want to see Morpheus's mural, if there was one at all. If the Fallen god living within him was a man-eater of all things, then he would've lost his will to continue further into the ruins.

Another consistent theme was an uncomfortable absence. At this point, he had seen at least ten to fifteen empty cells and no sign of prisoners at all. He examined every cell aside from the first one, eventually arriving at the end of the corridor. What he saw there was more disheartening than any of the preceding murals: another set of stairs.

He descended the stairs with more haste than before. Unlike the first set of stairs, however, he found ancient scripts scribbled on the walls of the stairway. He couldn't read them, but the messy way they were written was like that of a lunatic. He intentionally ignored them.

Near the bottom of the second set of stairs, there was one coherent and neatly written phrase, which he did take the time to translate: "*Memento quod cecidit: hi quia non adjiciet ut resurgat.*"

"Remember the Fallen," he read aloud, "for they will rise again."

No, no, no. I don't want those man-eaters roaming Gaia again, even if they were once gods and goddesses.

A sharp clang brought him back to his mission. He fumbled through his pockets for Master Felix's notebook. Squinting his eyes and holding the notebook up to the illumination crystals, he scribbled down the strange words.

He then cautiously tiptoed down the stairs until he

reached flat ground. The noise seemed to be coming from the cell at the end of the corridor.

He approached the cell, which was hidden in shadows. He couldn't tell whether there was an occupant inside or not. Unlike the first set of cells, this one didn't have any black mist or a ghastly stench exuding from it.

As he inched toward the cell, he fumbled for the key in his pocket. He pulled it out and nervously stuck the key into the lock, twisted it, and carefully opened the cell's door. He tried to withdraw his hand. But it was too late. Far too late.

A moving shadow—a dark figure—lunged at him. Lucian reflexively shut his eyes out of fear. A bony hand caressed his neck. He jumped backward, falling to the ground. Lucian opened his eyes to find a skeleton with its arms wrapped around him. Withholding a whimper, he threw the godsawful thing off him.

Before he could gain any composure, the outsider came out of the cell. In a split second, a rather intimidating expression on the outsider's face transformed into muted laughter.

"Hahaha!" the outsider snickered. "You can't be serious! What a coward! Are you crying!?"

"You—You!"

"Now that I've had my fun, let me get straight to the point. I don't know who you are or why you're releasing me, but thanks," the outsider said. "Oh, that's right. You don't know who I am, do you? I'm Aaron, Aaron Knight. You?"

The outsider offered his hand to Lucian. Lucian hesitated, still leery of the suspected attacker. He grabbed his hand, letting Aaron lift him to a standing position. Lucian then offered to shake hands as a courtesy rather than gratitude.

"I'm Lucian Roux. Master Felix said to come and save you. He made it seem like saving you was important. I don't know why. You looked pretty content in that cell over there."

"Come on! That's not even a funny joke. How could a lovable and bright person like *me* live in such a gross place like *that*?" Aaron replied, obnoxiously batting his eyelashes.

Lucian sneered and said, "Says the person who wrecked my house and hurt my family."

"Listen, it's not like I wanted to ransack your house. I was, well, forced to. And I didn't attack anyone. The house was empty when I arrived," Aaron defended.

"Then, what about my sister?" Lucian asked. "She's been missing for the past few days. If you didn't kidnap her, then *who* did?"

"Maybe the same twisted freaks that locked me up in that fine-looking cage over there." Aaron brooded. "I swear, having a skeleton as my inmate isn't a dream come true, you know?"

Lucian refused to believe him. Even if The Var and the Elders were lying weasels, they had no records of kidnapping lest they direct suspicion on their absolute authority and tarnish their good standing. He had lived long enough to know that their greatest fear was to lose their prestigious reputation.

If the culprit wasn't the outsider, then Lucian had to consider other options. After whittling down the list, there was only one evil mastermind that could construe such a convoluted plan. But exposing that person would be too much of a gamble... After all, Lucian couldn't risk falsely accusing the most regarded and beloved idol of the village.

Lucian held on to one hope: If it really was *him*, then Rosalie was safe...for now.

7

THE SUCCESSION CEREMONY

 *Caelum*

The morning of Lucian's Succession Ceremony, Rosalie returned. As if coming back from an errand, Rosalie entered the house when Lucian and Melinda were eating breakfast in silence. Upon seeing her daughter, Melinda's gaunt expression turned to a bright, relieved smile. While Rosalie's return was cause for celebration, her behavior was *weird*.

At first, Rosalie seemed emotionally distant. However, almost as if a spell had been lifted, Lucian watched as she regained her senses. Tears welled in her eyes, falling and pattering against the floorboards. Her tears startled and yet relieved him at the same time.

Rosalie's perfectly timed return in time for his ceremony and her memories regarding the situation were concerning. When he asked her where she was taken and who had abducted her, she appeared puzzled. She told him she couldn't remember anything after the day of the attack or the identity of her kidnapper.

Her memories had been completely erased, leaving her kidnapper's identity unresolved.

What's going on? If my theory is correct, then Elias should've been the kidnapper, but he can't use that type of complex mind magic, can he?

The ominous toll of The Holy Chapel's bells forced him to put aside his speculations, as the time ticked on leading to his sentence of eternal damnation. He was overwhelmed with a terrifying feeling—a feeling that induced a cold sweat.

With nothing but negative thoughts, he headed upstairs to put on his ceremonial robes.

Instead of the muted grays and blacks that he normally wore on less auspicious occasions, today, he wore an outfit specially bestowed by The Var himself. Like The Var's own garb, the robe was a pure-white color with two vertical gold lines running down the shoulders. Lucian had no idea what the Grand Elder was thinking, giving him such a luxurious garment, but he couldn't complain.

Tying the silk sashes that adorned the robes was a pain since his arms couldn't stretch that way. Unexpectedly,

Melinda offered to tie them herself. Since this was most likely the last time he would see her in his earthly life, he accepted her assistance. He noticed she was especially careful not to tie anything too tight or tug too harshly. It was like she was apologizing to him but without saying a single word. He felt unexpected gratitude through her care.

But this kind gesture wasn't enough to quell his nerves.

A mixture of emotions squirmed in his stomach and pressed on his heart. No tears fell. No anger welled up. He had partially given up on everything. He had known from the start that this would happen. He had no future. His thirst for adventures and want for happiness was too much to hope for.

A Fallen life was no life at all. It was akin to a death sentence. He was to fade away and rot like the rest of them. But before he completely disappeared, he needed to ensure that his family didn't follow in his footsteps.

"Melinda, I know we've never been on the best terms, but I need to ask you for a favor," he said, his voice slightly shaking. "Once I'm gone, you're the only one who can protect Rosalie. She's your flesh and blood, and I know you love her. You can't let him break her. You can't let that barbarian and drunkard hurt her again. Promise me that you'll protect her in my place."

His stepmother finished tying his sashes and straightening his robes. For the first time, her facade slightly cracked. He didn't press her any further. He didn't expect her to answer or promise anything. Now that he had prepared himself for his inevitable fate, he allowed himself to forgive her. Even though, he used to resent her in his heart.

He realized something so fundamental that altered his stance toward her: Her choice to stand in silence was all she could do. She was powerless as an outsider. He was cursed in his circumstances. They were both just unlucky. Ultimately, it was neither of their faults.

Instead, it was *his*.

Lucian's wandering thoughts about his future and his relationships were disrupted by a comforting hand squeeze. He looked down expecting Rosalie's hand to be holding his, but, to his surprise, it was Melinda who wrapped her palm around his hand, giving him a final sense of assurance. A sense of security. His expression softened, and he lightly squeezed her hand back.

With a slight nod, he thanked her and departed for The Holy Chapel. If his future was set in stone, then there was nothing that he could do to avoid it. He accepted everything with a melancholic smile. This was his resolve. This was his punishment for his predecessor's past. It was time that he finally gave up and followed his fate.

As Lucian walked, his lips tugged into a small smile at the thought of his last act of defiance: He had released the outsider. That Aaron kid was safe. He clearly remembered the events at the ruins. When they escaped the cells and fled from them, Lucian hid the outsider in Master Felix's observatory. Even though Master Felix was away when they arrived, Lucian was certain that his mentor would protect Aaron. After all, Master Felix was the very one who pleaded with Lucian to rescue Aaron, and Master Felix had both the position and power to protect him.

When the last toll of the bells rang, Lucian reached the entrance of The Holy Chapel. His mind was filled with conflicting thoughts so much so that he hadn't even noticed the piercing stares of the villagers stationed outside their houses tracking his every step.

Since they couldn't attend, they made it their mission to express their thoughts about the ceremony. Fortunately, the villagers weren't armed with physical weapons, as the Succession Ceremony was considered a sacred ritual.

One of the Elders stood outside The Holy Chapel, verifying the identities of the permitted attendants. As soon as the Elder recognized him, Lucian was ushered into the preparation room located behind the high-rise platform. It was a spacious room with only a few pieces of furniture.

Elias hadn't arrived yet, so Lucian used his last moments to reflect. He deeply regretted his previous interactions with the inhabitants of The Fallen District. Lucian had spent most of his life in a discriminatory and judgmental atmosphere, so he hadn't realized he too had played his part as a hypocrite. He had used their pitiful existences to make himself feel better.

At least, he had a roof over his head.

At least, his family talked to him.

At least, he had food to eat and water to drink.

All these thoughts were now disturbing reminders of his foolishness and immaturity. He had to apologize to them when he transferred to The Fallen District, if their souls hadn't already been sent to The Fallen Realm.

The door creaked open, revealing not his expected counterpart but rather The Var's assistant: a scrawny, crazy-eyed, elderly man. Bereft of final words, Lucian followed the assistant to the platform. Since Lucian was short for his age, the bottom of his robe dragged across the marble-tiled floor.

Lucian ascended the stairs, scanning the seats to see the attendees. Remus, Melinda, and Rosalie were seated in the third row. He didn't recognize anyone else. Elias's parents, whom he had only seen once by coincidence, weren't present. He wondered what could've been more important than their son's ceremony, but it wasn't his business where they were or what they were doing. Nothing mattered anymore. Neither the jeers of the villagers nor the dreadful days with his abusive father. Everything was coming to an *end*.

The Var wore a superficial smile. The curl of his lips sent shivers down Lucian's spine. Directed by The Var's assistant, Lucian was forced to stand right next to The Var. Bony fingers grasped his shoulder blades. It reminded him of his previous encounter with the skeleton in the underground prison cells. He repulsively jerked away, causing a disturbance in the congregation. Forcing himself to relax, he suppressed his overflowing emotions.

It's just a hand, he reasoned. *You're fine, Lucian. Everything's fine.*

The Var whispered into his ear, "I didn't mean to frighten you. I'm often told that I'm quite a sneaky fellow. Before we begin, do you have any final questions?"

"Where's Elias?" Lucian asked, curtly.

"He will arrive shortly," The Var said, "But his absence is *not* your concern."

With that evasive explanation, The Succession Ceremony started. Similar to Silas's ceremony, The Var's ceremonial speech preceded the ritual. However, unlike the previous ceremonies, Lucian decided to pay special attention to The Var's traditional garble.

"From Gaia's breath of life, which constructed our magnificent world, to Leon's courageous decision to descend to The Earthly Realm, we are gathered here today to pay our respects to the ancient gods who still live among us," The Var recited. "I, The Var of Caelum, am but a mere messenger of the gods. I've been bestowed with the role of the translator and human judge. In the history recorded by my predecessors, we've never had either Morpheus or Adonis born within the same generation. Nay, not even in the same era. This is a symbolic sign of the village's prosperity and welfare. Morpheus, the infamous god of destruction, and Adonis, the revered god of creation. Now, I shall translate The Aegis's will into our language."

Once The Var's speech ended, Lucian was directed to where The Aegis stood. Lucian was handed the bejeweled dagger, slitting his right palm, following custom. The moment the sharp blade ran across his palm, Lucian flinched. He then stepped toward The Aegis. The closer he was, the more entranced he became by the fire that burned everlasting without wood or a catalyst. It was truly a miraculous entity.

He nervously gulped.

He slowly raised his hand and watched as the blood ran down along the creases of his palm. The trickle of blood turned into droplets and fell into the goblet, where the flames of The Aegis were to consume every drop.

Like with The Placement Ceremony, The Aegis violently reacted. Its normally captivating and calming blue hue transformed into a ghastly, pitch black. The flames grew at a startling rate, and they seemed to cackle at him with each crackle.

Lucian's body wouldn't retreat. His muscles locked into place. The entity's aura seemed to envelop him, drowning him in a familiar darkness and feeling exactly like his nightmares. He heard cries of agony resounding throughout the room.

A low but soothing voice said, "You—who have inherited my Master's soul and will—you must survive. Remember the Fallen, for they will rise again."

"Who are you, and why do you know those words!?" Lucian cried out.

Before Lucian could press again for a reply, flashes of light broke through the darkness. His consciousness and his scenery reverted to the ceremony.

When Lucian opened his eyes, he witnessed absolute chaos.

The black flames that had initialized the panic were nowhere to be seen.

Instead, a woman's cry was amplified by the screams and curses of the crowd.

"He really is cursed!" the woman shouted. "Did you see that? He absorbed the black flames! He extinguished The Aegis!"

Lucian's mind froze, and his body violently shook. He suddenly felt extremely cold, and his teeth chattered. The only place that didn't feel frozen was his chest, where he remembered the charred stone was tied around his neck. To the onlookers, Lucian's motions mirrored someone who had been possessed.

Lucian looked at The Var, whose face curled into a disturbing smile. No one saw the old man's vile expression but Lucian. While Lucian didn't have time to process what had happened, he knew the villagers would surely beat him to death regardless of the reason.

Without question, distinguishing the flames of The Aegis was an unforgivable sin in this superstitious village. Being labeled a Fallen One was no longer his biggest concern, but rather it was surviving this situation. His earlier thoughts of acceptance turned into a struggle for survival.

The Elders and Mages were on their way to seize him on the stage, but the sudden opening of the main Chapel's doorway suspended their approach. Racing into The Holy Chapel was a guard, who yelled his report to The Var, "Elder Felix has disappeared along with the intruder!"

Now, there was no redemption for Lucian, who had connections with both fugitives. Among the long list of sins that were deemed inexcusable was desertion: Master Felix had fled with the outsider. Being both the apprentice of Master Felix and the culprit who released the intruder from prison, Lucian was doomed.

His situation couldn't seem more dire.

Realizing that his garments were slowing him down, he ripped them off, revealing his father's murky green cloak. He frantically reached around in the cloak's pockets, searching for something—anything—useful.

There it is! he thought, triumphantly.

The scepter with the purple jewel was still snug in the cloak's inner pocket. Before anyone could approach him, he pulled out the scepter and latched onto the closest person, using them as a hostage. It just so happened that the closest person to him was The Var, the most important figure in the entire village.

Lucian pointed the scepter at The Var's chest. While this was a blatant bluff, it worked. The Elders and Mages retreated and pocketed their weapons. Lucian used their fears against them: For what could be worse than a berserk Fallen One killing their beloved Var?

Legend went that if a Fallen One was driven to insanity, the black flames of The Fallen Realm would materialize and burn the corpses of his aggressors. It was a convenient superstition.

The Var's usual, calm and collected expression, however, refused to budge.

"You can't escape your fate, Lucian Roux," The Var hissed. "Even if you escape now, your bloodied past will resurface and haunt you for eternity. Even if you kill me, nothing will change. You are bound to rot away, like the little devil that lives inside you!"

"Shut up!" Lucian shouted. "Enough with your lies. Leave me alone!"

"You sure know how to plan a party, Lucian Roux!" a familiar voice chuckled. "Let's end this farce with a bang!"

A sudden deafening crash and a cloud of smoke made the entire Chapel unnavigable. Amidst the chaos and confusion, someone grabbed Lucian's wrist and pulled him. A sliver of light revealed his snarky savior.

"Why are you here, Aaron!?" Lucian huffed, short of breath.

"No time to explain!" Aaron said, laughing like a maniac. "We need to get to the observatory, now! I found an escape route out of this crummy village."

After a frantic run through the streets leading to The Fallen District, they collapsed at the observatory's entrance. Master Felix was nowhere to be found. Lucian sat in shock, as the thought of Master Felix abandoning him lingered in his brain. He gasped for air, sweat drizzling down his face. While Aaron kept laughing and shouting about some irrelevant story, Lucian tried to recover his sanity and stamina.

"They'll be here any minute, now," Lucian said, wheezing out the words. "If we're going to leave, then we need to do it soon. The Sorcerers of this village are experts. They can track anyone, anytime."

"You overestimate their abilities." Aaron scoffed. "Besides, I told you that I already have a reliable escape route. You'll need to leave first, though. I still have something to do, but I'll follow you soon after. Unless you need someone to hold your hand like a little child?"

"I don't need a babysitter," Lucian pouted. "I'm worried about my family. What will happen to them?"

With a more severe tone, Aaron replied, "They'll be better off without you! This is for their good as well as your own. Stop thinking about something so selfless. Stop thinking too hard, in general. It doesn't suit you."

Without another word, Aaron guided him into the observatory, revealing the passageway hidden behind a stack of books. The thickness and heaviness of the books threatened to topple the stack over at any moment.

Aaron climbed over the unstable books, and Lucian followed closely behind. Then, Aaron pointed at a faded but familiar circle.

"Put your hand here, and infuse it with your mana," Aaron ordered.

"What's mana?" Lucian inquired, unfamiliar with the term. "Do you mean my energy?"

Lucian's question was ignored. He reluctantly placed his palm onto the circle and infused as much energy as he could manage with his worn-out state. It seemed to be just enough. The wall shook, causing some books to fall off the stack, which had been concealing the secret passageway's location.

Once the secret passageway fully opened, Lucian peered inside. Although seemingly impossible, it was even darker than the underground cell's staircases.

"If you're that frightened, then use an illumination spell," Aaron teased.

Lucian was about to retort, but it was of no use.

The brute of a boy shoved Lucian into the passageway, the entrance closing in response.

Squinting to see anything, Lucian yelled, "How are you supposed to follow me if you can't even activate a magic circle!?"

Silence answered.

He sighed.

Lucian cast the suggested illumination spell and walked forward. Wherever he was headed, he didn't know, and he honestly didn't care. He didn't even know if he could trust Aaron's words.

What he did know, however, was that his fate was no longer in the hands of some aloof, distant gods anymore: It was in his own.

8

MADAM OF THE MIRROR

 *Caelum*

The farther he walked, the more fear seized him. The scepter's radius of light extended only a few feet in front of him, and the stench of something rotten, or moldy, messed with his senses. He couldn't tell the time of day or where the end of the passageway was, and he was on edge like stalked prey.

After a while, his body began unnaturally heating—a scathing type of heat spreading through him. It felt like a severe sunburn. The strange sensation was at first concentrated in the center of his chest, but then it gradually flowed through the rest of his body. He thought it was a result of overexerting himself, but he was wrong.

Lucian touched the fabric covering his chest. It burned

as hot as the heat stones used in his village. Quickly, reaching from above, he pulled his collar down to reveal the source.

"What the—!?"

Without hesitation, Lucian ripped the cord off his neck and chucked it to the ground. The flesh directly beneath the stone had turned a grotesque purple-red color. After rubbing the raw area on his chest, he tried to regain his composure.

Casting his fears aside, he warily approached and closely examined the stone. Upon hitting the ground, the charred encasement, previously wrapped around the stone, had cracked open, revealing an alluring, dark-blue, and rose-red, triangular gem. From the gemstone, waves of purple energy emanated.

Not knowing what to expect, Lucian stood at the ready with his scepter. Out of nowhere, the stone started ascending upward, floating in the air. He backed up, giving it some space. The gemstone seemed to have a mind of its own, flitting back and forth erratically.

Master Felix's warning resurfaced in his mind... At all costs, Lucian had to keep its existence hidden. He couldn't let it escape.

With gritted teeth, Lucian braced himself and ran toward the stone, grasping it with his bare hand. He instantly regretted his decision, letting out a painful cry.

The energy pouring out of the stone was too strong, the heat not abating in the slightest.

"Crap!" he wailed, releasing his hold.

After a few more futile attempts, Lucian resorted to the only thing that he could think of: He fought the energy that forced its way out of the stone, using his own mana to subdue it. However, there was one problem. The more mana he infused into the stone, the hotter the stone became.

He stifled the urge to scream and smashed it onto the ground.

"What else can I do!?" he screeched while saying, the flesh of his palms sizzling. "C'mon Lucian, remember what Master Felix taught you! What would Master Felix do in a situation like this? He'd say, 'Seal it, Lucian.' That's right, I can seal it!"

During his tutelage, Lucian had only *read* about a single type of Sealing Spell, but he had to try lest his palm melted like cheese on a coal-burning stove.

"*Revincio!*" Lucian chanted, the heat rising to his forearm and then rapidly returning to the source.

It worked. It actually worked!

The stone had been successfully sealed.

After retrieving the stone from the air, Lucian assessed the damage. Ripping off a part of his cloak, he wrapped his affected hand and tightly fastened it into a makeshift bandage. He let out a long sigh of frustration, knowing his hand may remain unusable for some time, but that would be a worry for the future.

Not even a few minutes had passed when the gemstone started moving again. This time, however, something was clearly different. The gemstone rose from Lucian's palm with purpose. Instead of releasing overflowing energy, it forcibly tugged him forward, leading him further down the passageway. The stone was guiding him but to where?

Is this the sign of the gods that Master Felix mentioned?

Due to the stone's erratic behavior, Lucian stayed in a state of heightened alertness. After what seemed like an hour, the gemstone jerked him toward one of the walls. He stretched out his hands, bracing for a collision. Unlike the experience at the barrier, his hands slipped straight through the solid wall, and the rest of his body fell forward.

With nothing to counter his weight, he tumbled downward and fell flat on his chest.

Thud!

"You homicidal stone!" he screamed while assessing the damage.

Quickly standing up, he swung the scepter around, trying to figure out where exactly the stone had led him. The space itself was dimly lit, so he relied on the scepter's light. After being battered and bruised, he jostled the gemstone in his other hand, taking out his frustration on the object.

Not so surprisingly, the gemstone retaliated, thrusting him toward another wall. He barely avoided the collision, when his body seemed to trigger something.

One by one, hanging torches were lit, revealing his surroundings.

"What have you done!?" he shouted, reprimanding the gemstone.

As his eyes adjusted, his body froze.

What stood in front of him were five lit hallways all separated by thick, brick walls. It was like a maze with a myriad of entry and exit points. Most curious was the centerpiece: an ornate, marble pedestal with a mirror resting on top of it.

The gemstone thrust him toward the centerpiece, almost knocking it over.

"You're quite the forceful bugger, aren't you!?" he exclaimed, flicking it once more for good measure. "What else do you want from me..."

Realizing that he was arguing with a rock, Lucian turned his focus back onto the object sitting in front of him: the mirror. He pocketed the gemstone, reaching out with his free hand to touch the mirror.

But nothing happened.

He waited, but still, nothing happened.

All of this buildup, and for what? Stupid stone...

After a few moments of making faces in the mirror to pass the time, he lost interest and went on to explore the rest of the area. Only when he started moving away did he see something move out of the corner of his eye: A silhouette swooshed across the mirror's surface. His head whipped around, trying to see it again.

Do it one more time, he internally urged.

His eyes were trained on the mirror for any sudden movements. He pointed his scepter at it as a precautionary measure.

A distant shadow in the background of the mirror that looked like a smudge slowly grew larger and came to the forefront of the reflective glass. It appeared to be a figure with a veil covering its face. He squinted, trying to discern *who* or *what* it was.

Friend or *foe.*

He couldn't tell.

Lucian turned and looked behind him to ensure it wasn't a trap. That someone wasn't sneaking up behind him. After confirming his safety, he tried to start a conversation with the figure. Before he could speak a single word, the figure took off the veil covering its face, revealing a hideous creature.

"Felix!" the wretched-looking figure cried, banging her fists against the glass divider. "Where have you been? Don't tell me you forgot about our promise! Eternity is not something you can forget!"

A bit disturbed, Lucian retreated a few steps backward. That monster was a woman. She had bony horns curling out from the top of her head, scaly, green-toned skin, and iridescent neon-yellow eyes. Her opened mouth revealed fangs and razor-sharp teeth. Lucian reflexively flinched at the sight of her.

The woman, at some point, stopped raving and took a closer look at him.

Pursing her lips and clicking her tongue, she whined, "You're not Felix! I thought I recognized his mana, but I was mistaken. Whoever you are, I don't want to talk to you! Leave before my patience runs out."

Lucian, recovering from his initial shock, thought to himself, *Master Felix really should sort out his personal affairs. She's a complete nutcase.*

"I HEARD THAT!" she exclaimed, banging the surface with her fists.

A wave of guilt washed over him, and he said, "I'm sorry, friend of Master Felix."

He then remembered the cause of this conversation. Retrieving the gemstone from his pocket, he asked, "Do you recognize this stone? It sure gave me one heck of an unexpected struggle trying to reach you."

"How did you get that? I haven't seen it since..." She

abruptly stopped speaking. After several seconds of silence, she piped up by saying, "Ah! I remember who you are now! You're Lucian, Felix's little apprentice."

"What do you mean?" Lucian asked, warily. "He certainly never mentioned *you*."

"Of course, he didn't," she protested. "Because I'm— No, I don't have to explain myself to you. But this makes things easier. You'll be able to release me."

He lifted his brow, staring at the gigantic mirror with a look of disbelief.

"Why should I release you, when you've been nothing but rude to me ever since I arrived?"

"Because I know the way out and where you need to go next," she stated with a snarky tone. "You're just a child. How do you expect to navigate the outside world by yourself?"

Weighing the options in his head, Lucian swiveled toward the exit, bargaining that whatever guidance she could offer was *not* worth the headaches.

"W-Wait, you can't leave me!" she shrieked. "Fine, fine! I'll do whatever you want! Just take me with you!"

Faltering in his decision, Lucian turned back around and walked toward her. "Promise?"

"I swear on my name, Eteria, the goddess of eternal beauty," she recited.

Aside from the disparity between her title and her form, he went along with the conversation.

"You said that I can release you, but how am I supposed to get you out of that giant mirror?"

"Well, that's the easy part!" Eteria proclaimed, excitedly. "Just recite the word, '*Translatio*,' and that pretty gemstone of yours will be my new home."

Lucian hesitated, intently staring at the stone.

"How do I know that I can trust you?"

"We ancient gods and goddesses are bound by our word," Eteria explained. "If we break a sworn agreement, then we'll lose our agency and our powers."

With a nod, he said, "Well, a friend of Master Felix's is a friend of mine, I hope."

Fulfilling his end of the deal, he recited the spell, "*Translatio*."

The spell invoked wonders: A whirlpool of wind and light swirled around the mirror, pulling Eteria out of it. Before she was transferred into the gemstone, her beastly form turned into a multicolored mist—a form easier to exist as.

Once she was successfully transferred and settled into her new space, she wouldn't stop telling stories about Master Felix, swooning over Lucian's eccentric mentor.

"And then, and then, Felix said—" she recounted, giddily.

"Are you done yet?" Lucian asked, dismissing her mindless rambling. "Master Felix taught me the basics of the world, but I want to know more. You said you would take me to where I needed to go, right?"

"That way!" she directed, tugging him to one of the entryways in the hallway. "No, not that way. This way!"

After a straight minute of back-and-forth dragging and pulling, Lucian entered the second, right-most entryway. He went through another straight and narrow passageway, but, this time, the exit was in view. True to her words, there was something at the end of the tunnel. The rectangular object glowed a vibrant blue and mystical energy swirled within.

He gulped.

"Are you nervous?" she teased.

"What *is* that?" he asked, skeptically.

"It's a portal," she explained. "Most Mages use portals to travel to anywhere in Gaia."

"Has anyone ever died while passing through a portal?" he asked, suspiciously.

"Only one," she replied, "but you'll be fine. You're young, full of mana, and have an excellent guide. So, you don't need to worry one bit!"

Yeah, very trustworthy...

"Hey!" she yapped. "Quit acting like a little baby and

use the portal! You were the one who wanted to go to the outside world."

Eteria's words stung. As much as Lucian hated to admit it, she was right... His desire to be free and to adventure outweighed any of his reservations or hesitations. Besides, there truly was nothing left to lose.

Well, it's now or never.

The portal wasn't as dangerous as it initially seemed. It had an oval structure constructed of the same metal and marble in Caelum. On both sides, there were two activation circles. He rested his palms, infusing as much energy as he could muster on an empty stomach and a lack of sleep.

The portal miraculously reacted, opening a gate. The faint scent of pine wood and freshly baked bread overtook his senses. The unpleasant stench of the passageway was overtaken by the aromatic scents.

Following his nose, Lucian approached the gate.

The gemstone tugged him forward, nudging him to move faster.

I know, I know! You're such an impatient goddess.

Before Lucian stepped through the gate, memories of his homeland filled his thoughts. Since everything happened so fast, he didn't have the time to process what leaving the village meant. This really was a farewell to the only world he had ever known.

And so, he went...

Into a world outside the barrier...

A world outside his stale and isolated village...

To find his own freedom...

To carve out his own destiny.

He, who had once been shackled by his past and by a hopeless future, finally had taken his first step forward. Through the gate, he went.

9

THE GUIDE

 ???

Past the portal, a brilliant sun embraced him. The sublime scents of freshly roasted meat and baked bread intensified, causing his stomach to rumble. Lucian was so captivated by the delicious aromas that he kept his eyes closed and subconsciously ignored Eteria.

In response to tuning her out, Eteria lifted the gemstone and brutally struck him in the chest. The blow to his chest was so powerful that he fell on his knees. The wind had quite literally been knocked out of him.

"What did you do that for!?" Lucian whined, wincing from the pain.

"You're NOT listening to me!" Eteria shouted, the

gemstone shaking with her voice. "You better start listening, or else..."

"Or else, what?" Lucian asked. "It's not like you can do anything if I decide to throw you into some random trash can and seal the lid."

"Ungrateful little—" she mumbled, her words trailing off. Her brief silence made it seem like she was weighing her options. Instead of fighting anymore, she tried a different approach. She spiked her tone high and said as peppy as possible, "Welcome to Lunaris, the Kingdom of Light. The portal we took seems to have sent us somewhere outside of the capital city, Solaris, but we can make do."

"Were there portals in the other hallways? Did we take the wrong one?" he asked. "Aren't you supposed to be an all-knowing goddess. So, where are we?"

She nervously laughed in response. "I mean, there were, but I had a feeling that portal was the one, you know? In terms of where we currently are, well, that's a great question!"

"So, you don't know where we are *at all*?"

Silence.

"Whatever," he mumbled. "Why am I not surprised."

Observing more closely where they had been transported, his sightline rose from the gemstone to the new world awaiting him. His eyes twinkled and flitted around, trying to absorb the new sights.

Tall, white, sparkly towers and smooth, ivory-colored buildings glimmered in the sunlight. Even the greatest structures in Caelum, The Sanctuary of Gaia and The Holy Chapel, paled in comparison. The pathway beneath his feet was exquisitely crafted and bespoke of luxury as specks of white marble had been used as one of the materials.

Everything shone brightly in comparison to the dullness of his hometown.

Lucian headed through the town square. From the store windows to the townspeople themselves, he had never seen such vibrant colors. The women wore long, pink-and-purple dresses with dabs of red and orange accessories adorning their hair, while the men wore mainly solid white tunics with gold pins and chains. Such luxuries were only afforded to the Elders and for ceremonial processions in Caelum, so it surprised him to see *everyone* wearing them.

A quarter of the way into his sightseeing, his stomach growled.

He had been so captivated by this new place that he completely forgot about his hunger. Letting his nose be his guide, it led him to multiple food stalls lining the busy streets.

This bustling marketplace reminded him of The Rebirth Festival.

Before Lucian went to buy food at the stalls, he counted how many Mons he had in his pocket. Although the amount wasn't enough to buy a full meal, he was sure it was enough to purchase a light snack, at the very least. Another grumble sent him jogging to the nearest bread vendor. He approached the stall, watching the vendor sell one of her loaves to a couple. He dug around in his pocket and latched onto the Mons, shifting around the coins in his palms.

Once the vendor finished with her other customers, he pulled the Mons out of his pocket and handed them to her. She seemed to be taken aback by the coins and spent a moment examining them.

"I can't accept these coins," she said.

His shoulders slumped, and he said, "Ah, I thought I had enough to at least buy some bread..."

She shook her head at him.

"That's not the problem, young man," she explained. "I haven't seen this type of currency since I was a little girl. These coins have been out of commission for many years."

"What do you mean?" he asked, baffled. "I used these coins all the time back where I lived."

"Well, they're worthless here," she stated. "Do you have anything else, by any chance?"

Rustling through his pockets, Lucian carefully took out the Credit Slip from Melinda.

"I don't suppose I could buy a piece of bread with this slip?"

He handed the slip to the elderly vendor. Her reaction was unexpected.

"I-I've never seen this amount on a Credit Slip before in my entire life," she said in disbelief. "Young man, who gave this to you?"

"It was a gift from my stepmother. Is something wrong with it?"

"Nothing's wrong, but..." She pulled him closer to her. "I don't know what noble's family you're from but having this much on a Credit Slip will get you killed. With 10,000 units on this slip, you could be as rich as a king. Hide this away before anyone finds out."

Following her warning, he hastily stuffed it back into his pocket.

A soft, mature female's voice interrupted their conversation and asked, "Are you troubling another weary traveler, Madam Morgan?"

Lucian sought out the voice's owner. He turned to the side to find a beautiful woman, who looked to be in her mid-to-late twenties. She had smooth and silky caramel-colored hair that hung halfway down her torso. Hazel-colored eyes greeted him with an unusual perkiness. She looked like a real-life goddess, unlike his beastly-looking traveling companion.

"Nothing of the sort," Madam Morgan said, dismissively waving her hand. "This old hag is just trying to do her business."

"Don't say that about yourself," the young woman said. "Your bread is the best in the entire kingdom."

"You're too kind, Miss Coral," the elderly vendor said, "but you needn't flatter me."

After the brief interaction, the beautiful lady turned her attention to him. Lucian's mind went blank. He struggled to find the right words to say.

"You don't seem like a local," she said, leaning toward him. "Sorry for not introducing myself earlier. My name is Salía Coral, but you can call me 'Sal.' I work as a seamstress during the day and run a traveler's inn at night."

"Nice to meet you, Sal. My name is Lucian Roux. How'd you know I was a traveler?"

"Your..." She paused, pointing at his chest. "...clothes."

He looked down at his dirty-brown shirt, which was out of place among the other colorfully clothed townspeople.

I'm an absolute idiot. Of course, my clothes were what gave me away.

"Now, Lucian, if I had to guess...you don't have a place to stay for the night and are short on spending money, right? If you'd like, you're welcome to stay at my inn. *Free of charge.* How does that sound?"

Hesitantly, he asked, "Is that okay? I don't want to burden you."

"Of course!" she said, sweetly. "I'll show you around the town and then find you a room."

She rested her hand on his shoulder.

Suzzt.

"Ah!" she burst out, retracting her hand.

"I'm so sorry!" Lucian exclaimed. "Are you alright?"

"Just a static shock," she said, laughing it off.

When she touched him, Lucian also felt the shock. Rubbing the affected area, he couldn't help but feel like something was off. On the outside, Sal seemed nice. On top of that, he didn't have anywhere to stay that night, so he dismissed his gut reaction. After that incident, however, she always maintained a fair distance.

After being shown around the town square and the shopping districts, they headed to her inn. Unlike the other radiant buildings, her inn was a small, quaint, wooden building located outside of the town near a surrounding pine forest. Apparently, she wasn't a fan of crowded places, so she asked the builder to construct the inn on the outskirts. The inn was two stories high with a front desk and a restaurant downstairs. Five rooms, in total, were on the second floor.

Sal welcomed Lucian inside and led him up the stairs to the second floor, directing him to the room closest to the stairway for *his* convenience. After giving him a mini tour of the second floor, she left him to his own devices until dinner.

Once Sal went back to the first floor, Lucian felt unusually tired and slipped into a daze. He was content with the free room, but he couldn't shake the unnerving feeling from earlier.

For some reason, his body became weaker and weaker, and his focus was fading rather rapidly. Upon reaching the bed, he collapsed, drifting into a peaceful sleep. He didn't dream, but something or someone kept annoyingly trying to wake him. At first, he tried ignoring the nuisance, but it kept shaking him and trying to warn him.

Warn him of *what*?

Lucian was aroused by the creak of the door and the squeaky floorboards. He opened his eyes to the sight of Sal tiptoeing into his room. She had a sweet smile on her face. For a second, Lucian thought he saw Sal lick her lips. But it must've been his mind playing tricks on him, right? He tried to ask her what she wanted. Nothing came out. He couldn't move. He felt hazy.

"Why...can't...I...move?" he struggled to say, shifting his shoulders. "Why..."

A wicked smirk crept on her lips.

"I didn't know you could still speak," she cackled while saying. "You're too naive, young man. But I guess you must have strong mana to resist the effects of my poison for this long."

Scared out of his wits, Lucian mustered enough strength to inch toward the edge of the bed. It wasn't enough to stop the crazed woman from immobilizing him. Hovering her hands over his body, she released a dark mist.

With how little strength he had, all Lucian could do was hold his breath. As the mist approached him, Sal licked her lips again, saliva drizzling down her chin. She caressed his hair, a terrifying expression forming on her face as she transformed.

Her beautiful, silky, caramel-colored locks turned into an inky-black thicket, extending down to the floor. Her fair skin was whitened to a ghostly white hue. Fangs protruded from her lips. She licked them with her tongue in anticipation of her meal.

Lucian shifted his shoulder, struggling to no avail.

Sal's eyes glowed a hellish red. She kissed his forehead. He finally realized what that sensation was from earlier: She was actively draining his mana.

"Let...me...go!" he cried out.

"Your soul is a delicacy—a once-in-a-millennium treat!" she exclaimed, giddily. "Consuming your high-grade mana will satisfy my appetite for a few centuries! Come here, my precious snack!"

Sal widened her mouth, preparing to dig in.

"Thank you for—" Her words were lost, as she was suddenly hurled off the bed. Hitting the wooden floor, she cried out in pain.

Lucian couldn't lift his head to see, but he knew there was someone else in the room. Friend or foe, he didn't know, but the unidentified stranger had saved him. After a few moments, Lucian harnessed enough strength to turn and see the fallen creature that had tried to devour him. She hissed and lunged at the mysterious stranger. Just like before, she was knocked backward.

"What a naughty Syras," a masculine voice scolded, clicking his tongue. "To think you would attack a child. Shame on you."

Sal spat up blood from the attack, and she said, "It's his fault for having such tempting mana."

"No," the stranger said. "It's yours for luring him into your nest and trying to drain his mana."

You go, random stranger! Lucian thought, trying not to distract his savior.

"You'll pay for ruining my meal!" she seethed, a red foam bubbling from her mouth. She jumped and spurted the poison at the stranger.

The mysterious man chanted, "*Revincio!*"

Sal was thrown back for a final time, writhing helplessly on the floor.

That's the spell I used earlier, Lucian thought to himself, as he watched the exchange.

Unlike Lucian's attempt, the stranger's spell was stronger—way stronger.

The man's spell perfectly restrained Sal into an unbreakable hold.

"Don't even think about escaping!" his savior shouted.

Lucian watched as Sal transformed into a scaly snake, trying to slither away from the seal. Her efforts were in vain. The magical restraints aligned to her new form and squeezed her so tightly that they suffocated her to death.

"Huh." The stranger sighed. "I was going to warn her that if she tried to use her mana, she would be squeezed to death. Well, no matter."

The stranger, who stood at the doorway the whole time, finally came into his field of vision. He was a tall, lanky man with ginger hair, freckles, and a thin beard that lined his jaw and proceeded to his upper lip. Thick-rimmed glasses sat on his nose, a wooden staff gripped in his hand, and a shiny, black top hat rested on his head. He was a very eccentric-looking person.

Almost as eccentric as Master Felix.

"It's better if you don't try to move," the man warned, "unless you want your muscles to tear. A Syras's poison is very apt at restricting her prey's muscles. If you move your muscles any more than you already have, they'll snap like rubber bands."

Lucian immediately stopped trying to move, emulating a stone statue.

"Good kid," the man said, tapping the wooden staff on Lucian's chest.

The moment the staff touched him, Lucian felt a heavy weight lift off his body. He sat up, still feeling slightly sore. He then looked at the ginger-haired man and wholeheartedly thanked him.

"It's no problem," the man said. "My name is Ferris Rode. I am a traveling Sorcerer. I noticed something was off about Miss 'Sal,' ever since I arrived in this town, but I needed proof. And you just so happened to walk right into her trap. Syrases are tricky creatures. They're said to be the minions of an evil god. You never know when or where they'll show up or whose identity they'll mimic to feast on your soul."

"What evil god?" Lucian asked, curiously.

"Hmm, that's a good question for future reference," Ferris replied while stroking his beard. In one swift swing, Ferris bonked Lucian on the head with his staff. A wave of information flooded into him. Fables, rumors, and images of the evil god transferred into Lucian's mind, but the name stood out above all else.

Akar was the name of the evil god—the god of deception.

Lucian waited until he regained his strength and then rose to a standing position. He shook the man's hand and officially introduced himself. "Thank you for saving me, Mr. Rode. My name is Lucian Roux, a Student of Master Felix."

"What a coincidence!" Ferris exclaimed. "To think I would actually meet Felix's student here of all places."

"You know Master Felix?" Lucian asked.

"Felix was a classmate of mine at The Academy," Ferris explained. "This is perfect! He told me you were interested in the 'outside' world, but I didn't think I would ever get the chance to meet you. If you want to know anything under Gaia's graces, just let me know!"

Before Lucian could ask a single question, the gemstone floated upward, producing a blinding light.

Something seemed to snap.

Eteria's shrieks resounded in his ears. "LUCIAN!"

"What is *wrong* with you? Do you want me to become deaf!?" Lucian yelled back.

"That evil woman sealed my voice!" she exclaimed. "I tried to warn you, but she blocked my voice from reaching you! And now, you're too busy talking to a complete stranger."

"Will you shut up for once?" Lucian stated. "This man just saved me from danger!"

Ferris scratched his head in confusion.

With an awkward tone, he asked, "Lucian, who are you talking to?"

"What?" Lucian asked, dumbfoundedly. "You can't... hear her?"

Eteria manipulated the gemstone to knock him in the chest with considerable force. "Of course, that man can't hear my voice, you dimwit! I can't believe you're *that* ignorant. Normal humans can't hear me! Only you, who has the gift of Interpretation, can."

"But my results were black—black as night! So, I shouldn't *have* any of the gifts."

Eteria let out a prolonged sigh, and she said more clearly, "You're a Reincarnate. This Ferris guy isn't. Regardless of whether you believe you have the ability or not, you're speaking to a goddess, right now. Use your brain, Lucian. Interpretation *is* the gift of translating the words of the gods and goddesses."

"I just told you that my results were black!" Lucian argued. "Why won't you listen!?"

"Who told you that you didn't have any gifts?"

"Well, The Aegis did... Its flames turned black," Lucian yelled.

"That's nonsense," she stated.

"What's nonsense?"

"I know The Aegis has no such power."

"How do you know that?"

"Because I know *him*."

"Know *who*?" Lucian asked, frustratedly.

"The god within the goblet."

10

DARK VISIONS

 *Orsus* ◆

Nearly two weeks had passed since Lucian and Ferris left the previous town and arrived in Orsus, the City of Oracles. Like the previous town, the buildings and the residents looked the same. However, the market and the atmosphere felt livelier and more magical. Like the magical goods in Caelum, the stores contained a variety of healing crystals and heat stones.

Lucian's initial excitement about arriving in Orsus was greatly diminished by his current reality. Instead of exploring and experiencing everything the town had to offer, Ferris made it his sole conviction to lecture him to death. Although the information was essential, Lucian wanted to let his imagination and his feet roam freely in the city itself.

Being stuck in an inn room wasn't on his itinerary.

On several occasions, Lucian attempted a stealthy escape from the inn. Every time he tried, he failed rather miserably. Ferris, his new teacher, even went so far as to tie him to a chair a couple of times. Ferris was a competent teacher but inconsistent in his lessons and his punishments. Disobedience was sometimes penalized by a two-hour lecture on ethics and respect, while, other times, it was a simple whack on the head.

Even so, thanks to Ferris's unyielding persistence, Lucian gained a wealth of historical knowledge about the three major powerhouses of The Earthly Realm: The Kingdom of Lunaris, dubbed the Kingdom of Light, with its monopoly on trade and politics; The Kingdom of Avrith, dubbed the Kingdom of Knowledge, with its unshakable defense system and monopoly on the production of magical tools; and The Terras Empire, dubbed the Empire of Warriors, with its monopoly on weaponry manufacture and military strength.

While the kingdoms possessed their own unique cultures and architectures, they shared one unified system: their currency. The value of credits varied between the individual lands, but the concept of a shared currency persisted. His 10,000-unit Credit Slip could purchase a small castle in Lunaris, a noble's title in Avrith, or a private army in Terras.

Learning about the currency system, Lucian started to question Melinda's *gift* and The Var's *choice*: Why would Melinda give to Lucian and The Var give to the Fallen Ones a currency that could only be used outside of Caelum?

LUCIAN FELT GIDDY. FERRIS FINALLY ALLOWED Lucian a trip into town. Once again, however, Lucian was sorely disappointed. Instead of a sightseeing trip, his new mentor endlessly babbled about The Terras Empire's current situation, revealing that its politics and economics were pretty much in shambles. Lucian tuned out the rest.

Even the talkative Eteria didn't make a peep, fearing Ferris would restart his hour-long lectures if he thought that Lucian wasn't paying attention.

Although Lucian believed Ferris was walking aimlessly, giving him an on-the-move lesson, Lucian noticed that there was a purpose in the man's step. Lucian interrupted his mentor's ramblings and asked, "Where are we going? Anywhere fun?"

Ferris finished the last sentence of his lecture and said with a frustrated tone, "If you weren't Felix's precious student, I would've already thrown you into The Portacle Sea. With your current capabilities, you would be eaten by a Giant Clam within the hour."

Lucian shuddered at the mental image emerging in his head. Flailing his arms like a fish, he said, "I'm sorry for interrupting you, but I've been listening to your lectures non-stop for the past two weeks. Can't we take a break?"

Lucian sped up his pace to match Ferris's and noticed a small smile appear on the man's face.

"There's one more lesson, and then you'll have as much fun and adventure as you wish," Ferris said, lightly tapping his staff on Lucian's head. "Felix was right... You're a very impatient little squirt, aren't you?"

Arriving at their destination, Lucian didn't have time to retort. Although he was happy to leave the inn, the shop —if you could even call it that—wasn't the type of place someone would willingly visit for fun. The welcome sign was heavily faded with pieces of wood sticking out every which way. The windows were cracked, and the glass was covered in dust.

Lucian was like a cautious cat on high alert; whereas, Ferris was chill as a cucumber, seemingly enjoying the atmosphere of eccentricity that exuded from the small shop.

Ferris entered first. Lucian followed, wincing at the grinding screech of the door and the rusty cry of the welcome bell. Once inside, however, Lucian was dumb-struck. Although the shop's exterior was shoddy, the interior was astonishing.

Polished to perfection, the wooden shelves were lined with many foreign items and neatly organized. The floors were so clean that they glistened. Inside the glass container were crystal-clear gemstones and powerful-looking staffs.

Ferris called out, "Master, are you in?"

Lucian expected a person to emerge from the back room, but instead, a tiny, scruffy creature raced out, scratching the floorboards with her long, curled nails. She leaped into Ferris's arms, licking the man's bearded face and caressing her head against his cheek. The creature's defining features included her fluffy, almond-colored fur, and her large, captivating, amber eyes. Ferris lightly stroked her fur, and the fluffball let out a satisfying howl.

"I've never seen a creature like that before," Lucian remarked. "What *is* it?"

From the back of the shop, a low, gruff voice answered, "*She* is a Titi. She may not look like much, but she's the strongest of her litter. I found her when I trekked The Talis Mountains a few decades ago."

Lucian searched for the voice's owner. His eyes rested on an elderly man with a full head of gray hairs and white strands. His back was arched, so he used a wooden staff for support. He greeted them with a wave.

"I'm surprised that she still remembers you," the old man said, shaking his staff at Ferris. "What I'm more surprised about is the fact you've finally found yourself an apprentice. I never thought you had it in you to settle down and teach a youngster."

With an awkward smile, Ferris corrected his master by saying, "He's not *my* apprentice, Master Maverick. This is Lucian Roux, *Felix's* student."

The old man, identified as "Master Maverick," stroked his mid-length beard. He had a very complex expression on his face, his wrinkles creasing deeper into his forehead. After a moment of silence, Master Maverick seemingly made up his mind, grabbing Lucian's hands and shaking them enthusiastically.

"I see, I see!" Master Maverick exclaimed, tightening his grasp. "If that's the case, then you'll need to learn about Gaia's fundamental properties."

Lucian reflexively rolled his eyes and asked, "Another lecture?"

The Master let out a hearty laugh. Master Maverick ruffled Lucian's hair while responding, "You're just like Ferris when he was your age."

"What do you mean?" Lucian asked.

"Well, let's just say, he was a pain in the a—"

"—Master!" Ferris exclaimed, cutting him off.

"Be quiet, you ungrateful rascal!" Master Maverick yelled.

Master Maverick turned his attention back to Lucian and said, "My lessons are *fun*, unlike Ferris's endless rants. Not only will you learn about what makes this world tick, but you also will learn about your magical attributes."

"But, Master, he's not ready—"

Master Maverick whacked Ferris's arm with his wooden staff.

"Stop trying to clip his wings! If he can't even try to fly, then he'll have no confidence for the future," Master Maverick scorned. "You've always been such a worrywart. Trust me. I am your Master and a Magus."

Ferris seemed to withdraw into himself, slightly pursing his lips.

Lucian found the whole scenario extremely amusing since he didn't know anyone could counter Ferris's eccentric nature.

Master Maverick moved toward the counter, snatching a pure-white gem out of the glass container and a small piece of paper with a strange symbol on it.

After handing Lucian the two items, Master Maverick led Lucian into the back room. Lucian followed, not waiting for Ferris, who stubbornly refused to move. The

Titi also stayed in the other room, curling up for her afternoon nap.

Lucian entered the back room, which looked even more impressive than the main area. At the furthest wall, there was a wooden board with an unfamiliar diagram with symbols etched on its surface. Sifting through his memories, he tried to identify the diagram but to no avail. Out of all the magic books in Master Felix's observatory, none of them fit.

Master Maverick seemed to notice Lucian's fascination with the diagram and eagerly urged him to move closer to the board. Upon a closer look, Lucian recognized that the diagram's outer layer formed a hexagram. Six symbols were connected by lines. Inside the hexagram were two unique symbols, linked directly to each other with a single line.

Although all of them were fascinating, Lucian's eyes fixated on a very specific symbol. Like the barrier, he felt a strong urge to touch it. Before he could stop himself, his fingertips were tracing the symbol's outline.

A pair of eyes burned into Lucian's back. Turning around, he locked eyes with Master Maverick, who had been closely observing his actions.

"I'm so sorry!" Lucian apologized, bowing his head.

Expecting a strike from Master Maverick's staff or a glare of dissatisfaction, Lucian braced himself. Thankfully, nothing happened. Master Maverick's focus wasn't on

Lucian but rather on the diagram. He tapped the head of his staff on the diagram and chanted a spell. With only a single word, the entire diagram started to glow, each symbol flashing a different color.

Eyes widening in awe, Lucian let out a rapid fire of questions. "What did you do? What do those symbols mean? Why are they different colors?"

Pointing his staff at the topmost symbol of the hexagram, which emitted a fiery red glow, Master Maverick began his lesson: "As you can see, there are six secondary elements: Fire, Ice, Wind, Earth, Thunder, and Water. Most Mages can wield at least one of these elements."

Moving his staff to the two symbols inside the hexagram, Master Maverick explained, with a more severe tone, "These two symbols, 'Light' and 'Darkness,' are what we call, 'the primary elements,' which serve as the foundation of the secondary elements. Historically, only the gods have been known to wield the primary elements."

Taking in a sharp breath, Lucian grimaced. The symbol that attracted him was none other than the primary element, *Darkness*.

After finishing his base explanation, Master Maverick asked Lucian to unfold the paper resting in his hand. Unfolding the paper as instructed, there was a similar yet smaller version of the diagram on the board.

"Now, what?" Lucian asked, examining the page with a mix of curiosity and apprehension.

"This tester is made of Papyrus, a material often used to script ancient documents such as magical books," Master Maverick explained. "The material can store and activate any magic cast onto it. In this case, a droplet of blood is the activator. Once the condition is fulfilled, the tester will guide the droplet to the individual's inherent attribute. Upon reaching its destination, the chosen symbol will glow."

Lucian gulped.

Master Maverick handed him a knife, and Lucian cut a slit in the flesh of his thumb. Enduring the pain, he steadied his finger, and his thumb hovered over the paper. The moment the first droplet made contact, the blood rapidly spread throughout like veins, moving toward its destination. Surprisingly, the veins split into branching paths, leading the blood to two symbols.

Fire and *Darkness*.

Upon seeing the two symbols glow, Master Maverick ripped the paper out of Lucian's hands. He seemed like a crazed old man, as he held the paper up to the ceiling's illumination crystals. The old man seemed even crazier when he started dancing like a fool around the room and singing out of tune.

Hearing Master Maverick's jovial outburst, the Titi

scurried into the back room. Soon after entering, the Titi danced alongside Master Maverick too.

"Uhm, Master Maverick?" Lucian asked, apprehensively. "Are my results *that* good?"

"Yes, they are! Of course, they are!" the Master shouted, a giant grin forming on his wrinkled face. "You have TWO magical attributes! Do you have any idea what this means? No, of course, you don't! This is a rarity even in the abundantly magic-centric Kingdom of Avrith. I expected you to have interesting results because you have such abundant mana, but this outcome is unbelievable!"

Master Maverick's celebratory wails and shouts were enough to summon Ferris into the back room. Ferris promptly asked what happened, and Master Maverick proudly showed off the tester. The glowing hadn't faded, at all. Rather, the two symbols seemed to intensify. Ferris stared at the results, strangely unfazed.

"Master," Ferris addressed the old man. "You should've expected these results. Lucian is from the legendary village of Caelum. He's a Reincarnate, for Gaia's sake."

"Oh, I suppose so... But still!" Master Maverick pouted. "This geezer has only read about this occurrence in books. He's never seen them before with his own two eyes! There hasn't been a Mage with both Fire and Darkness magical affinities since the ancient god, Morpheus!"

Ferris fidgeted at the reference.

After another five minutes of singing and dancing, Master Maverick moved on to the next item, the white gem. Lucian was instructed to sit on the ground to be as close to the earth as possible. Closeness to the earth would supposedly synchronize him with Gaia's spiritual core. Master Maverick told him to steady his breathing and infuse small amounts of mana into the gem every minute or so. Lucian's former sorcery training slightly helped him, but precise mana control never was his forte.

"Imagine yourself slowly descending into the abyss of your mind," Master Maverick instructed. "This gem will provide you with a glimpse of your spiritual path. It will either dive you deep into your past or spiral you to your future. Neither of which is set in stone. Allow the mana to flow through you. Feel it. Sense it."

LUCIAN SLIPPED INTO THE DARKNESS WITH EASE. His eyes were closed, making it easier to focus on his other senses. His body seemed to be floating somewhere. His nose slowly recognized the smell of burning metal. His skin felt waves of heat crashing against it, intensifying with each passing second. His ears homed in on a muffled sound—small cries transforming into bloodcurdling screams.

He opened his eyes.

His mouth dropped.

He closed his eyes.

He reopened them.

The same scene of death and destruction played out. He was floating in the air, high above the ground. Flaming boulders shot at him from below. He quickly dodged them. The all-consuming flames filled his eyes, blinding him.

Littered on the ground, there were burned crisps as far as the eye could see. They were *corpses*. There were so many of them that they completely covered the terrain, stretching out to the horizon.

Lucian froze, but his body continued to move forward. He wasn't in control. He kept ascending upward alongside one of The Heavenly Pillars. When he reached the apex, where the pillars breached the upper stratosphere, a figure approached him at the speed of light, hurdling him backward. His back crashed against one of the pillars.

Lucian coughed up blood—black blood.

Two hands firmly wrapped themselves around his neck and thrust him toward Gaia's crust. Although his vision was blurry, Lucian automatically knew who had attacked him. The figure that was choking him was Adonis,

Morpheus's younger twin brother. Adonis's long, azure hair grazed his face, and they plummeted downward. Pure rage and hatred filled Adonis's eyes. Lucian struggled to break free of Adonis's grasp, but his body was too weak.

Just like the time the Syras had drained his mana.

"Why, Adonis?" a male's voice deeper than his own asked. "How could you betray me!?"

"Brother!" Adonis yelled. "You betrayed us! You broke the pact! You cursed us all, and now, we are doomed to live as Fallen Ones without any hope of returning to The Heavenly Realm. You are our curse!"

•············••✦ *Orsus* ✦••············•

LUCIAN ABRUPTLY SNAPPED OUT OF THE VISION. Streams of sweat trickled from his forehead to his neck. All of that stress invoked a cold sweat. Master Maverick was speaking to Lucian, but it took him a while for his mind to process what he was saying. Lucian felt a surge of powerful emotions—emotions that weren't even his own. Tears trickled down his face. After collecting himself, he looked down at the white gem, which had turned an ugly black.

"Lucian," Master Maverick said, "what happened?"

Lucian's watery eyes turned to Ferris. The eccentric man looked like he was in pain as well but for a different reason. Although Lucian would've normally questioned Ferris's peculiar reaction, he was far too overwhelmed with the vision.

"I-I..." Lucian paused. "I can't remember..."

Lying to Master Maverick was the last thing that he *wanted* to do, but Lucian had to hide his connection to Morpheus at all costs. Although Ferris already outed that Lucian was a Reincarnate earlier, he didn't want to be treated like he was in Caelum...as a *monster*.

Master Maverick rubbed his back and gently said, "That's alright. I didn't know you would have such a painful experience. Most people experience relatively harmless visions related to their elemental attributes, but yours must've been quite scary. I sincerely apologize for putting you through that..."

Master Maverick hesitated and then stated, "However, there is one good thing that came out of it."

"What?" Lucian asked, recovering from the shock.

"Like the tester, the gem is also a magical tool. While the tester's purpose is to reveal your affinity, the gem is to stimulate your awakening. Since you've awakened, you'll be able to use your mana for much more than a few basic sorcery spells. Now, you can use elemental-specific magic,"

Master Maverick explained. "From your awakening, there was another important revelation... The gem turning black is evidence of that."

"Evidence of what?" Lucian asked.

"*You* are the one we've been searching for."

Ferris interrupted by saying, "Master, just to confirm, don't you think we should go visit, well, you know, *her*?"

Master Maverick jumped upward and yelled, "Why do I have to see that old hag!?"

"You know very well why," Ferris argued. "From the start, you should've been the one to suggest he see her. Like it or not, you can't help Lucian any more than you already have."

"Why can't you do it, then?" Master Maverick countered. "You're capable enough to—"

"End of discussion," Ferris snapped.

"See who? Go where?" Lucian asked, shooting up like a sprout.

"The Oracle," Master Maverick groaned. "We're going to see The Oracle."

II

THE ORACLE

 *Orsus*

On the way to The Oracle, Lucian was trapped between two stubborn, crazed lunatics in their march of madness. His first impressions of the easygoing, knowledgeable Ferris and the grandfatherly, sage-like Master Maverick had been crushed.

They were like two wild animals that were fighting over a piece of meat.

Blah, blah, blah, thought Lucian, mocking his childish companions.

Phrases such as, "You always were as stubborn as a mule" and "Why would you throw your precious Master into a viper's nest?" were flung over him from his right side. To his left side, Ferris's words fell into one of two categorical responses: "It's not my fault that your midnight tryst was a failure!" or "You're an old man, so stop acting like a child."

Both men were utter disappointments.

Lucian clamped his hands over his ears, praying for the squawking to cease. Even with the external noise blocked out, Eteria seized the chance to start internally spewing complaints.

Even my own mind isn't safe.

Keeping his hands on his ears, Lucian jumped forward a few inches to shake the gem into submission. It didn't work. He didn't know why, but she had been oddly quiet for the past week or so. It felt like a blessing. But now, the silence had been broken, and a wave of whining washed over him, drowning his inner thoughts.

Why do I even try? Lucian thought, cursing his misfortune. *Can't I have one minute of peace and quiet?*

He had a serious choice to make: risk another hour-long lecture or be tortured with the ear-splitting arguments passing over him like a flimsy fan. His sanity couldn't take it anymore. To garner their attention, he brought his hands in front of him and clapped them together as hard as humanly possible.

With a forced smile, Lucian said, "I want to know more about the magic system. Master Maverick, you keep referring to the terms, 'Magus' and 'Mages,' and Ferris considers himself a 'Sorcerer.' Are they different from each other?"

Master Maverick's eyes sparkled with childlike excitement. All traces of the recent bantering seemed to completely fizzle away.

Honestly, Lucian thought. *This old man has the memory of a goldfish.*

The Master slapped his thigh and exclaimed, "You're a fairly ambitious one, aren't you? I like curious brats like you!"

Oh, no, Lucian thought, instantly regretting his decision. *Here it comes!*

The elder's back straightened, and his voice changed to an overly exaggerated scholarly tone, as he said, "Before I can talk about what a Magus is, I must first clearly verbalize that Mages and Sorcerers are two entirely separate entities."

Ferris unnaturally coughed, adding, "For the most part."

"Oh, hush you! You never let me finish!" Master Maverick scolded Ferris.

Master Maverick regained his former stature and continued by saying, "Mages are individuals born with natural magical attributes. They can communicate with the Elemental Spirits as well as manipulate their mana without intermediary tools such as magic-inscribed scrolls and mana-infused weaponry. Sorcerers are individuals born without a magical attribute. They are limited to common-place spells, including simplistic offensive and defensive tricks. They can't freely use their mana, so they rely solely on magical tools created by Mages, who infuse their mana into them. Like poor Ferris, over there. Pity that boy couldn't become a Mage. He had so much potential when he was younger. What a shame. What a waste..."

Ferris reached overtop Lucian's shoulder and pretended to whack the old man with his wooden staff.

"To think you would hit an old man," Master Maverick whined, pleading for Lucian's pity. "See, see? He's the bad guy, not me!"

"I like these two!" Eteria proclaimed, snickering. "They're too funny!"

Ignoring them, Lucian asked, "What about the 'Magus' you spoke of?"

Master Maverick straightened his loose, ruffled black robe and explained, "Each Kingdom appoints its own Master-class Mage, a 'Magus.' On the surface, it's an honorable title. However, in the past, Maguses were abused as weapons of mass destruction. When wars broke out, they were the first to be deployed and expected to end the war by themselves. Even if the royal military was deployed, they would unfortunately only be slaughtered by the enemy Magus's high-level spells."

Master Maverick pivoted by saying, "However, the

tides have recently turned. With the creation of high-grade magical weapons, Maguses no longer need to fight wars alone."

"Why are you a Magus, then?" Lucian asked, with innocent intentions. "They can't really expect a single elder to defend an entire kingdom?"

"Well..." Master Maverick said, averting his gaze and shrugging his shoulders. "I'm actually retired, but it doesn't hurt to bolster my reputation with a valuable title, now, does it? Besides, my other former student, Felix, is the current Magus of Lunaris."

Lucian's eyes widened, realizing just how powerful Master Felix truly was.

Lucian's head turned to Ferris, who was surprisingly quiet during the old man's lecture. No, that wasn't it. Ferris wasn't even humoring their conversation. He appeared to be wary of something. His walking pace alternated between fast and slow, and his eyes were vigilant to some unidentified shadows lurking within the distant alleyways.

Almost too naturally, Ferris pulled the green cloak's hood over Lucian's blond head.

Lucian tapped the ginger's shoulder and whispered, "Ferris, what's wro—" He was cut off mid-sentence. Ferris vertically touched his lips with his index finger, signaling silence and a look that meant, "Don't Ask." Since Master

Maverick didn't react or notice, Lucian followed along with Ferris's abrupt request.

Lucian feigned ignorance and continued walking. He refocused on Master Maverick, who had moved on to a new topic: the history of magical theorems and ancient relics.

The *real* or *perceived* threat seemed to have backed off by the time they had arrived at their destination. As a result, Ferris returned to his normal, whimsical state. Ferris stated that they had reached The Oracle's abode. Or, as the Master liked to call it, "The Viper's Nest."

THE VIPER'S NEST WAS DIFFERENT THAN HE HAD expected. Lucian imagined a dark, lowly building, where tree roots and vines entangled, blocking all passage. He assumed an elderly woman would greet them at the door, who had thick white hair, crooked teeth, and a fat wart stuck on her dry and cracking skin.

However, upon entrance into the actual abode of The Oracle, his ideas were uprooted.

Where their destination lay was astonishing; violets and daisies danced in the wind with fresh soil as their fodder;

the glistening whiteness of the smooth, marble edifice mirrored The Holy Chapel; the sun trickled off the sides of the surface, reflecting a golden gleam.

"Stop gawking," Master Maverick said with an irked tone. "Let's get this over with, so I can return home and eradicate this awful memory from my mind."

The doors, which were as white as the building, possessed speckles of an emerald shimmer. The beauty of it all nearly blinded Lucian. He was forcefully strung along by Ferris, who led him and Master Maverick inside. Master Maverick stubbornly dug his heels in, while Lucian's gaze lingered on the architecture.

As soon as they were inside, the doors closed behind them. Descending the spiraled staircase, which was in the back of the main entry, a woman who seemed around eighteen years of age welcomed them with a warm smile.

As she continued down the steps, her ocean-blue hair flowed down her back like a waterfall. Her eyes glistened a golden hue, her lips dipped in rouge, and unlike most women of Lunaris, she wore an elegant ivory dress with a floral brooch adorning her chest and a blue-and-gold headband nestled atop her head.

Master Maverick snorted at the sight of her. "Lucian, don't let this temptress fool you. She's old enough to be your great-grandmother."

Those words echoed in Lucian's ears. It took a whole

minute for that information to sink into his brain. *Great-grandmother?* thought Lucian, thoroughly shaken. *But she's so beautiful!*

"If you only rely on your sight, then you're doomed," Eteria snickered while saying. "There is more than meets the eye, in many cases."

Once the woman was on level ground with them, she said, "Welcome, Lucian. My name is Evangeline Drayton. In this form, please refer to me as 'Eva.' Additionally, thank you both for joining him. It's been several months since I've last seen you, Ferris, and a decade since you came skulking in, Maverick."

"Humph." Master Maverick sounded in response. "If you think I've forgiven you, then you're completely wrong."

Ferris bowed to her, lightly kissing the backside of her hand. "It's been far too long, Madam Evangeline."

"Eva." She repeated. "You *must* call me Eva."

"Very well then," Ferris said with a gentlemanly tone. "Miss Eva, will you administer the test for Lucian? We've determined his attributes, but we want to ascertain their authenticity."

Ferris handed her the tester with Lucian's results on it. Unlike Master Maverick, who happily celebrated Lucian's results, Eva pursed her lips. Her welcoming smile dropped into a concerned frown. She surveyed Lucian before she responded to Ferris's request.

"Ferris, you very well know what this means...for him and you," Eva cryptically said. "Are you certain that it's the awaited time?"

He shot her what appeared to be a warning look. "He'll only be tested on his current capabilities. His magical capacity equals that of an Apprentice Mage. Like the ranking exams, your test will determine his powers and potential in that area. As a Mage yourself, aren't you curious to see what'll unfold?"

Eva's forehead creased, and she said with a lowered, concerned tone, "But those Mages are *not* fifteen, and they are *not* expected to pass the test without a partner. If anything happens to him—"

"—I'll take full responsibility," Ferris assured. "This is what *Felix* would've wanted."

The mention of Lucian's mentor, Master Felix, seemed to convince Eva to reluctantly concede.

Lucian had a gut feeling that this test would be neither fun nor an easy task. From their brief conversation, he grasped that this "test" would either make or break him. In his case, with the scrawny body of a fifteen-year-old and the skills of an Apprentice Sorcerer, he prescribed himself a set of broken bones and some nasty bruises.

I'm so dead.

Ferris looked at him with an eased expression. "Don't worry, you'll never be truly alone. Neither for this test nor in the future. Just relax and let yourself rise to the challenge."

With that simple reassurance and a slap on the back, Lucian went with Eva into the center room, which appeared blocked off by magical seals and physical metal bars. It only took a moment for her to undo all of them with the flick of her wand. She guided him inward to a dimly lit room.

When the doors creaked shut, Lucian followed Eva down a flight of stairs that led even deeper into the edifice. He shivered. His arm hairs shot straight up, and goose-bumps rose on his skin.

Brr... He shivered. *Why's it so cold down here?*

Eva's breaths spiraled out to form visible puffs of air. She seemed unfazed by the sudden drop in temperature. She didn't even shiver. He, on the other hand, tried to muster and preserve his body heat the best that he could.

"Don't worry," Eva said, comforting him. "You'll only feel cold for a few moments."

Lucian watched as she walked toward a ginormous goblet of water. It looked like a mini pool, one large enough to fit several people. She beckoned him toward the goblet, telling him to imagine himself traveling through the water.

At first, the water was so murky that he could only faintly recognize his blurred reflection. As he focused more, his reflection grew clearer. Lucian fixated on his reflection that drew nearer to the water's surface by the second. The moment his nose barely touched the water, a light push sent him headfirst into the goblet.

"Good luck," Eva's voice whispered in his ear, as he was pushed and sucked into the goblet. "You're going to need it."

With those parting words, his body rushed through several spirals of water. He fell, steadily drifting toward what seemed like a portal wrapped in water. Sprays of water droplets hit his eyes. He tightly shut them.

The sensation of passing through the portal and his body landing on a solid surface made him certain he had arrived at his destination. He slowly opened his eyes, surveying the area for any immediate danger.

When his eyes fully adjusted, his heart dropped at the familiar scenery. His mind froze. He had returned—returned to the place that he so desperately tried to escape from. He had been dropped in the middle of The Sage's Forest.

He was in *Caelum*.

12

TO KILL A BEAST

 *Caelum*

After an initial moment of disbelief, Lucian regained his senses. This place was everything he had feared and so much worse. Making his skin crawl, a disconcerting wind weaved through the forest. His stomach tangled into tight knots, and he felt his breakfast trying to wind its way up his throat. With a concentrated effort, he forced the food back down.

Tiny rays of light poured through the lapses in the foliage. Seeing where the sun sat in the sky, it was either noontime or around one o'clock. Luckily, he wouldn't have to navigate The Sage's Forest at night. But Lucian didn't have the time to waste idly standing in one spot. He had to move.

This was neither a dream nor a joke.

This is a nightmare.

Remembering his previous venture into the forest, his ears tuned to the faint, buzzing sound, which he assumed was the barrier.

Lucky me, Lucian thought. *At least I landed far away from the village.*

After considering his options, Lucian determined the barrier was the only reasonable means of escape. The other exit, the underground tunnel, was too far away. Not wanting to draw any further suspicion, he headed to the barrier. He listened vigilantly, letting his ears direct him. But where his ears led him wasn't where the barrier lay.

No matter how much time passed or how much further he walked, his outstretched hand never collided with the slippery surface of the barrier.

After exhausting a fair portion of his strength, he collapsed on the forest floor and gazed upward through the trees. He saw sections of the clear blue sky that alluded to unattainable freedom. He saw a few crows cross the sky. He envied winged creatures. He too wanted to fly away from all of his problems. He too wanted to be free.

"What a stupid wish," he mumbled, clenching his fist and gritting his teeth.

At the loud crunch of dead leaves near his ears, he jolted forward and jumped to his feet. He turned around to find a familiar face with an unfamiliar boy in tow. Seeing her face in this place made the entire situation seem surreal.

Lucian approached the familiar figure, ascertaining that she was a real entity, not just some constructed figment of his imagination.

"I didn't know that you could freely leave the gem at will," Lucian commented, curiously. "Aren't you supposed to be cursed?"

The female figure who stood before him was none other than Eteria, the self-proclaimed goddess of eternal beauty. Unlike her title, in person, she looked even more frightening, the tips of her fanged teeth poking out from under her green-skinned lips. She curled them into a not-so-welcoming smile.

"Little Lucian, everything you said about me is correct," Eteria said, tugging her small companion closer. "I've never lied to you. Right, Aerus? Tell him I've never lied."

The unfamiliar boy sent a glare in her direction. He looked to be around seven or eight years of age with disheveled jade hair and piercing crimson eyes. What stood out more so than his unusual features were his eerie silence. Even with Eteria's taunts, this "Aerus" kid didn't say a single word in response.

Additionally, out of the boy's body pulsated barely visible waves of a coral-blue light—a captivating color that felt familiar. Lucian rubbed his eyes with the back of his hand, ascertaining that Aerus's peculiar condition was neither a visual illusion nor a fragment of his imagination.

Eteria clasped her hands together and excitedly exclaimed, "I haven't introduced you two yet, have I? Aerus, meet Lucian. Lucian, meet Aerus, the god of strength and protection. I think in your village they referred to Aerus as 'The Aegis.'"

A child as small as this is supposed to be the god of strength and protection? Lucian scratched his head. *On top of that, he's The Aegis, the ancestral flame of my village?*

"Not exactly," Eteria corrected him. "While my curse is this monstrous appearance, his curse is that of vulnerability, to live in the form of a child. His true form is that of a seasoned warrior and protector."

Wagging her index finger, she continued by saying, "Also, his existence in your village was more of an accident. His godly soul was trapped within the soul-bonding goblet and turned into a tool of worship and an everlasting flame. Aerus told me that he only managed to escape because he consumed your blood and formed a contract with you."

"I keep forgetting that you can read my mind," Lucian muttered in an annoyed tone. "If he's truly the god of strength and protection, then why was he used in a ritual determining one's fate? Isn't there a 'god of rituals' for that role?"

Averting her eyes, Eteria answered, "Hah. You'll have to ask The Var himself if you want the answer to that question. As mankind doth not know the truths of the gods, the gods doth not know the schemes of mankind."

"What is that supposed to mean?" Lucian asked.

The faint, buzzing sound transformed into an ear-splitting, high-pitched noise. He started to ask Eteria what the sound was, but both she and the child suddenly vanished. Like an illusion, they faded away. In a mental state between confusion and trepidation, Lucian braced himself.

Then, the sound stopped.

The forest became devoid of sound, so much so that he was able to hear the lightest crunch of leaves behind a bush and a low growl. This time, his stomach wasn't the culprit.

Rather, it was a predator, stalking him and waiting for the optimal chance to strike. Lucian kept himself from letting out a pathetic squeal or cry. If he died, then he would die as a man, not a mouse.

With each additional crunch, Lucian retreated backward, coordinating his steps with the predator. By the time the crunches ceased, he had put some distance between himself and the rustling bushes.

Hoping to spook the predator, Lucian grabbed a broken tree branch lying on the ground and hurled it into the bush. The branch passed through the bush and hit something solid. The predator, which lurked and stalked him for the past few minutes, barreled out of the bush with great vigor.

Imposing and terrifying were the two words that precisely defined the creature. The predator was a ginormous, black-furred beast with razor-sharp teeth, a mouth wide enough to hold and chomp down on two men in one bite, and paws that could easily trample him to death. Glowing bright blue eyes mirrored his own but with malicious intent.

When the beast stomped, the ground started to tremble beneath its paws.

Sparks of lightning danced between the beast's needle-like strands of fur. The beast was preparing for its first strike.

Lucian frantically felt around in his pocket for Master Felix's scepter.

It wasn't there.

I'm so screwed.

His life flashed before his eyes.

I don't want to die. I don't want to die. I don't want to die, he recited in his mind like a mantra.

The beast, with incredible speed, launched itself at him with one leap and easily closed the distance between them.

Lucian tried to throw himself to the side, but he wasn't fast enough. The beast bore its fangs into his left leg with an inescapable grasp. Lucian screeched in pain, feeling the fangs tearing into his flesh.

Knowing that he would die if he didn't act, Lucian gathered as much strength as possible and funneled a dangerous amount of mana into his fist.

He punched the beast's nose with a sickening *thud!*

The black beast shot backward, scraping at the forest floor to regain its balance. However, the force was too strong and sent the beast flying through the forest. The beast's backward momentum only stopped when its spine slammed against a tree. It yelped upon impact and then growled with a thunderous roar. It slammed its paw on the ground, sending a wave of lightning bolts straight at Lucian; however, they luckily fizzled out before reaching him.

"Angry, aren't you?" Lucian taunted, putting up a brave front. "What a pitiful creature to be outdone by its prey."

Although Lucian seemed confident, all he had was bluffs. Not only was he confused about where the surge of mana came from, but he also didn't have a plan. Master Felix had never taught him how to fight a wild beast; he only knew a few basic sorcery spells. And any pain tolerance that he possessed was from his human father's beatings.

Sadly, Lucian neither had the time to search for

answers nor formulate a plan, as the beast was already preparing for its next attack. Returning to its original spot, the beast stood its ground, opened its mouth, and summoned lightning.

This beast wasn't dumb. It learned from its failed strike. Now keeping a safe distance, it aimed its lightning-filled mouth at him. Lucian might've had a chance with a close-quarter fight, but his lack of long-range skills would lead to his defeat.

To make matters worse, Lucian couldn't move his left leg. It was dead weight, profusely bleeding and staining his left pant leg with a bright red hue. He tore off a piece of his shirt and wrapped it around the wound. He tried not to look at it too much, as he was keeping one eye trained on the beast.

Lucian inched toward the nearest tree, dragging his limp leg. Making the tree trunk his support, he inched his body upward. Using both his arms and hands to claw his way to a standing position, he managed to regain some sort of balance. He put a good portion of weight on his good right leg. Lucian's mind and body were strained beyond belief.

Time was running out.

The beast wasn't so patient to allow its prey to gain a more favorable stance. As Lucian fought with his body to stand, the creature began to shoot concentrated balls of lightning at him. They exploded near Lucian's head, breaking a nearby branch and forcing him to unnaturally bend his torso to dodge every shot. Managing to dig his right leg further into the dirt allowed him to maintain his balance.

"Is that it!?" Lucian shouted, his focus waning. "I won't be defeated by a cowardly creature like you!"

The beast snarled and flashed its bloodied teeth at him. Lucian's strength was rapidly depleting so much so that he almost blacked out. However, he refused to let himself fall. He dug his nails into the bark. He refused to die a coward's death. He refused to let the beast defeat him. He refused to give up, no matter what.

Not like this, Lucian repeated in his head. *I won't die until I prove everyone wrong.*

Another ball of lightning hurtled at him. A sharp pain shot through his left leg, causing a delayed reaction. Too slow to react, the ball crashed against his right arm, destroying flesh. He screamed. However, he didn't fall. Securing a clear hit, the beast drew near him, calling him on his bluff. Soon everything would be over. Lucian believed he was doomed until a deep voice within him broke through its restraints.

"Arise, arise, O Fallen soldier," a deep voice bellowed.

Shaken by the sudden sound, Lucian flinched. Assuming madness had seized him, he laughed. His delirious mind was surely playing tricks on him, right? Breaking through his doubts, the internal voice repeated itself with an even greater force.

After several seconds of adamant denial, Lucian lost to the internal presence, who seized control of his body. Like in the vision, his body felt lighter than a feather, and a sadness as deep as the sea consumed him.

"You are my Reincarnate, and I am thy progenitor," the voice said, using Lucian's mouth. "You shall not die so long as I live."

The throbbing pain from his leg and his arm were alleviated.

Out of his left palm, a titanium spear emerged.

Cloaked in darkness, black flames arose from its metal base.

Welling up within him was a certainty that he wouldn't die. A certainty that he would surmount whatever fate threw at him. A confidence to win against any odds. Almost immediately after the spear materialized within his hand, the internal control dissipated, releasing him.

Before the internal presence completely vanished, the voice added to Eteria's previous words: "If you only rely on sight, then you're doomed. There is more than meets the eye, in many cases."

Lucian tightened his grip on the titanium spear, emitting black flames. Shutting his eyes, he tapped into his sixth sense to locate the beast. Through his closed eyelids, the flow of mana appeared as golden lines stretching out like branches in front of him. All of the threads of mana were concentrated at a specific spot.

Upon opening his eyes, he threw the spear with all his might. From his lips, he incanted: *"Impensius atque deleret."* The titanium spear twirled through the air, the flames intensifying and striking the beast directly in its mana core.

When the spear cracked its core, the mighty beast let out a bloodcurdling cry. As a last-ditch effort, it shot several lightning strikes in Lucian's direction but to no avail. Soon after, the beast collapsed to the forest floor, and the sparks of lightning fizzled out from its mouth.

Examining the beast's corpse, it reacted strangely to death. Only a few seconds after dying, the beast's body transformed into a puddle of inky, black water. While Lucian was perplexed by the transformation, he was too exhausted to react.

Adrenaline dying down and legs giving out, he fell flat on his back. His right arm and left leg burned like a blazing fire. His mind wavered between consciousness and unconsciousness.

"Bless the gods!" an angelic voice praised, pouring from the sky.

Eva...?

The water spirals that transported him to the forest returned. The scenery surrounding him turned into wide pillars, and streams of water lifted him into the sky. Tears formed, slowly dripping from his lashes. He survived. He *won*. A sparkling concentration of water wrapped around his body, closing his wounds and fully healing him.

He passed through the portal and then was thrust out of the goblet and onto the basement floor. Several minutes passed until he regained his senses and realized where he was. After awakening alone in the room, he raced up the stairs and burst into the main entrance area to see where Eva was. Upon seeing Lucian, Eva raced toward him, wrapping her arms around him with a warm hug. Strangely, Ferris and Master Maverick were nowhere to be seen.

"Thank the gods that you passed the test," Eva exclaimed with a relieved expression. "I honestly don't know what Ferris was thinking. Even though everything worked out in the end, you were very underprepared."

"Where are Ferris and Master Maverick?" Lucian asked.

"Ferris had to escort Maverick back to his shop due to an emergency, so they won't be back for a while," Eva said with an uneasy tone. "They said that they deeply apologize for their absence."

"Oh, right! Ferris and Maverick wanted me to give you these items," Eva exclaimed, swiftly changing the subject.

She rummaged around in her pocket and handed two items to him. Placed into Lucian's hands were a small, brown leather box and a flimsy piece of paper with text written on it.

He first opened the box, which had a magnificent signet ring inside; its band was pure gold, and it had the insignia of the moon engraved into the center stone. He awkwardly slid the ring onto his index finger. As for the note, he searched for his notebook and stuffed it into its binding, choosing to read it later when he could find some time for himself.

With the images of his recent test flooding to the forefront of his mind, Lucian said, "They're both untrustworthy, those irreconcilable dimwits."

"Hah," a familiar voice chuckled. "I've never heard that one before."

Based on the sarcastic tone, Lucian instantly recognized who it was.

From one of the rooms downstairs, a boy with jet-black hair and violet eyes emerged.

With a snarky tone, the boy said, "I'm surprised you made it this far, Lucian."

"It's about time that you arrived," Lucian said, in a serious tone. "Because you have a whole lot of explaining to do, *Aaron*."

13

THE OUTCAST

 *Orsus*

The sleek, style, and onyx sword thumped when Aaron set it on the wooden table. With a triumphant tone, Aaron exclaimed, "THIS is what I was looking for!"

Lucian's eyebrows furrowed, as he slid the sword away from his steaming food. "I asked you a question, 'Why didn't you follow me?' But we're eating, now, so don't you dare bring that filthy thing anywhere near my precious meal."

"Glutton." Aaron insulted him, sheathing the sword in a leather-bound encasement. "You should praise me for my stealth and ingenuity. It only took me a few weeks of staking out your village to retrieve my stolen sword."

"Confiscated."

"Stolen."

"It's been over three weeks," Lucian said, rolling his eyes. "If you were that ingenious of a person, then it wouldn't have taken half a century to retrieve a stupid sword."

"Ahem." Aaron cleared his throat. "It's not a stupid sword. *It* has a proper name, Phantom."

The overwhelming pride that Aaron exuded while talking about his Phantom sword worried Lucian.

He even named the chunk of metal.

"Well, isn't it cool?" the boy babbled. "The sword's swing is so fast that no one can see it. That's why I named the sword, *Phantom*."

"Hah..." Lucian remarked, chowing down on a scrumptious biscuit covered in gravy. "You certainly are a real sword fanatic, I'll give you that."

Eva emerged from the kitchen. In her hands were several more drool-worthy dishes: a plate of fresh greens with a light seasoning of salt, a sweet-and-sour soup peppered with spices, and a slab of imported boar meat. Lucian licked his lips in anticipation. The mouthwatering aroma filled his nose to the brim.

Aaron waved his hand in front of his face, blocking Lucian's perfect view of the delicious dishes. "Didn't you want to know where I was?"

"Not anymore." Lucian pushed Aaron's hand away, eagerly scooping out the right portions to eat as the plates were placed on the table.

"You're no fun," Aaron whined, flicking Lucian in the forehead. "All you think about is eating, sleeping, and yourself."

Lucian winced at the flick.

Eva, rounding the table, bonked Aaron's head with her fist. "Let the boy eat! He took the test today and nearly died."

"Oooh." Aaron mocked him, flashing a devious smile. "Little Lucian over there took the beginner-level Mage test and is exhausted. What a poor and unfortunate soul."

"No," Eva said, pinching the boy's ear. "He fought a member of the Lychnus."

"Haven't heard that name in a while," Aaron said with a subdued, darker tone. He turned to Lucian and remarked, "Seems like I was wrong. You fought a high-level beast by yourself. What trick did you use? Speaking from personal experience, they're one of the nastier kinds."

Finishing the hearty meal, Lucian wiped off the bits and pieces of bread crust and greens sticking to his upper lip and right cheek. He thanked his hostess, Eva, who had a knack for cooking and magic. Her healing technique had done wonders for his fatigued body.

Lucian didn't so much as glance in Aaron's direction,

as he asked Eva, "You're The Oracle, right? I assume there's a reason that I had to meet with you. Is there some 'oracle' or 'fortune' that you can tell me?"

"Tsk, tsk, tsk," the sound resonated from her tongue, hitting her upper gums. "I divine neither fortunes nor fairytales. I divine prophecies. Since you're so impatient for yours, I'll reveal what the gods have shown me."

Urggh, thought Lucian, sick to his stomach. *Why does everyone only talk about the gods and their selfish wills?*

"Don't you need your crystal orb?" Aaron asked, referencing an object not in the room.

Puffing up her chest with pride, she said, "Not in this form—this beautiful, youthful form."

What a strange thing to say about yourself, Lucian thought.

"Lucian, can I ask you to shed some blood for me?" Eva asked, pulling out a needle from her pocket. "It'll only hurt for a second."

He leaned backward, dodging the approaching tip of the needle. "I've lost enough blood in the last couple of weeks—from the beast, the magic circle, and my Succession Ceremony. I'd rather not lose anymore."

"Tch."

"Stop fooling around," Aaron said, snatching the needle away from her. "Blood isn't necessary for what you're trying to do. Water Mages use their own mana to reflect these prophecies—not the blood of their subject."

"I wanted it for my personal collection." She pouted, picking up Lucian's half-emptied glass of water. "Alright, fine."

Dipping her middle finger into the water, she lightly touched the tip of the glass, moving the tip of her finger in a circular motion.

Resonating, the glass echoed a high-pitched ring. She whispered something inaudible. The water rose in response, small bubbles forming and floating in the air. The clear, blue water droplets reflected the overhead light and produced images within them.

"What do you see?" Lucian asked, anxiously tapping his finger on his thigh. "Is it bad?"

"Patience, young one," Eva said. "My prophecies are neither bad nor good. It's up to you to decide what the results mean."

Eva enlarged the images, interpreting the results with a steady eye.

Within the air, the water, which reflected the images, transformed into words. Eva's interpretations went as so:

"Find the sword that slays the gods, the tree that alters life's time, the one who manipulates memories, and the heart that hath been lost."

One by one, the words deformed, the water splashing

onto the wood. More pronounced than the rest was the final phrase that materialized:

"Then, you shall find the Regulus."

Eva looked as though she had exhausted her energy supply. She heaved in the air and then puffed out muffled curses. She bent over, using the chair's head and the table's surface as her support.

"Don't overexert yourself," Aaron said, sarcastically.

After seeing Eva struggle more than usual, Aaron stated, out of concern, "Your current form may look young, but it can only wield a fraction of your mana."

"I know. I know." Eva waved his comment off. "You can at least let me pretend."

Tugging at her sleeve, Lucian asked, "What does any of it mean?"

Eva regained her composure and said, "That is for you to find out. But I'm not heartless, so I'll give you a hint. Aside from the last command, all of them are located across The Earthly Realm."

"Where do I find them?"

"They'll find you."

More riddles? Lucian thought while sighing.

"Aaron, you and Lucian should walk around town and prepare to leave. It'll be a while until you come to Orsus again. I have a new mission for you," Eva said, switching to a serious tone. She handed Aaron a miniature, paper-wrapped parcel. "Deliver this package to Leon Alastair in Avrith. He must receive it *before* the Regulus is found."

"Another day, another tiresome request," Aaron said, stretching his arms out. "Hey, Lucian, this is perfect timing. During our journey, I'll teach you how to fight since you're weak and as helpless as a baby bird."

"What do you mean, 'our' journey?" Lucian asked with a suspicious tone. "I never said I would go with you. And *who* are you calling *weak*?"

"You have to," Aaron responded, cheekily. "Eva is returning to The Terras Empire soon, and Ferris and Maverick are on an important mission. Besides, you were the one who wanted to know your prophecy, so you must fulfill it, right?"

"You sound so confident that I'll dutifully obey your commands," Lucian said, with a caustic tone. "It sickens me."

"You have no choice in the matter," Aaron said, pompously crossing his arms and legs. "I heard about your run-in with a Syras. If you were left to your own devices, then you would've been skinned alive before you could even cry out the words, 'Save me, Mommy.'"

"You jerk."

"Thanks for the compliment."

Eva whacked them both on the back of their heads and sent them off to run errands at the marketplace. With a list of items to buy, Lucian and the arrogant, fickle boy named Aaron exited Eva's abode and went on their way.

For the most part, their casual, slow pace was natural for them. Lucian trailed slightly behind his raven-black-haired companion.

When the density of people increased, Aaron acted unusually, picking up the pace. From personal experience, Lucian figured out what was happening almost instantly. He sensed the prying stares trained in their direction. It wasn't just one or two stares either; no matter who they passed, they all turned to look at Lucian—no, it wasn't him that they were looking at—they were looking at Aaron.

While Lucian habitually covered his head with his cloak's hood, due to Ferris's prior instruction, Aaron's strands of messy, black hair flowed freely in the breeze. The more they walked, the more Lucian understood why they were staring with such fervent expressions painted on their faces.

It was due to Aaron's natural appearance.

This was the first time Lucian really looked at the boy. With hair as black as night and eyes that shone like a mystical gem, it was no wonder they gawked at him. He was like a living, breathing, mythical creature walking among them. But that didn't seem to be all.

Although some townspeople were fascinated with Aaron's unique qualities, they were few and far between.

Most of them sent vicious glares in his direction and spoke behind his back.

Quite openly so, in many cases.

"Mum, look, it's a Terrasian!" a passerby girl exclaimed, bouncing up and down. "Can I meet him? Pretty please?"

Her mother shuffled the girl along, initially ignoring her silly question. After the onset of a tantrum, the mother said, "Of course, you can't. I've told you time and time again that talking with Terrasians is a sin. You shouldn't speak with those whom the gods abandoned."

What did she just say? Lucian wondered, absentmindedly bumping into Aaron, who had stopped in his tracks. *Oomph!*

Aaron swiveled around, plastering a cringe-worthy smile on his face. "You shouldn't look so surprised. If you do, it only makes you seem foolish. I've already given up on caring, so you should too."

"What was *that* all about?" Lucian asked, startled by the overt discrimination. "Why do they care if you're a 'Terrasian' or whatnot?"

Aaron pulled Lucian aside. Inhaling a deep breath, he thoroughly explained, "You seem to have some fantasy about the world outside your village. Let me tell you this: Life is neither rosy nor fair. You've heard about The Terras Empire's failing economic condition from Ferris, right? What that woman said is correct. I'm just a lowly Terrasian who escaped that poverty-stricken land due to a stroke of good luck. Not only that, but there are also rumors spreading across The Earthly Realm that The Terras Empire is under an unbreakable, nasty curse. For a good reason, too. Something's tearing that kingdom to shreds from its seams. I swore that I would return to save those who couldn't leave and start a new life. Until then, I just have to deal with the idle rumors of ignorant foreigners."

"Woah," Lucian said. "So, you're not just a simpleton with a fetish for swords."

Aaron glared at him.

"Just joking," Lucian awkwardly said. "Your sense of humor can be fickle, you know."

After a shopping trip of silence, the two headed back to Eva's residence. Aaron held the purchased items, while Lucian acted as the line leader since he felt uncomfortable with their previous conversation. During the remainder of the shopping trip, he had been walking on eggshells.

Lucian was the first to approach the grand, milky-white doorway. Surprisingly, he didn't have to push it open forcefully; the door had been left ajar. Something seemed off.

While Lucian tried to analyze the situation in his head, a hand tightly grabbed his shoulder. He attempted to jerk away but was confronted by his companion's voice behind him.

"Don't move," Aaron whispered. "I don't sense anyone inside the house, but we need to stay alert."

"Not even Eva?"

"Not even Eva."

Lucian stopped and watched, as Aaron unsheathed his black sword, which previously hugged the boy's hip. Aaron tiptoed toward the door and kicked it open with his heel. He pointed his sword center to the entrance. Once the door fully swung backward, making a *thud!* against the internal wall, the sword Aaron brandished fell to the floor.

Aaron cursed under his breath.

Lucian peeked through the doorway. Now that he had a full periphery of the room, he couldn't believe his eyes. No, he didn't want to believe them. For what he saw was the tragedy that seemed to succeed him.

He felt like the harbinger of death himself.

Puddles of blood soaked the blue tiles. The doors had been broken, indicating a violent struggle. There were also holes in the floor and on the walls. In the kitchen, broken glass pieces were scattered everywhere.

Nearest to the entrance to the basement room where Lucian had taken the test was the fallen victim of an unprecedented attack. It was *her*.

Eva's corpse lay motionless, hollow eyes looking onward with a blank expression ruining her pretty face. Streaks of blood covered her hair, her face, and her gown.

Lucian almost fainted upon seeing her, smelling the permeating stench of burned iron in the stagnant air.

"Grab your belongings," Aaron ordered, retrieving his dropped sword with an infuriated look. "We're leaving immediately."

"Where are we going?" Lucian asked, glancing back at the corpse. "Shouldn't we...at least bury her?"

A blankness seemed to fill Aaron's eyes, as he muttered to himself, "No. The more evidence we leave, the easier they'll be able to find us."

"Them?" Lucian asked, piecing together the almost inaudible phrase. "I don't know who you're talking about. Who *are* they?"

"None of your concern. Just pack your stuff. If you're not ready within the hour, then I'm leaving without you."

"To where?" Lucian asked, irritated by the boy's insensitive tone. "Where in Gaia's name are you planning on dragging me!?"

"A place that'll test whether you really are *him* or not," Aaron said, leaving out much-needed context clues. "If you are, then this trip will be well worth Eva's sacrifice."

"Stop with the riddles and tell me where we're going!"

Sliding the sword back into the sheath, Aaron replied, "We're headed to the Land of Barbarians and Monsters, The Wastelands."

14

THE WASTELANDS
(PART 1)

 *The Wastelands*

The calmness shrouding the outskirts of The Wastelands was chilling. Lucian heard the wind singing, the sand gently rising and falling, and the distant howling of the unknown. He held his words, waiting for his companion to make the first move and to take the first step into the moonlit territory.

Aaron appeared relaxed as if he was on a simple midnight stroll. He appeared apathetic, as he crossed the border from stone to sand. His attitude befuddled Lucian, who cautiously followed, each step as light and quick as possible. After several minutes of Lucian tiptoeing across the sand, Aaron abruptly stopped.

Lucian thought Aaron was preparing to lecture or laugh at him, but he was wrong. "I just remembered something," Aaron said. "I need to repair my sword."

"Is the only thing you care about your sword?" Lucian let out his inner thoughts.

Aaron glared at him.

"Aren't we supposed to deliver Eva's package?"

"That can wait," Aaron stated. "My sword's repair comes first..."

"Where are we supposed to go?"

"I forgot my map back at Eva's place," Aaron sighed while saying. "Do you have one?"

Rummaging around in his cloak's inner pockets, Lucian said, "Ferris left a note for me. Maybe there are some directions or clues that we could use?"

He pulled out and revealed Master Felix's weathered notebook, which he had yet to investigate. Inside, Lucian flipped through the pages, searching for the tiny note from Ferris, which he had stuffed into the book for safekeeping.

"Aha!" he exclaimed. "Here it is! The answer to all our problems...probably."

Lucian unfolded the creased piece of paper to find a mess of scribbles and poorly drawn symbols. The scribbles were actually names, and they each correlated with a symbol. He handed the paper to Aaron, who was more likely to recognize them.

Even Aaron had to take a minute to decipher Ferris's awful handwriting: "The first name is Korakk with a picture of a snake; the second one is Faeran with a picture of a pig; the third one is The Talis Mountains with a picture of a tree; the last one is Avrith with a picture of a shop called, 'The Broken Latch.'"

"So, it's not a map?" Lucian asked with a dispirited tone.

"Yes and no," Aaron corrected. "Although the drawings suck, they're placed in the correct general location."

"Great!" Lucian said.

"You revealed that note at a perfect time," his companion remarked. "Korakk is located at the southernmost region of The Tribal Nations, so we can stop there to repair my sword on our way to Avrith."

"How badly is your sword damaged?"

Aaron pulled out Phantom, showing the blade to Lucian. Squinting his eyes, Lucian identified a small sliver of a crack near its hilt. He wondered why something as small as a scratch warranted a full repair job. But when it came to weaponry, Lucian was a novice, so he tried to withhold his judgments.

Wow, Lucian thought. *We're going to reroute our whole journey for a single scratch on a sword...*

The two of them resumed their trek through the endless sand. The moon had already reached its peak in the sky. Lucian dragged his legs, as they were already sore. Since Orsus was in the southernmost portion of Lunaris, the pair had already been walking for several hours before they reached The Wastelands.

Apart from Lucian's physical exhaustion, the conditions of The Wastelands weren't as terrible as Lucian had thought they would be. There was a slight, cool breeze, and the moonlight illuminated his path.

When the sun peaked its shiny head out from the depths of the nightly abyss, Lucian saw that they made considerable ground. The Kingdom of Lunaris was miles away, by this point. Walking alongside his brooding companion, Lucian noticed a bright smile appear on Aaron's face. He knew something was brewing in his comrade's devious mind.

"Now that the sun has risen," Aaron said with an ecstatic tone, "and you can see the dunes... It's time for training!"

"Training *what* exactly?"

"Your stamina and endurance." Aaron winked.

"Is that all?"

"Haha! Once I determine your physical stats, then I'll know where to start!"

"Tch."

"You wouldn't want to be eaten by the malicious creatures slithering and sneaking in the predator-ridden Wastelands, would you?"

"What dune?" Lucian monotonously asked, fearing his death more than muscle pains.

"That one, right over there!" Aaron pointed at the tallest dune in sight. It was so large that they couldn't see over the top.

Of course, you picked that one, you sadist, thought Lucian, dragging his legs while lazily walking over to the mountain of sand.

"Hey, Lucian, one more thing!" Aaron yelled from a few feet away. "Here's a little treat to boost your energy. I wouldn't want you to die from overexertion."

Flying through the air came a shiny rose-colored gem. Lucian snatched the gem midair and examined it in his hand.

"What am I supposed to do with this!?" Lucian yelled back, following the absurdity of the exchange.

"Suck on it!"

"What did you just tell me to do?"

"It's a mana crystal. If you place it in your mouth, its stored energy will restore your strength," Aaron instructed. "Treat it like a piece of candy."

Skeptical but fatigued, Lucian plopped the crystal into his mouth and used his tongue to place it in the pouch of his left cheek.

"Hoo lon thiz goin tak?" he asked, the crystal obstructing any attempt at articulate speech.

"Pfft!" Aaron burst out in a fit of laughter.

A few seconds passed, but the gem's restorative effects eventually worked. Lucian felt a renewed sense of strength and peppiness. He felt like he could beat a boar with his bare hands. He spat the crystal out of his mouth and let it sink into the sand. He bounced up and down, and then he sprinted up the dune. He clawed at the sand with his fingers and dug in his feet, but sadly, he made no progress.

"This time, concentrate the flow of mana into your feet!" Aaron ordered. "Don't bother using your hands. Your feet are what we're working on. Understand?"

Who died and made you king?

Several failed attempts later, Lucian collapsed face-first into the bottom of the dune. Out of breath and out of patience, he glared at Aaron, who had been the instigator of his pain. He tried to mimic the flow of events when he had faced off with the Lychnus, but it didn't work.

The stream of mana in his body was noticeably

constricted, and he had barely managed to reach one-third of the dune's height before helplessly sliding back to the bottom. He expected everything to magically work out and was sorely disappointed when it didn't. He had been too reliant on favorable circumstances and otherworldly assistance.

"Ready to give up?" Aaron asked, approaching him. "I see that your physical strength pales in comparison to your mana potential."

"Well, how do I fix it?" Lucian asked, saying each word as if it were a staccato.

"Practice," his comrade said. "That and these pearly-white bracelets."

Out of his pocket, Aaron revealed a set of bracelets and anklets with an unfamiliar pattern inscribed on them. Without Lucian's consent and too fast to protest, Aaron clipped the restraints on Lucian's wrists and ankles. The moment the devices snapped on, the tiny dots, located in the middle of the accessories, lit up.

"What are these?" Lucian asked, struggling to stand. "What did you do to me?"

"I restricted the flow of your mana," Aaron replied. "Well, that's not entirely true. I made it so your mana doesn't try to leak from its container—your body."

"Why would I need something like this?"

"You don't seem to realize it, but the reason you're such

a yummy target for predators and Syrases is due to your inability to conserve and suppress your mana. Most humans are built with monitors that output a certain amount of mana based on conscious and subconscious controls," Aaron explained. "Sadly, you don't seem to have any sense of control. It's like you're an endless production factory of mana that'll burn your body up if you can't control it."

"Essentially, you're like the sun," Aaron stated, matter-of-factly.

"That sounds more like a curse than a compliment."

"Long story short, these magical devices will adjust to your individual mana output and help your body grow accustomed to its maximum capacity," Aaron continued. "If you don't take corrective steps, then eventually your body will burst before you naturally can acquire stability."

Lucian gulped. "How do you know all of this?"

A look of painful remembrance crossed the boy's face. "That's for me to know and for you to follow. By the time you master your mana, these restraints will be no more than mere accessories. Unless, of course, you prefer to prematurely explode."

Lucian lifted himself off the ground. Still fatigued but strangely light, he rose to a standing position. "That was a fast recovery," Aaron remarked.

"Alright, let's practice with them," Aaron said. "You

seemed to struggle with releasing your mana, right? Try again, but this time, don't worry about mitigating your output. That's what these devices are for."

Lucian approached the dune once more with a "You're insane" and an "I'm going to die" kind of look plastered on his face.

"Just try one more time," Aaron said. "The more failed attempts you make, the easier it'll be to know where you currently stand."

Great logic, Lucian thought, rolling his eyes. *If I die, then I'll know exactly where I stand.*

"...dead on the ground," Lucian finished, not knowing he had said it aloud.

"What?"

"Nothing."

Like a good, obedient trainee, Lucian challenged the mountain of sand. He haphazardly released his stored mana, watching as the devices blinked on and off in rapid succession. He dug his foot into the rising sand and pushed off. Each step upward propelled him even farther. By the time he realized what happened, Lucian found himself firmly standing on the top of the dune looking down at Aaron. Even Aaron was surprised, as he had an impressed look on his face.

"Nice work!" Aaron shouted from the bottom. "Once

you can fully control your mana, it'll only take one or two steps to reach that same height."

As if he were mocking Lucian's struggles, Aaron jumped off the ground and landed next to him. With exactly three steps, the boy had ascended to his height.

What a show-off.

Looking at the vast expanse of The Wastelands, Lucian experienced a sense of childish wonder. Although mostly covered in sand, The Wastelands had its name for a reason. At night, he couldn't see the scattered objects wedged in the sand, but now, in the vibrant sunlight, everything was visible.

"See that small rectangle in the distance?" Aaron said, pointing a tad northeast. "That's where we'll make camp for the night. It'll provide us with overhead shelter, and it's a place I stay often when I need to rest."

"How much longer until we reach...Ko—"

"Korakk," the boy finished. "It's normally about a day's trip, but that's when I travel alone. With your speed, it'll take another day and a half before we see a single Tribe."

Although sore and slightly sour from his recent failures, Lucian earnestly asked, "Why are you helping me? There doesn't seem to be any benefit for training or teaching me."

"There is. A pretty good reason," Aaron said. "Let's

call it a conviction. Along with saving Terras from the grips of decay, I've also vowed to help anyone in need. And you definitely look like you need all of the help you can get."

"Hey!"

"I'm just ruffling your feathers," he said, revealing for a second an expression laced with sadness. "I guess you should know I'm a fairly selfish person. The main reason I'm helping you is that I never had anyone do the same for me. It's like I'm reliving my past through you. I apologize if that makes you feel 'used.'"

Images of Lucian's suffering in Caelum weaved their way into his memory. "I've been used all of my life," he said, saying it more to himself than to his companion. "If you can find solace or happiness living through my accomplishments, then do it. I see no reason not to feel pride or self-worth by doing a good deed. I wish more people were like you, then I wouldn't have to..." His sentence trailed off into silence.

Slapping Lucian's back with his hand, Aaron exclaimed, "Enough with the sob stories! Now, it's time for the real fun to start."

A bead of sweat formed and trickled down Lucian's forehead. "What do you consider to be real fun? I think our definition of fun differs greatly."

"Don't worry!" Aaron assured him. "This'll be fun for both of us. I haven't tried this activity since I was a child."

"What is it?"

Aaron quieted Lucian with a finger to his lips. They quietly slid down the dune and tiptoed to another mountain of sand, peering around the corner. "There," Aaron whispered, pointing north of them. "Perfect. There are two of them."

Lucian's gaze followed Aaron's finger to a pile of faded and broken refuse. Poking their heads out from beneath the pile, two creatures with the heads of lizards and the bodies of cheetahs emerged.

"That's the fun I was talking about," Aaron giddily said.

"What *are* they?" Lucian asked. "And what are we going to do with them?"

"We're going to ride them, of course. It's a tradition for those who trek The Wastelands to ride a Venari."

"How do you expect us to tame one of those things!?" Lucian whispered, emphasizing each word.

"Oh, it's very simple," Aaron said. "It's called bait-and-tackle. One person attracts their attention since they're carnivorous, while the other one jumps and ties them down when they attack. It's a commonly used strategy."

"But that means I'll have to be the ba—"

"Bait," Aaron said with a devious smile. "You also don't have a weapon, so you technically can't be the person who tackles."

"But I—"

Unprepared and scared of the sharp claws ferreting through the waste, Lucian was prompted to draw their attention. Since Lucian's legs refused to move, Aaron did what any great friend would do in the same scenario: Aaron pushed him.

15

THE WASTELANDS (PART 2)

 *The Wastelands*

Like a sacrificial lamb, Aaron sent Lucian to be slaughtered. Lucian clutched the edge of his cloak so tightly that his knuckles whitened. His knees buckled at the sight of the Venaris' curved, pointy daggers for teeth. Their seemingly perky disposition on his arrival sent shivers rippling down his back like ocean waves.

With a cracked voice, he yelled, "Aaron, hurry up! I don't want to be these Venaris' fodder."

His companion didn't respond. Aaron appeared to have already rounded the opposite corner of the dune from which they had descended. Lucian assumed that Aaron was planning to attack from the rear, where the piles of refuse would hide his movements.

Bait, Lucian thought. *I have to buy him time... I'm so done for...*

To defend himself, Lucian infused more mana into the devices, feeling an irksome backlash from his exhausted body. The devices around his ankles whirred and buzzed, while the ones on his wrists beeped and flashed.

The orchestra of sounds resounded throughout the surrounding area and seemed to aggravate the creatures standing atop the mounds of waste. They peered down at him like lofty conquerors. Their glowing neon-green eyes, which were encircled with scales, widened; the matted fur that covered their hind legs stuck upward, as they stood to their full height.

The Venaris' slimy, bristly tongues hung loosely outside their mouth, which was wide and long enough to wrap around his entire neck and suffocate him. He positioned his body in a fighting stance. Although he physically looked prepared to engage, he mentally wasn't even close. Infusing one-third of his remaining mana into his lower legs and feet, he was ready to make an emergency escape, if necessary.

"Come on, you small-brained lizards!" Lucian shouted, prodding them on. "Fight me!"

I only have to distract them for a few minutes... Come on, Aaron! Any day, now!

As if on cue, the two Venaris leaped off the refuse and

barreled toward him. Their speed, though not comparable to the Lychnus, was faster than he had expected. Their first target appeared to be his neck. He hurtled himself past them with the explosive power of his mana-infused feet. Upon realizing that he needed the Venaris to have their backs toward the refuse, he rounded them up again.

"You slimy salamanders," Lucian said, huffing out the words. "You'll never catch me!"

Ah, I spoke too soon! Lucian internally lamented, as one of the Venaris nipped at the end of his cloak, tearing the bottom half off completely. *If only I had a weapon! Why don't I have a Phantom at a time like this?*

"Not even a weapon can cure your clumsiness," Eteria mocked.

"Not the time, Eteria!" he yelled, momentarily glancing down at the gem.

"I guess you don't need my help, then," she said, sassily. "I know a way you can subdue them, but I suppose you want to do this alone."

The Venaris were closing in on him.

"Eteria, help me!"

"What's the magic word?"

"Do it!"

"Oh, alright," she relented. "Infuse the two-thirds of your conserved mana into your fist and punch their throats."

"You think such a simple plan will work?"

He dodged another attack from the flank.

"Of course, it'll work!" Eteria exclaimed. "The Venaris, while known for their exceptional speed, have a major weakness: the tender, thin flaps around their necks. Punch them, and you'll see and hear the tear of the soft muscles."

What a revolting image. He shivered. *But the purpose isn't for me to kill them. It's for me to distract them long enough for Aaron to...*

"Too late!" Eteria shouted.

The bulkier of the Venaris tackled him, its front scaly feet pinning his shoulders to the sand. Its tongue swung side to side, and its mouth stretched wide. Lucian couldn't move, let alone punch the Venari's neck. Its companion circled the two of them, most likely waiting for its turn to partake in tearing apart his flesh.

The Venari's tongue dripped with saliva, making a pitter-patter noise, as the slimy substance hit his face. Lucian sealed his eyes and mouth shut. *Ew, its breath wreaks!* The pungent smell of rotten meat and decomposing garbage was overwhelming.

Lucian whipped his head to the side, trying to avoid the stench. He unintentionally exposed his neck. He had to. It was his only option. Saliva mixed with the bitter chunks forced their way out of his stomach and swished into his mouth. He spat them out on the sand and then stared into the eyes of the scaly-eyed creature.

Just get it over with already!

His hands clutched the surrounding sand, awaiting the sharp teeth to sink into his neck and tear him to shreds. His chest rapidly rose and fell. Each breath was perhaps his last.

The creature's pointy snout neared, tongue drooling excess saliva onto his face and sliding down his forehead. His mind went to his family, his new friends, and his fate.

Am I really going to die in such a pitiful state?

The first contact that the Venari made with his face sent his body into a panic and his mind into a state of confusion. Its tongue slurped Lucian's face like a lollipop.

No teeth bared into him.

No blood was drawn from him.

Every second that passed, he grew more confused. Instead of death, he was met with an amiable, full-face wash. The slime coated his skin in a thick film.

A strikingly familiar laugh sent him into a frenzy of frustration. "Did you enjoy your bath?" a voice that he had recognized as Aaron's howled, wheezing from enjoyment. "You never cease to amuse me!"

With one whistle from his obnoxious companion, the Venari hopped off his body.

The moment he was set free from its grasp, Lucian used the last two-thirds of his mana to land a right hook into Aaron's stomach. Aaron lurched over, spitting out saliva.

The boy, recovering from his fit of laughter, collapsed, seemingly only affected by the momentum of the punch's force but not the actual punch itself.

Lucian grimaced.

He's a monster inside and out. How could I have fallen for such a novice prank?

Rising to his feet, Aaron asked, "Did you honestly think that punch could hurt me?"

"I hoped it would, you wretched fiend."

Aaron patted the head of the other Venari, who nuzzled its face into his side.

"Now that we have a means of transportation, we should head out," Aaron said. "Our destination is the same —we're headed to that speck of a rectangle in the distance. It should take about a full day's ride. We'll arrive by dusk."

"Are you even human?" Lucian asked, cautiously patting the head of the bulky Venari, who was supposedly his "ride."

"You can't blame me for your naivety," Aaron said. "I have another mantra that I follow: Those who fool should never be fooled, and those who are fooled should never fool."

"Nonsense."

Aaron concluded the conversation, mounting onto his

chosen Venari. Lucian mimicked his movements, climbing the back of the bulkier Venari and wrapping his arms around its neck.

Eteria was right. Its neck is soft and squishy.

Another whistle from Aaron sent the Venaris gliding across the sand, picking up pace at a rapid rate. Their feet barely touched the ground, as they flew past the dunes.

Ah, I understand now. If they had run at their full speed, my corpse would've been resting in their jaws within seconds.

There were no immediate threats to his person, but he felt queasy. His stomach writhed and swished in pain. He figured out the cause of his upset stomach. In Caelum, caravans were the only source of transportation. The Council of Elders regulated the speed of them as well.

Therein lay the problem. He had never ridden anything, whether caravan or creature, that went faster than the running speed of a human. While Aaron reveled in the pace and exhilaration, Lucian had to restrain the slosh of fluids in his stomach threatening to surface once more. He spat several times to the side to slow its dangerous progression.

I hate this. I hate him. I hate this. I hate him, he internally recited.

Lucian's discomfort turned to distress when he realized that he had to endure this torture for several more hours.

His shoulders slumped, and he buried his face in the back of the Venari's neck.

I might as well sleep. Even if I fall off at this point, it's just sand.

Within a matter of minutes, the rhythmic pounding of the Venari's padded feet against the sand lulled him into a half-awake, half-asleep state.

GIANT IVORY PILLARS TOWERED OVER THEM. Although in a ruinous state, its magnitude and magnificence conveyed a level of dignity and refinement to its creation and form. Lucian gawked at the ruins, which had such detailed and refined architecture. Unlike the ruins in Caelum, these pillars, though chipped and crumbling, were glorious.

"What *is* this place?" Lucian asked, filling his eyes to the brim with its regal image.

"Oh, that?" Aaron said with a look of disinterest. "That's a glorified pile of rubble."

Lucian shot his companion a dissatisfied look, but Aaron wouldn't budge on the topic. Entering the circle of pillars, Aaron made a makeshift campsite out of items found littered in the sand. Either out of pure luck or survival ingenuity, Aaron created a medium-sized tent, tying random fabrics together and propping them up with sticks.

Then, there came the obstacle: the fire.

Aaron had gathered wooden sticks and piled them on top of each other, but there was no way to light them. "Don't you have the Fire attribute?" Aaron asked. "Can't you make it burst into flames with the touch of your hand or something?"

"Of course, I can't. At least, not that I know of. Who do you think I am?" Lucian responded. "Plus, aren't you supposed to be the survival expert?"

"Let's add 'lighting a fire' as part of your training," Aaron said with a wide grin and impatient tone. "Now, make a fire."

Easier said than done.

"I think I'm out of mana," Lucian said. "I used the last bit punching you."

Aaron snorted. "You're not out of mana. You can't be out of mana. It's been long enough for you to restore your mana, so you'll be fine. With your mana recovery rate, you should be at full capacity, now."

"What am I, a god?" Lucian joked.

"You very well may be," Aaron mumbled.

After Lucian shot him a strange look, Aaron said, "Okay! Time for you to light the sticks and create a fire!"

Lucian smoothed his fingers over the bracelets and anklets. He closed his eyes, concentrating on the sound of his breath and the mana flowing from his core to his fingertips. He also felt the restriction of the devices, which, in turn, assisted his control over the mana slowly defusing from him.

When Lucian was younger, Master Felix told him to construct an image of what he wanted to happen in his head. To "visualize" the world around him and to create something out of nothing. A concept that he had not understood until this very moment. He released the mana, letting the streams swell at his fingertips.

Tsszzt!

A spark! He opened his eyes, directing the mana to the stacked sticks. What he had imagined was sorely off the mark from reality. The conjured flame was tiny—so tiny, in fact, that it fizzled out completely before reaching the sticks. He sighed, allowing the mana to disperse.

Looking over at Aaron, Lucian shrugged his shoulders. "So, Mr. Wise Guy, what now?"

Out of Aaron's pocket came two heat stones. The boy struck them together, creating sparks that then lit the sticks and produced flames.

"If you knew how to create a fire, then why did you

make me do such a silly and useless thing!?" Lucian exclaimed, irked at Aaron's lies.

"It's not useless," Aaron said. "Remember that feeling the next time you try to manipulate your mana. Everything is an experience."

"You sound like Master Maverick."

Warming themselves around the fire, Lucian conjured up a modicum of courage. He wanted answers. His mind swam with questions about Aaron and everyone he had encountered so far: Master Maverick, Ferris, and Eva.

Why help me? Why make me stronger?

Before a single question left his lips, Aaron said, reminiscing, "It's been a long time since I went on a journey with another person. You probably won't believe me, but I've been a loner for most of my life. My mother died when I was a child, so I was left alone in a poverty-ridden place without any relatives or allies. That was when I decided to leave and find my place in the world outside of The Terras Empire."

"I'm so sorry," Lucian said, recounting his mother's death. "To lose your mother is like losing a piece of your soul. If I may ask, how did she pass?"

The memory seemed too heavy for the words to come out of Aaron's mouth. He apologized to Lucian, and they spoke of other subjects.

"Why Caelum?" Lucian asked. "More specifically, why did you ransack my house?"

"I apologize for your house," Aaron said. "I'd heard a rumor of a land where special mana crystals were abundant. I stumbled upon your house by accident and noticed no one was home, so I decided to search for some. But it seems that I was wrong and was falsely labeled as a criminal for the supposed attacks. I don't blame you for your anger, but I wasn't the one who attacked your family. I was long gone before anyone was even near the house. Meeting you was probably the highlight of that trip."

"Me?" Lucian asked. "What's so special about meeting me?"

"A lot of things," Aaron mumbled, lowering his head in contemplation. "More than you could ever know."

"How did you meet Ferris and Eva?"

"They once visited The Terras Empire when I was a kid," Aaron recalled. "They came across me in the slums and offered their help. I accepted and left my terrible conditions. Everything that I've learned in the past ten years is thanks to their training and teaching. Who would've thought that a street rat from Terras could live a life of adventure and freedom?"

The moonlight was dimmer than the previous night, and the fire crackled brightly. Lucian and Aaron, after that brief conversation, sat and enjoyed the warmth that heated and comforted them.

After a while, Aaron said, "I'm going to patrol the area. I've heard some concerning rumors about bandits and ambushes late at night in these parts."

"Do you need any help?" Lucian said, eagerly.

"Not now," he said, sharply. "I'll wake you if there are any disturbances."

With those last words, Aaron ventured into the darkness. His figure disappeared into the distance to a place where even the moonlight couldn't reach him. Lucian climbed into the tent and rested his head on a makeshift pillow. He had napped for an hour or two on the way to the pillars, but his mind and body were still riddled with exhaustion and soreness.

A small smile crossed his face, and he whispered before sleeping, "I suppose I owe the gods appreciation for one thing...my first friend."

16

A NEW FRONT

 ???

"Y ou must choose." Three distinct objects encased in transparent, glass boxes sat before him: a key, a dagger, and a rose. Neatly filed in a row, his hand grazed the top of each box.

Although unable to choose, his eyes lingered longest on the dagger. He had a powerful urge to release it from its encasement. He untied the ribbon draped around the box, which kept it closed.

With the box now open, he hesitated but ultimately wrapped his fingers around the dagger's hilt and hugged it close to his heart. The dagger pulsated, a black mist emerging from its blade. With it came a stream of emotions flooding inside him: fear, disappointment, anger, resentment, and loss.

Overcome by these volatile feelings, he shoved the dagger back into the box and threw it and its container onto the white space several feet ahead. He watched as it bounced on the tiles, not shattering as normal glass should have. Instead, it sank into the floor, disappearing into the black abyss beneath the tiles.

Repeating the same steps, the other two items infused him with varying emotions. The rose with its thorns expressed excitement, joy, affection, envy, sorrow, and acceptance. The silver key conveyed a feeling of helplessness, despair, shock, disillusionment, and pride.

"YOU MUST CHOOSE."

Defiantly, he chucked the two glass boxes away, watching them sink into the floor.

Far off in the distance, three blurred figures emerged: a male figure cloaked in black, a female figure cloaked in blue, and a male figure cloaked in white. He squinted his eyes, but the images only blurred further.

Then, they disappeared into the black mist that consumed them. Their figures writhed in agony, as they were sucked into the abyss. They reached out their hands to him. He ran toward them: determined and desperate. He didn't know why he ran. His feet moved of their own accord. He chased after formless phantoms in the darkness.

The shadows overtook him, the figures long gone.

He let a whimper escape him.

"*SAVE ME.*"

"*REMEMBER ME.*"

"*KILL ME.*"

Cries and screams inundated his head, causing him to collapse to the floor.

"Stop it!" he shouted at the darkness. "Leave me alone!"

The light vanished within the presence of darkness. Another figure formed before him, a familiar voice filling her mouth with words that didn't quite fit: "Who could ever love a Fallen One like you? Who could ever forgive a criminal, a murderer?"

"*YOU MUST CHOOSE...*" a fading voice ordered, "...Lucian."

"Lucian, Lucian, Lucian," a muffled voice repeated, adding to the screams of the shadows. "Lucian..." The voice broke through like shattering glass.

 *The Wastelands*

LUCIAN'S EYES OPENED TO AN AGGRAVATED Aaron, who kept yelling in his ear and two impatient Venaris stomping their padded feet on the sand. Yawning, Lucian remembered loosely falling asleep *again* while traveling on his Venari. His garments were drenched in sweat from his nightmare... He searched his memory for its contents but to no avail.

His companion seemed to assume Lucian was purposefully blocking him out, so the raven-haired boy clawed at his shoulder. Aaron shook him so hard that he almost knocked Lucian off the Venari's back.

"Lucian!" the boy shouted, still shaking him.

Trying to maintain his balance, Lucian angrily shouted, "What's wrong with you!? Can't you see I'm awake already?"

With a worried look, Aaron said, "It's already past noontime. Are you okay?"

"What do you mean?"

"You were mumbling something in your sleep. You seemed to be having a nightmare, so I woke you up. Also, your sleeping patterns are gradually becoming...well, irregular."

"What about you?" Lucian countered. "I haven't seen you sleep at all. Isn't that *irregular*?"

His companion's forehead creased. "I wasn't trying to pick a fight with you. I just—"

The eruption of sand and wind forced the Venaris and their riders backward. The creatures dug their claws into the sand, resisting the gusting winds that were pushing them. Aaron's words were lost in the deafening sound.

What's happening? Lucian wondered, panicking.

He covered his eyes with his forearm and clamped his mouth shut to avoid the incoming waves of sand. Even with those precautions, some sand still managed to find its way into his eyes and mouth.

He squinted, looking to his side, watching Aaron wrap a beige woolen scarf around his face. Aaron's attire matched perfectly with his surroundings: He wore an extended, dark brown cloak with sturdy, hefty, bear-skinned boots.

Suddenly, the sandstorm stopped.

When the sand settled and the wind died down, Lucian looked ahead and then back at Aaron while saying, "You didn't tell me we were here."

"You didn't let me finish," the boy replied, snarky as ever. "But you're right. Welcome to the southernmost Tribal Nation, Korakk."

What had produced the swirling winds was the enormous granite gate sliding open and scraping up both sand and waste. Even without peering through the passage, the tops of the pointed and rectangular buildings were visible, seemingly reaching the skyline. It was a scene unlike any other with the region's primary structures made of limestone and sandstone.

Upon Aaron's whistled command, the Venaris ambled toward the gate. When they reached the entrance, a middle-aged man with long, dark brown hair and silver eyes halted them. He wore what looked like a guard's uniform with a sword sheathed on his right hip. In his hands, he held a wooden roster with names on it and an unsharpened pencil.

With a bored expression and a dull tone, the man asked, "Reason for travel and length of stay?"

Uncovering his scarf-covered face, Aaron sarcastically said, "Nice to see you too, Caspar."

The guard seemed to recognize Aaron, his frown turning into a jolly smile. The immediate change caught Lucian off guard.

"Aaron, what a pleasant surprise!" the guard exclaimed. "How long has it been since your last visit?—a year, three years? This old man can't seem to keep track. Time runs too fast here. Way too fast..."

The boy unsheathed his black sword, pointing to a small crack in the blade. The guard, letting out a laugh, said, "Coming to Korakk for such a trivial reason, you must be kidding!"

The grave look in Aaron's eyes said otherwise.

The guard seemed to take the hint. "Oh, well, whatever

the reason, I'm glad you're here. Seeing as you need a quick fix-up, Barren is your man! We've been frequenting some local pubs, and he mentioned your name. Something about a run-in with The Royal—"

"Ahem! Pardon my manners, it seems that I've been babbling..." An unknown signal had been exchanged between Aaron and the guard unbeknownst to Lucian. The guard changed the topic and turned to acknowledge Lucian. "So, who's this bright-looking fellow with you?"

"I'm Lucian Roux," he responded, politely. "It's nice to meet you, Mr. Caspar."

"What a respectable youngster," Caspar praised. "When I first met Aaron, he was just a little thing—a rascal with a fighter's blood in him."

"Let's go," Aaron said, indirectly silencing his old acquaintance. With another whistle, the Venaris lurched forward. Lucian had just witnessed a new side to his comrade—a side very different from his trickster self.

"You seem close," Lucian said, careful not to aggravate him further. "He knows a lot about you."

"He's just a busybody," Aaron said, curtly. "What you'll learn about this world is that the only one you can truly trust is yourself—no one else."

Lucian noticed the boy's scrunched-up face. It was unlike Aaron to express such sullen words. He wasn't sure whether he liked his friend's new side as much as the other.

The cold, heartless words reminded him of his father. Words that only someone who experienced true suffering could speak of. He waited until the moment passed.

Taking his mind off the sour atmosphere, his eyes fixated on the scenery. The streets of Korakk bustled with people. On his Venari, he passed by several stalls with enthusiastic men and women selling their handcrafted goods and wares. What surprised him most about Korakk was the people themselves, specifically their peculiar physical features and outer attire.

Unlike Caelum and Lunaris, the people had naturally tan skin and muscular builds. Their clothes were very foreign to Lucian. The women wore colorful, cotton tops that covered the top half of their bodies and were adorned in multicolored jewelry that glistened in the scorching sun. The men were dressed in loose-fitting pants with dark brown oversized shawls covering their necks down to their waistlines.

Occasionally, he spotted some of the men wearing thin, rectangular hats with the insignia of an eye on them. He also marveled at the men who easily towered over him, standing at around six-foot-ten or higher. Unlike the other townspeople, they wore black, woolen shirts, which exposed their shoulders. They looked like warriors set off for a hunt or a battle with unique symbols painted on their bodies.

Before Lucian could fully take in his surroundings, they arrived at their destination. The Venaris slowed to a stop, and Aaron jumped off his ride's back. Lucian followed suit, wondering if their garbage-eating traveling companions would patiently wait until they returned. He assumed they would since Aaron didn't seem too concerned about them.

Aaron and Lucian entered a small side store with the emblem of two crossed swords on a sign bolted to the wall. Since there was no door, Aaron nonchalantly walked in, and Lucian tailed closely behind. Lucian instantly noticed the variety of weapons displayed on the inner walls of the doorless shop and the long, central table.

I didn't even know some of these weapons existed...

"Welcome to Barren's," a voice said, almost mechanical sounding.

In the innermost part of the store, a burly man sat, who looked to be in his mid-to-late forties. He had bronze-toned skin, magenta eyes, and waist-length, coarse-black hair. An engraving of a black dragon coiled around his right, muscular arm, and his clothes matched the ones Lucian had seen on the street. The shopkeeper appeared to be wiping the lustrous sword with a cloth dipped in a thick, glossy oil.

He appeared highly focused on his task, not even glancing up at them, as he said, "Anything you see in the shop is up for grabs. Feel free to look around. If you need a repair, then put your name on the front roster, and I'll call you when it's ready."

Curiosity compelled Lucian to grab and lift one of the displayed swords lying on the steel table. Due to his unfamiliarity with swords, it was much heavier to hold in his hand than he had expected. He accidentally dropped it.

The sound of the sword hitting the metal table reverberated throughout the shop. Still not looking up, the man said, "Aaron, if any of my swords get scraped or chipped, you'll be the one paying for 'em."

"Looks like your senses have been dulled by too much drinking, Barren," Aaron mocked. "If it was *you* from four years ago, then you would've sensed my presence the moment that I approached the store."

"I still can, you cheeky brat," Barren said, finally lifting his head to examine his customers. "It's called customer service. Ever heard of that? It's polite."

"You? Polite!" Aaron clapped his hands together, practically falling over from laughter. "Never thought the day would come when I'd hear the mighty Barren, the Killer of Wasteland Beasts, mention politeness. What, do you also believe in forest pixies, now?"

Turning his head toward Lucian, Barren said, "What sorry sucker have you scammed this time? No, wait, he looks too young to have anything valuable on him unless you're meaning to exploit him...no, not even you would stoop to that level."

"I'm his friend," Lucian stated.

Barren seemed to search Aaron's face for a change in expression or a nod of approval, but the raven-haired boy's face didn't reveal anything apart from a tiny tinge of annoyance.

"I didn't know you made a new friend, Aaron," he bluntly said. "After that incident with your other friends, I thought you would've—"

"Barren," Aaron snapped. "I'm not here to reminisce. I'm here to get my sword repaired. Lucian is my traveling partner, not my friend."

Eteria, who acted mostly as an observer, broke her silence and vocalized his emotions better than Lucian could have. "Ouch. Says the person who claimed his life's mantra was to help people. What a hypocrite."

"Aren't we all hypocrites?" Lucian spoke internally to her. "No one can perfectly wield their convictions like a sword and uphold their ideals like a saint. Eteria, let's give him a chance. He gave me one."

"I can't tell whether you're sweet or just plain stupid," she hissed, her voice dissipating into silence.

The black sword made a clanking sound, as it was placed on the front metal counter. Barren eyed the "repair" needed and scoffed. "All of this trouble for just a scratch? It looks like you're the one who's gotten weaker. Not me."

Pretentiously, Aaron said, "Whatever...any news on the thing that I requested?"

"Still pending," Barren replied. "Your request isn't that simple. No matter what the payment is, no one wants to venture into a dragon's den for mana crystals, which may or may not even exist."

"Wusses."

"I don't blame them. The dragons inhabiting The Talis Mountains are said to be deadly. If you're that concerned, why don't you retrieve them yourself? You're strong enough to..." He paused at Aaron's anguished expression. "...I heard there's a new request offering 150 crystals to anyone who can take down a high-grade creature."

"Hah, there must be some catch," Aaron said, regaining his composure. "No one's suicidal enough to offer up 150 crystals of their own mana to slay a single beast..."

"But there is," Barren affirmed. "A foreigner has been roaming around Korakk challenging all of last year's BOTB participants."

"So what?"

"Not just challenging them. He's beaten them...*all* of them."

"Even the runner-up from several years back?"

Barren nodded.

"What do you think he wants?" Aaron asked, crossing his arms in disbelief. "What's in it for him if someone takes up that ridiculous request?"

Lucian followed the conversation for some time, but one term befuddled him. "What's a BOTB?"

Like Master Maverick, Barren's eyes twinkled at his question. "Oh, right! You're new here, so you don't know about the BOTB. Short for 'Battle of the Bronze,' it's an annual tournament of strength for a high-level prize. Aaron was the BOTB champion four years ago."

Lucian's eyes lit up.

"Can I—"

"No," Aaron said, sharply. "Barren, don't fill this boy's brain with garbage. He's not here to fight. He's here to learn."

"Then, isn't experience the most important thing for him right now?" Barren countered. "He's not a child. Let him taste the fresh air of Korakk and amplify his fighting spirit. You were in the same situation when you first arrived. I see no issue with it."

"Where's the man you referred to?" Aaron changed the topic. "I want to meet him and gauge his intentions. I want to see if his request is crazy enough to be the real deal. I'm in dire need of a mana refill."

"He's at the southern pub. You know, the one where

you nearly beat that poor drunk to death over a simple misunderstanding. When was that—the summer of—?"

Aaron glared at the man. "Just do your job."

Aaron then looked over at Lucian. "Stay with Barren until I come back, understand?"

"Yes, Your Highness," Lucian said, bowing his head like a vassal.

Aaron didn't respond. He simply walked out, mounted his Venari, and departed.

Once Aaron's figure disappeared in the distance, Lucian looked at Barren, who started fiddling with the sword again. "You know," the man said, "he wasn't always like that. He used to be such an endearing little squirt. After *that* happened to him, it's no wonder why he locked his heart up as tight as a safe. Probably for the better too with that disposition of his."

"You keep saying 'that' incident," Lucian mentioned. "What happened?"

"It's not my story to tell," Barren shrugged with an unchanging tone. Lucian looked extremely disappointed, so he said, "Ask Aaron. If you're as close to him as I think you are, he'll tell you... Until then, let's find you a sword!"

"A sword?" The words spilled out of his mouth. "Why would I need a weapon?"

"For the BOTB, of course!"

"Wait, did you just say the BOTB? But Aaron told me..."

"What Aaron doesn't know won't kill 'em," Barren said with a wink. "You know how he is. He'll skewer me alive if he finds out I let you participate in the tournament behind his back. He's too overprotective of you, so it wouldn't be such a bad thing to let you spread your wings a little, right?"

Lucian jumped up and down like a little kid. "When is the BOTB?"

"Tomorrow afternoon," Barren said with a broad smile, the wrinkles on his forehead softening. "You'll have to sneak out fairly early, so Aaron doesn't catch you. After you leave, come to my store, and I'll have your sword ready for you."

"But, for now, until Aaron returns," the man continued, a devious smile playing on his lips, "I'll answer any question about Aaron, no matter how gruesome or embarrassing it is. Well, except for the one that I can't tell you about."

Before Lucian could ask a single question, Barren said, "Since we might chat for a while, let's move our conversation to a more *suitable* location."

Leaving the shop, Barren led Lucian into the one place that he hated most: a bar.

17

WHAT MAKES A MAN

 *Korakk*

Barren Yeriel Xanthus was the name of the man sitting before him. His worn profile spoke of a lifetime of man- and beast-hunting. He had scars that would never fade and a look that could pierce through the hardest of hearts. His broad, strong physique spoke of many years of intense training and endurance. He looked like a warrior in every sense of the word...or not.

Not this man, who stuffed his face greedily with globs of goulash and wore an expression unbefitting a hardened warrior. Swigging another pint of what Lucian could only assume was an alcoholic's dream, a vodka shot, the man swayed back and forth.

Lucian pinched his nose, the wafts of a familiar stench

breaching his senses. *What a merry fellow,* he thought, observing Barren. *Not much of a warrior in speech or action, but he's a kind soul all the same. And the alcohol doesn't affect him the same as...*

"May I ask my first question?" Lucian asked.

"Oh, right!" the man said, signaling for another pint from the innkeeper. "Ah, I'm so embarrassed! I got you all excited and then my thirst took over. You know how that is?"

Barren slid an apology across the table in the form of a glass of liquor. Lucian recoiled, sickened by the very smell and look of it. He pushed the glass to the side, accidentally letting it out, "Reminds me too much of my father."

The man quickly retrieved the pint and apologized, "I didn't know your father was... I'm sorry. I didn't mean to be insensitive."

"No, that wasn't meant to be said aloud," Lucian said, backtracking. "But like the scars etched onto your body, the scars in my heart will surely never fade."

"You're so young too."

"You said you would answer any question about Aaron, right?"

"Ah, yes...I did say that..."

Don't chicken out. Lucian clasped his hands together. *Ask him...ask him...*

"About Aaron's unique disposition," he started to say,

240

"I've noticed that he sometimes... How should I put it? His personality becomes a bit all over the place. I can't tell which one is his true self."

Barren subconsciously smoothed his fingers over his tattooed arm, an action Lucian assigned as a nervous tic. "It's not normal, but it's also not strange given his circumstances. His mother died when he was a kid, which would be traumatic for anyone. Thrown out into a world of spite and solitude, I can only assume that created the gap between his old and new self. A defensive mechanism for protection. I don't know all of the details, but from my time with him, I can tell that he's hiding something more serious than he lets on."

"His friends," Lucian mentioned, breaching the topic again. "What about them? What happened?"

Barren let out a long sigh and said, "Kid, look, we discussed this."

Lucian's eyes pleaded for an answer.

With a look of resignation, Barren conceded.

"The Dragonian Curse, that's what," Barren said while gulping down more of his drink. "Once inflicted, the infected person lives the rest of his life not knowing when the ancient dragon's curse will activate. His former friends cut ties with him once they found out."

"The Dragonian Curse? Why would he have something like that?" Lucian asked, eyebrows furrowing. "Why does everything have to be so complicated?"

"Mind you, I've never seen a living, breathing dragon in my lifetime. Not even in my prime. The curse is a nasty thing that drains the infected of all his mana. It's like a virus. It's spreading as we speak, trying to erode his body."

"The El Stone embedded in his back seems to be doing its job, but it's not enough. Not nearly enough. What an unlucky person, he of all people getting slashed by the dragon's poisonous claws. There's a reason why no one wants to travel to The Talis Mountains..."

"Why The Talis Mountains? How did he even contract the curse in the first place?"

"I think Aaron mentioned something about traveling with his mother while she was picking herbs or mining crystals," Barren said, sounding uncertain. "The dragons are fabled to be deadly but harmless to humans when undisturbed. To have aggravated the legendary being to such an extent, I don't even want to imagine what happened. Either way, you know why Aaron seems so tightly knitted together, now."

Crash!

The sound of a glass bottle shattering on the floor caused Lucian to jump. After calming himself down, he went back to pressing Barren for more answers. He refused to let this opportunity escape.

"What are The El Stones you mentioned?" Lucian asked. "How do they impede the curse from spreading?"

"Short for 'Elemental Stones,' The El Stones are said to be Gaia's greatest creations. They aren't all-powerful, but they are all-storing. Unlike human-made mana crystals that can only hold a certain amount of mana, one El Stone can store mana equivalent to a person's life force. Since the Dragonian Curse feeds off mana and activates when the infected person's body is weakest, The El Stone slows its progression by maintaining a stable mana flow. But that's still not enough. Once the infected person's mana runs out, it's over. The progression of the curse is swift and lethal, killing the infected person within the day."

Barren waved over the innkeeper. He seemed to be rummaging in his pocket for something. He pulled out a nail-sized, light-green crystal and handed it to the man. "And this, Lucian," he explained, "is Korakk's and The Tribal Nation's currency. Since the inhabitants of The Tribal Nations are born with a naturally higher mana capacity, we use these stones as bartering chips."

"Why would you lessen your own lifespan?" Lucian asked. "If you run out of mana, won't you die?"

"In a sense," Barren said, nodding his head. "Even though we trade with our mana, we can restore it with someone else's. That's why we barter. Equivalent exchange is part of our culture. Unless you're one-sidedly giving out crystals left and right, then you're a dead man. In all my years, I've never seen anyone agree to that type of trade. Even if that were the case, I would never accept that exchange."

"Do you have a spare, empty mana crystal?"

"Well, I do, but why do you need one?"

"Aren't mana crystals the currency here?" Lucian asked, rhetorically. "I'll need one sooner or later... I have something I want to buy, no matter the cost."

Barren's mouth curved upward into an approving smile. "I see, I see. You're at that age where you want to try out many things. Alright, here you go. I keep some with me just in case."

The crystal, which was placed into Lucian's hand, looked like a lush forest. It reflected the color of life, and its beauty captivated him.

Recollecting himself, Lucian wrapped his fingers around the crystal. He practiced what he had done with Master Felix in training and then with Master Maverick in Orsus. His mind moved to images of his mother—serene and gentle memories.

The crystal's light broke through his closed palm. His arm tingled as the mana successfully flowed into it.

Ah, so this is what it feels like. So soothing.

Aaron was right. Even with the devices regulating his mana flow, he had far too much for his untrained body. He sensed when the mana crystal reached its full capacity. He stopped in time, gauging Barren's reaction.

"Wow, well, aren't you good at that!" Barren praised, slapping Lucian's shoulder.

Lucian carefully laid the crystal in his pocket alongside the weathered Credit Slip. "It's not my first time, after all. I think those lessons paid off."

"They sure did," Barren said. "I forgot to tell you one more thing about mana crystals. There are different grades of 'em like there are different grades of monsters. They're divided into three categories: low-grade, mid-grade, and high-grade. Usually, low-grade crystals are used solely for customers to buy minor goods; mid-grade crystals are used for adventurers to restore their mana; and high-grade crystals are used for basic healing and long-term storage."

Remembering Caelum's hierarchy of healing crystals, Lucian inquired, "Aren't the healing crystals separate from the mana crystals? Where I lived, there were different grades of healing crystals too."

Cocking his head to the side, Barren stated, "I've never heard of such a thing, but I can't dismiss your claims. You said your homeland has different grades of healing crystals? What are they like? What do each of 'em do?"

Counting on his fingers, Lucian said, "Third-grade crystals can cure minor illnesses like colds, second-grade crystals can cure bruises and external injuries, and first-grade crystals—owned and used primarily by the Elders—are rumored to heal debilitating diseases and incurable illnesses."

Barren stroked the black scruff on his face and said, "I work off complete confidentiality with my customers, so I won't dig any deeper, but what you're saying contradicts my knowledge of the properties and uses of crystals. I've never heard of a crystal that can cure an illness that Healing Mages could not."

"*What you'll learn about this world is that the only one you can truly trust is yourself—no one else.*" Aaron's cautionary words resurfaced.

Am I too trusting? Lucian wondered. *Just in case, I shouldn't reveal too much, even if he is someone Aaron knows.*

Acting as if he was uncertain of his own words, Lucian causally brushed the topic aside saying, "Ah, well, I might've been mistaken. To be honest, I've never really seen those crystals to begin with, so they might just be a rumor."

"That's too bad," Barren said, frowning. "If those crystals really do exist, we could fix what's going on in Terras."

"What do you mean?"

"Aaron didn't tell you?" Barren asked, his jaw dropping slightly. "I thought everyone knew about Terras's condition."

"I've heard that it's under a curse."

"Not just any curse," Barren said, gravely. "There's a deadly plague in Terras. No one is allowed in or out without a travel permit. Even the nobility in the inner regions is affected. It's a death sentence living in a place like that. The only known cure comes at a hefty price: one life for another. And when people are that desperate, they just might do something insane."

"Is there anything that can be done?"

"Pray for them," Barren said, his eyes filling with an inexplicable sorrow. "If anyone can help, it's the gods. We, warriors of The Tribal Nations, once fought in their platoons. As mercenaries, we were hired to salvage Terras during its transformation into an Imperial Empire. However, the way Terras is headed, there won't be anything left to save."

Foreign words popped into Lucian's head, translating into familiar characters. Words that weren't his own escaped his lips, but they too were understood in an instance of miraculous translation. "The old shall fall; the new shall rise. When the world is rid of its fraudulent king, the true king shall arise from the ashes like a Phoenix in the dead of night. That is when true freedom will reign."

Taken aback, eyes widening at his words, Barren stuttered, "H-How do you know those words? That's the oral prophecy passed down to Korakkian children, speaking in the ancient language of Ion. Who told you that prophecy?"

With a blur of frantic hand movements, Lucian lied, "On my way here, I heard the little children singing something similar on the streets. I just copied them... I'm sorry to hear about Terras."

"Y-Yeah, I am too..." the man said, still processing Lucian's explanation.

The slam of the inn's door sent Barren to his feet. A messenger, who looked around twenty or so, carried a parchment scroll with a red crest. Out of breath, the messenger collapsed, hands and knees pushing on the floor to keep himself from passing out.

Barren barreled toward the fallen man, helping him to his feet. Quick words were exchanged between the two in the same language Lucian had spoken earlier. A look of desperation crossed his new comrade's face. His worried eyes turned quickly to a glare.

Barren returned to the table, grabbed his scattered belongings, and said, "Kid, I need to tend to some things, but I'll be back by morning. Until then, stay in the room upstairs. I already paid for a night. Aaron knows where this place is too. I'll notify him."

"But what about the—" Lucian's words fell on deaf ears.

Barren had already bolted out of the bar with the

messenger in tow. Lucian was stuck between confusion and worry, but he decided not to cause the man any more trouble. Apparently, the building served two functions: as a bar on the first floor and an inn on the second floor. Going up to the second floor, he checked in with the innkeeper, who handed him a silver key. He headed down the hallway, reading the room numbers as he walked.

Once Lucian spotted the sign, "Room 4," he unlocked the door with the silver key. After heading inside, he stuffed the key into his pocket next to the other miscellaneous items that jangled about.

He surveyed the room: It was a decently sized space with two twin beds, a nightstand, a lamplight, and a mirror on the opposite wall. Since the darkness had overtaken the sun, and nighttime had fallen, he lit the illumination crystals lining the walls.

He removed his battered and torn green cloak, resting it carefully atop one of the wooden chairs on the opposite side of the room. He hopped onto the twin bed closest to the window, lay on his back, and stared at the pale ceiling. Ideas danced in his head.

A mixture of fear and elation filled him.

"What do you think, Eteria?" Lucian asked.

With a yawn, Eteria replied, "About what? Oh, about Aaron? I think you hit the jackpot of unluckiness. Your first friend is cursed too. You two really do fit the phrase, 'Birds of a feather flock together.'"

"Do you think there's a way to help him?"

"Help him!" Eteria cackled. "You can barely take care of yourself. How are you going to help him? You would only make things worse."

"Don't say that!" Lucian exclaimed. "There must be something that I'm good for!"

"Well, there is one thing you're 'good' at," Eteria said, emphasizing her pronunciation of each word.

"What's that?" he asked, enthusiastically.

"Being a clown!"

He shook the pendant several times, before she yelled, "I'm sorry! I'm sorry!"

"You're such a baby sometimes, Lucian," she said. "I might as well call you baby 'Luce' from now on. It's cute and girly. A perfect name for you, right?"

He shook it again; this time, using a force so hard the gem continued vibrating even after he had stopped. "I don't want a pet name," Lucian snarled.

"Hey!" she cried out. "Don't forget that Aerus is in here too! Don't forget about him! You don't want to make him hate you, do you?"

"He probably thinks it's well deserved," Lucian said, defiantly.

A day's worth of travel and talk made him drowsy.

Sleep came naturally to him, as it was one of the only times he had to himself when he lived in Caelum.

THE UNNATURAL CREAKS OF WOOD ALERTED HIM. Still half-asleep and not wanting to move, his eyes remained shut. He heard the steady sound of breathing. *It's only the wind*, Lucian convinced himself, trying to sleep. A strange tingling feeling came over him like a wave. His body reactively tensed to a chill in the air.

It wasn't the wind.

Even with his eyes closed, Lucian could feel a malicious mana steadily approaching him like a tiger stalking its prey, waiting to pounce. His muscles tensed; he dared not to move, quietly praying that the moment passed without incident. The cold breaths of the figure blew against his face. Pretending to be asleep was no facile task. He had to relax his limbs, trying not to shake under the sheets.

He couldn't do it. His curiosity and fear overtook him. He slightly cracked his right eye open to see a dark shadow with glazed-over eyes staring right at him.

The figure's eyes shone even more sinister in the darkness of night. Fortunately, the person didn't seem to realize that Lucian was awake. If the figure had noticed, it wasn't apparent on his face—a cold, expressionless look characterized him.

A shiny object rested in the figure's hand, a dagger Lucian assumed, but it was too dark to see it clearly. The figure slowly inched the object toward him. As a cloud moved from in front of the moon, the unknown object, a knife, was revealed. Put to his neck, the blade pressed down hard enough to summon a trickle of blood.

Unsure as to whether he was dreaming or not, Lucian endured the pain.

Short, quick breaths were followed by long, leaden ones, escaping from the mouth of the shadowy figure. The stranger's profile came into view.

It was Aaron.

The raven-haired boy, whose presence synchronized with the shadows, seemed to hesitate, ultimately recoiling his hand. He dropped the knife onto the floor next to the bed.

Lucian heard a reassuring *thump!* as the knife hit the floor, easing his fears.

He softly sighed in relief, careful not to draw attention to himself. He watched as Aaron sunk to the ground, the boy's back bending over in anguish, as his knees and hands trembled uncontrollably. Aaron began to sob, as he mumbled to himself. Lamenting his actions, he cursed something or someone under his breath.

Then, in a fit of indescribable resentment and rage, the boy left the room, closing the door behind him with an audible *click!*

Lucian convinced himself he had been trapped in an awful nightmare—the type that one would wake up and completely forget about the next morning.

Eteria, who was silent throughout the entire exchange, didn't make so much as a peep. Lucian reasoned that it must've been a nightmare. His worries faded to tiredness. His will to sleep surpassed his worry.

The motherly embrace of sleep brought him back into her comforting arms.

18

BATTLE OF THE BRONZE (PART 1)

 *Korakk* ◆

The sound of merry giggles and metallic hooves clattering on cobblestones permeated the air. Lucian's eyes fluttered open, his hand rubbing over the small swell on his neck.

"Hm?" Lucian questioned, drowsily.

He slid his legs to the side of the bed, bent forward, and then checked the floor beneath his feet.

No sign of a knife...

And no sign of Aaron.

The bed next to him was in the same state as when he had arrived: tidy and unused. This could only mean one thing: Aaron didn't return after last night's events.

Still confused, Lucian scoured the room for any indication of Aaron's presence, any sign that his friend had returned, perhaps by chance. None.

That'll make my plans to participate in the BOTB a lot easier... Lucian thought, a fleeting feeling of guilt washing over him and quickly fading away. *It might be for the better that he's not here... It'd only make things more awkward.*

Attempting to focus on something else, Lucian retrieved the beat-up cloak and slung it over his shoulders. He slipped the front black button near his neck into its hole, attempting to smooth out the wrinkles. A bulge in the cloak's pocket revived one of his fleeting thoughts.

I still haven't read Master Felix's notebook, he thought. A fleeting thought indeed, as the moment it occupied a space in his head, it left, all the same, reduced to nothing but a forgettable afterthought.

He shook his head, his unkempt blond hair brushing his face. He grasped one of the strands between his thumb and index finger, thinking, *When did it get this long?*

Before departing, Lucian unclasped the window's lock and opened it. A light breeze swirled into the stuffy room. It caressed his cheeks and pushed the loose hairs covering his eyes to the side. He savored this precious moment of respite.

Well, it's now or never! He decided.

Down the stairs, through the door, and to Barren's blacksmith shop, Lucian ran. The light breeze grew stronger, threatening to rip the hood off his head. A back-and-forth struggle occurred, and Lucian lost. Thus, his hair was bare for the world to see. He resigned to his fate.

It's such a nice day, he thought, in a laidback manner. *Keeping my hood off should be fine every now and then.*

Halfway to his destination, the peculiar expressions that the passerby wore perplexed him. Their stares were unlike the ones he had witnessed in Orsus. They were neither glaring nor gossiping about him. They simply stared. Mouths parting slightly, they stood as still as statues until he had passed.

It's like they've never seen a foreigner in their lifetime, he thought, scoffing at himself for such a foolish thought. *Right...I'm a foreigner!*

Ever since Ferris made him overly concerned about his appearance, he unknowingly covered his head with his hood on every possible occasion. And just as Aaron's appearance starkly contrasted with the citizens of Orsus, so too did Lucian's appearance contrast with the citizens of Korakk.

Of course, they'd be surprised!

Carefully observing the citizens caused him to be even more certain of his conclusion. Not a single soul apart from himself had lighter features. They had dark, brown hair with purple or brown eyes or black hair as deep as night with silver or maroon eyes. Their skin tones ranged from lightly tanned to warm-toned.

Mimicking Aaron's motions in Orsus, Lucian quickened his pace to a jog, hurrying to Barren's shop. Covering his head with the hood didn't change anything, as the fabric surrounding his head had a tear. He didn't know how or when the cloak was torn, but what he did know was that he surely needed a new one.

Arriving at Barren's, Lucian called out, "Good morning! I'm here to pick up that sword!"

Heading inside, he pushed the shabby, thin fabric hanging over the entrance to the side. Nothing had changed since the other day. Not even a single sword had been sold. Everything was neatly organized and arranged on the central, metal table. Barren sat at his spot, tinkering with another weapon.

Lucian approached his counter.

"Hello, Barren," Lucian said. "I'm here, as planned. What should I do?"

Barren's eyes looked up, meeting his own. With the blade's tip, the man pointed and waved the sword toward one of the side tables, hugging the animal skin-covered walls. "Choose any sword on that table. They're easier to use. Perfect for beginners like you."

"How did you know I was a beginner?"

"The way you pitifully handled that sword yesterday

was proof in and of itself," Barren laughed, setting the sword down on the table with a *clunk*. "Did you happen to see Aaron last night? I sent him to your place, but somehow, he decided to stay at The Shed."

"Shed?" Lucian asked. "You have a shed?"

"No, not a real shed... *The Shed*," Barren repeated. "It's a cheap inn on the eastern side of Korakk. It's close to where he met with that potential client. So, did you see him or not?"

Unable to accept the truth, Lucian lied through his teeth while saying, "I must've been asleep when he arrived." He dared not meet Barren's gaze, as he felt the man would've known that he was lying.

"That's too bad," Barren said, shaking his head. "I thought that his sleeping patterns would've improved by now, but it looks like I was wrong. Ever since the incident with the curse, he hasn't been sleeping. He's practically an insomniac. It's not healthy. Have you ever seen him sleep?"

"No," Lucian said, shaking his head. "Why, is it that bad?"

"Not exactly bad. Just..."

Lucian made his way to the side counter, testing each sword down the line. He tried picking a few of them up, but he failed to lift any of the hilts higher than five inches. Every time, he dropped the sword, watching it clatter on the table.

He roamed to the end, where a slim sword sat with a rough, scratchy hilt and a shiny but short blade. He wrapped his fingers around the hilt and picked it up with ease. Not knowing how to hold a sword, he awkwardly kept turning the handle over in his hand, trying to find a comfortable grip.

This looks good, he thought. *I wonder what kind of sword this is...*

Laughter from the back of the shop drew Lucian's attention away from the weapon. Barren wheezed uncontrollably, staring straight at Lucian's selected sword. Like a madman. "Y-You just had to pick that one, didn't you? I meant to put that one out there as a joke, but you've taken to it! I'll gladly give you that one."

"What's so funny?" Lucian snarled, not in the mood for mockery.

"That ain't a sword!" Barren burst out, slapping his knees and tottering on his chair.

"If this isn't a sword, what exactly is it?"

"Try slapping it against the table," Barren suggested.

Lucian felt like a vein was about to pop on his forehead, as his patience was running dangerously thin. Drawing his arm back with the sword poised in the air, he hit the table with all of his force, watching as the blade deformed right in front of his eyes.

Disbelief spread over his face. Not only was the sword,

well, not a sword, but it also turned out to be a useless weapon. When the sword whacked against the metal table, its blade flattened like putty or clay. It was malleable: a trait that no normal weapon should ever have, even as a joke. He could've been killed fighting with this sword.

"How could you try to sell something so useless!" Lucian exclaimed. "You're a conman!"

Rising from his seat, Barren walked over to him and took whatever the thing was out of his hands. With his bare hands, the man rubbed the object between them, shaping the blade into a spear-like structure. Taken from his back pocket, Barren wedged a yellow crystal into a small hole in the hilt.

How's a crystal going to help? Lucian wondered, somehow hoping for a miracle to occur.

"And there you go!" Barren exclaimed, handing the object back.

Before Lucian's very eyes, the malleable object hardened into its new form, a stream of light emanating from the weapon. Lucian tapped the edge of its spear-shaped form and pricked his finger by its sharpness, blood dripping from the freshly made wound.

Contrary to his earlier statements, Lucian's shoulders lifted in excitement. "I'm sorry for calling it useless... I didn't know that it could change forms so easily! Can I have it?"

"Of course, you can!" Barren exclaimed. "But only if you promise me one thing... You have to return it to me after the BOTB's over, okay?"

Taking the weapon in his hand, Lucian eagerly responded, "I will! I promise!"

"Good, good!" the man happily said. "If you bring it back in one piece, I'll give you one of my newer products. It's expensive but worth its weight in gold. The material that I used is called, *'Dragonite'*—its blade is coated in Dragon's blood and its hilt is wrapped in Dragon's skin."

"Will you really let me have something that pricy for free?" Lucian asked, with a sparkle in his eye.

"Yes, but only if that weapon you have in your hands is left intact."

"I understand!"

"Alrighty then, let's get going, shall we?" Barren said, switching the outside sign from "open" to "closed."

Excitement welled within him. *It's time*, Lucian thought. *It's time...*

WHEN THEY ARRIVED, HIS WORDS FELL FLAT. THE immensity of the arena's aura and atmosphere overwhelmed him. Screams of pain, cheers, and curses clogged his ears. Barren led him through the hordes of people, who practically pushed others over to peek into the expansive arena built of iron and concrete.

It looked like the fabled Colosseum he had read about in one of Master Felix's ancient textbooks. Unlike the book's description, no wild, untamable beasts lurked within ready to devour humans. It was only a human-to-human brawl. The *clangs* and *clunks* of metal hitting metal reverberated, catalyzing another wave of screams and cheers from the crowd.

They entered what appeared to be the participant's entrance. Barren spoke with several guards, fighting off waves of regular folk trying to push their way through. Even amongst the chaos that erupted, Barren leisurely spoke to them, amiably too, Lucian noted.

Once past the people and the passage, they walked through a maze of curved tunnels, reaching a set of stairs leading upward to the inner section of the arena.

He clutched the weapon tightly in his palms, blood rushing to his head and face. He looked like a ripe tomato. Nerve-racking wasn't the right word to describe the drop in his stomach and heart. No, it was something more. For the first time, he felt a stomach-gurgling, heart-wrenching fear stir inside him. Unlike his father, who had a clear limit to his strength, these contestants were complete mysteries.

What stood before him was a battlefield of unknown possibilities. A place where simply having some smarts and more mana wouldn't save him.

Why did I do this to myself? he wondered. *What am I going to do?*

Unintentionally, he had tuned out a significant portion of Barren's explanation of the rules and regulations enforced in the arena. Not like those would've helped him escape the impending doom that he would inevitably face. His knees felt weak. He felt weak. He was weak.

I am weak, he thought. *Too weak...*

"Don't worry, Lucian," Barren said, setting a reassuring hand on his shoulder and squeezing it. "You're starting in the preliminary rounds. You shouldn't be facing off against someone too strong. You'll be fine. The participants in the BOTB are soft on newbies. Trust me."

Lucian slurped in a single breath, repeating the same words, as he exhaled, "Everything will be fine. I'm not going to die. I trust him. I trust him. I trust him."

Barren ascended a set of stairs, peeking inside the arena to assess Lucian's first opponent. Lucian anxiously awaited the words, "See, your opponent's not that scary, now, is he? You'll be fine." But those words never came. Barren stood frozen on the top step.

Since Barren wouldn't come down, no matter how long that Lucian waited, he decided to see what was so shocking. Gulping down his fears, he climbed to the top. The blaring sunlight momentarily blinded him, his eyes needing time to readjust to the brightness. Once adjusted, he saw the source of Barren's distress. He was slightly shocked but for an entirely different reason. His opponent stood at the ready, awaiting him.

The gleam of gold and silver armor shimmered in the sunlight, only covering the upper half of his opponent's body. The bottom torso, mainly the belly region, had been left exposed. Leather straps clasped the fabric beneath the armor to mid-thigh compression shorts with strips of animal skins covering most of it.

Along with a broad sword with the tips of its blade slanted, the opponent donned a white cape with the giant emblem of a golden knight riding a black horse. As the wind whirred, the cape flowed like smooth waves, threatening to fly away, if not for the rope tethering it in place.

He looked to Barren, who stood frozen in his place, gawking at the girl.

Slipping out of his mouth, Barren said, "Forget everything I said. You're screwed. You're completely done for. I'm sorry, Lucian, if I had known you'd be going against *her*, I would've never signed you up. Please forgive me!"

"Barren, what are you talking about—"

What type of opponent could've made the imposing, intimidating Barren, the Killer of Wasteland Beasts, cower like a child? Especially since the person standing in the arena's center was shorter and slimmer than Lucian.

Why is he so afraid? thought Lucian, dumbfounded by the man's absurd statement. *That person—my opponent—is just a little girl!*

Truly, the opponent who stood anchored in her spot was a girl of ten or eleven years of age. Her layered, wine-colored hair barely reached her shoulders. Petite and pretty were the words that characterized her, not terrifying or fearsome.

"You've got to be kidding, Barren. She's only a tiny little thing—a girl," Lucian said, his words matching the ignorance of the men in his patriarchal village. A habit he had neither known was discriminatory nor false.

Lightly resting his rough, scarred hand on his shoulder, Barren said, "If you think so, then you're going to be in a world of pain when you face her. I wouldn't test her if I were you."

"Who *is* she?" Lucian asked, skeptically. "She can't be that strong with those tiny arms of hers..."

"Angelique Maroon," Barren stated, subduing a squeak. "Youngest reigning Elder Warrior of The Tribal Nations and the second strongest fighter of Terras's elite group. Lucian, you don't seem to understand that her presence here could summon the deaths of many people if she isn't satisfied with today's duel."

"An elitist warrior?" Lucian repeated. "What is this organization that you're talking about anyway? A band of jesters for the king to entertain himself with?"

"No," the man said, in a grave tone. "They're the reason why Terras can maintain its dominance over Gaia. They are the ones who slaughter men and beasts alike, the ones who leave nothing but rivers of blood in their wake. They are...The Royal Guards."

19

BATTLE OF THE BRONZE (PART 2)

 *Korakk*

The thunderous stomping of feet from the crowd surged forth, inundating Lucian with their overpowering energy. Vile demands of blood mixed with rains of spit hurdled downward at the arena: a blend of gray granite, yellowish clay, and red soil, producing a dusty climate.

Lucian coughed, clearing his airway, sucking in both red sand and dry air.

"Angel of Death!" the crowd chanted. "Angel of Death! Angel of Death!"

From Lucian's perspective, the Angel of Death, whom they so enthusiastically cheered for, was no more than a small girl feigning strength. No matter how hard that he tried, all he could see was a scrawny child wearing uncomfortable armor and holding onto a big sword several times her size.

His obvious expression of disbelief seemed to alert her, since she shot back a cocky smirk, mouthing the words, "I'll crush you," with specific emphasis on the word *crush*.

The match's official stood squarely between them, holding a thick roll of parchment in one hand and a charred-black wand in the other. He was a scrawny-looking man in his mid-sixties, and his outer attire consisted of a pitch-black robe with silver tassels. Atop his head sat the same hat that Lucian had seen before... The eye-shaped insignia creepily stared at him.

"Welcome to the first match of The Battle of the Bronze!" the official's voice boomed, temporarily quieting the rowdy crowd. "Give a round of applause for Ms. Angelique Maroon and Mr. Lucian Roux!"

Not again, Lucian sighed, plugging his ears.

What he had expected didn't occur. No screams, no bellows, came from the crowd. Instead, the onlookers synchronized their claps, mechanically, eventually dissipating to silence. None of them deviated, making Lucian even more suspicious.

Just like The Var's power, he thought. *I wonder...*

His train of thought was cut off, as the official started to weave signs in the air with his wand and shoot off a round of fireworks. He covered his ears, crouching and expecting the remnants to fall back down and hit him, but they fizzled out before making landfall.

They lingered in the sky, producing myriads of strange colors—a mix of blues, reds, and greens. Even when he thought that they would crash into the crowd, they simply faded. Their existence fizzled away, taking with them the vibrant colors that held his gaze.

He then turned his attention to his opponent, who had been skillfully swinging her sword. She did so with considerable ease for someone of such a small stature.

Am I really going to have to fight her? he wondered, a bit guiltily.

With the same pitch and force, the official announced, "Let the match begin!"

The girl, whose eyes were mainly focused on her sword, finally met his gaze with an uncontrollable fire of excitement. *Wham!* the sword went as she plunged it into the earth.

Being a seasoned warrior, she pulled the blade out with only one hand on the hilt. She waved it around like a flag, showing off her precise control and her overwhelming strength to handle such a monstrously sized weapon.

Her eyes sparkled at the sight of his sword.

"Hey, kid!" she called out to him.

He recoiled at that word, slightly offended. She didn't seem to mind when he gritted his teeth at her. Rather, she seemed to enjoy it.

Sliding her tongue over her pearly whites, she confidently proclaimed, "Let's make a deal! If I win, I get that funny-looking sword of yours. And if you win, well, let's say that I owe you a *favor*. How does that sound? A fair deal, don't you think? I *am* Vice Captain of The Royal Guards, after all."

Lucian looked over to where Barren had been standing. His acquaintance had vanished, probably off placing bets against him. Even so, Lucian was a man of his word.

He turned back to her and said, "I have no interest in receiving any favors from a child."

Her face turned as red as her wine-colored hair, a few snickers echoing from the crowd. Her malicious glare silenced them. At that moment, he knew he had made a major blunder.

"You'll pay for this!" she shouted, her eyes glowering with rage.

I'm screwed, he dismayed. *Why did I run my mouth and offend her?*

Using one step to propel her forward, Angelique shot straight at him. Her dainty fingers were wrapped firmly around the hilt of her sword, raising the blade to a level position on her right side. She looked ready to skewer him. She was faster than anything he had ever seen. Faster than even the Lychnus, who had nearly devoured him.

He jumped sideways, rolling like a barrel to avoid her attack. Another quick follow-up attack sent him rolling to the other side, and he barely avoided a puncture in his chest.

Before Lucian could collect himself, she appeared above and drove her blade down. He dodged, using his mana-enhanced legs to launch himself out of harm's way. He landed awkwardly, the brunt of the motion falling on his limbs.

"You're pretty light on your feet, aren't you?" Angelique heaved. She used both hands to retrieve the sword wedged deep into the dirt. Unlike her previous attacks, this next plunge would surely skewer him.

In between huffs, she cried, "Too bad you're a filthy rat!"

After a moment of resistance, she successfully tore her blade out of the ground. Pieces of rubble and dirt flung outward, hitting Lucian's face. In the interlude to Angelique's next attack, Lucian took the chance to scurry away.

Comparing his tiny sword to the bulky weapon that

she wielded, Lucian hopelessly thought, *My sword won't even be able to scratch her...*

Her quickly approaching figure dragged him out of his brooding. She clutched the sword in her left hand, dragging up loose dirt as she moved. It made a scraping sound as its heavy blade slid through the ground.

She's coming! he internally screamed. *What am I going to do!? Calm down, Lucian! Think...think!*

Then, an idea hit him like a bolt of lightning.

Angelique compressed her legs and sprung upward, lifting the blade high above her head.

If I can't beat her, he thought, *then I'll block her.*

He flipped his sword to its side, gripping the hilt with his right hand and the flat side of the blade with his left. She descended, metal hitting metal. The two swords colliding sent reverberations through his arms.

The use of her full weight and the downward thrash nearly broke his block.

He was pushed backward, his heels scraping against the sand beneath him. He barely regained his balance, letting out a pitiful imitation of a warrior's cry.

She pushed harder, her sword denting his blade.

He tightened his grip.

He only had two choices: bear the full brunt of her attacks or be slashed into two by a girl several feet shorter than him.

His pride wouldn't allow it.

His will to survive wouldn't allow it.

The tighter Lucian's grip became, the more his right palm dug into the hilt's engravings. Where his left hand held, blood dripped down his arm as his knuckles brushed against the blade.

After a struggle of wills, Lucian managed to fend her off, overtaking and pushing her backward. She slid away from him, slightly stumbling as she went to regain her balance.

Finally.

"I can do this," he whispered. "I can do this."

He lifted his right palm off the hilt, a stinging sensation coursing through his flesh. To maintain his grip for future attacks and blocks, he wiped the blood and sweat off his hand on the front flap of his cloak. Each stain, each tear, became a symbol of his struggles.

He twisted his sword back to its original position, relying heavily on his right hand.

He lifted the blade while yelling, "At least a rat knows how to fight!"

Shaking the dust out of her hair, Angelique shouted, "Yes, and like a rat, I'll exterminate you!"

She was mad, completely mad. Her eyes, reflecting a tinge of gray, analyzed him. She licked her lips, a crazed expression distorting her innocent-looking face. She cackled, revealing the full extent of her insanity.

She brought the sword above her head, readying for another attack. But she didn't instantly charge him. Her motions slowed a bit.

This is my chance!

Mimicking her movements from the start of the match, Lucian propelled his body forward at an incredible speed. With his momentum, he closed in on her, smacking the side of his blade against her ankles.

She was swept off her feet, a sickening *thud!* affirming the hit.

"Now, who's the rat?" he asked, watching her squirm on her back like a capsized turtle.

One of her hands reached down, clenching her injured ankle. Her condescending smile, however, didn't fade. It grew wider at the sight of her own blood, exciting her.

His eyebrows creased in confusion, and his expression turned into disgust. For good measure, he did another *whap!* to her stomach with the flat edge of his blade. Even when her body curled inward, her throat spitting out blood, she cackled like a hyena.

"That's enough!" Lucian screamed, her crazed voice driving him insane. "Let's end this!"

He drove the sword down at her. She swiftly rolled out of the way, regaining her balance, and took advantage of his missed swing. Lucian's sword, now wedged into the ground, gave Angelique enough time to counterattack.

Part of the Angel of Death's counterattack was to punch Lucian's sword. She was small, but the impact released his sword from the ground and threw him backward. Oddly enough, she avoided attacking Lucian's body directly.

Why isn't she attacking me? Why isn't she—oh, no!

The composition of his sword had changed. The hilt remained the same, but the blade was deformed, stretching like a beast's entrails. It had been elongated by every block and attack during this match, slightly trailing in front of him like a rope.

What the—it's gone!

His eyes focused on the spot where the yellow gem should've been. The gem had been completely shattered, tiny glass shards sticking out of its mount. A look of panic arose on Lucian's face, shaking the confidence he had just accumulated.

"That's dirty!" Lucian shouted.

She stuck her tongue out while saying, "You haven't seen anything yet!"

During his moment of hesitation, the girl drew her sword back like a club and swung it sideways, crashing the blade against the right half of his body.

Lucian was flung across the arena, falling and slapping

onto the arena's unforgiving surface. Like a piece of paper, he crumpled.

She's a monster!

Crunch!

Lucian writhed on his side, struggling to move due to his possibly broken ribs. The taste of iron swam in his mouth, and the liquid's sickening smell inundated his nostrils.

His opponent limped toward him.

Come on, Lucian! Move, move! She's just a little girl! Get up!

It was neither grit nor adrenaline that pushed him. It was just a sheer will to survive. Lucian stood up, legs shaking, and ribs cracking in excruciating pain.

His shaky periphery narrowed in on her.

Rustling around in his pocket, he pulled out the green, mana-infused gem that he had borrowed from Barren in the bar. He bit down, holding the gem between his teeth, reshaping the rope-like putty into the shape of a spear.

Taking out the crystal, he hammered it into the holder with his palm. He watched with pride as its light engulfed the malleable-shaped spear, hardening into metal.

He was thoroughly surprised that she didn't attack him in the interlude between his fall and the remolding of his weapon. All the while, he had assumed that she was limping toward him with the same fury burning in her eyes.

Instead, she stood stiff in her spot about a quarter-length span away from him. Even with a limp, she had an unnatural strength and could've easily reached him in no time. So, why?

Her eyes communicated a mix of coldness and terror.

Aren't I the one who should be afraid? he thought, taken aback.

With the metal spear in his hand and the odds stacked against him, Lucian envisioned the forest. He remembered the feeling of the mana flowing through his veins and everything surrounding him. He remembered his pinpoint precision when he threw the spear into the beast's core and shattered it.

Clutching the spear, he closed his eyes, letting the unseen become seen. The golden streams spread out before him. They connected to other life forms, but the other mana cores were far too weak to matter.

His opponent's mana was distinct. His heart hurt as he delved deeper into her mana.

It's like when I met Aaron, he thought, his hand clutching his chest.

It was similar yet different. There was a familiar pain, but the wave of recognition didn't entirely submerge him.

What is this feeling? Who is she?

Reopening his eyes, Lucian assumed a throwing stance. Every single movement caused his broken ribs to dig deeper into his flesh. He winced, the pain temporarily stalling him. The golden streams converged at a single point, shining as bright as the sun. Even though his vision was blurry, he locked onto her core.

"Y-Your eyes!" she cried, pointing at him. "Why are *you* here?"

"Stay focused," he mumbled, concentrating on the spear's trajectory.

I have only one chance, he thought, as his body was on the verge of collapse.

Excruciating pain shot through his side as Lucian pulled back his arm and released the spear with a powerful thrust. The spear spiraled at her, picking up speed on its path. Instead of the black flames he had used against the Lynchus, a green glow enveloped the metal weapon.

Even as highly skilled as she was, Angelique couldn't fully avoid the incoming spear. It tore through the air, the way lightning parts the sky, dredging up a tornado of dust and dirt. All she could do was block. The pressure of the spear hitting her blade thrashed her backward, her body slamming against the furthest wall.

A revolting *crack* resounded.

Lucian approached her. Fear had no claim over him, even as he had to drag his legs forward. He was shocked at how calm he was. The muscles in his face relaxed with each step, even as his ribs threatened to break through the soft flesh covering his torso.

His steps were firm, enduring the agony. He wouldn't show her any weakness. Not when victory was close at hand.

"Y-You can't be *him*!" she repeated.

"Looks like the rat won," he said, striking the sword into the ground.

Once Lucian had affirmed that she couldn't move, his legs turned to jelly. His shoulders sagged. His insides sloshed around. He lost his balance. His feet faltered, slipping out beneath him. He braced his body to slam against the ground.

Something...Someone had stopped his fall.

Sweat drizzled down from his forehead into his eyes, stinging them and skewing his already dizzying vision. His strength had already left him. The back of his head hit the figure's firm chest.

Ah, I'm dead either way. Aaron's going to kill me... Wait, what is this feeling?

With what little strength he had left, he swiveled around and faced the figure. His vision gradually focused into an unstable clarity. His eyes rested on the man who had caught him. The man had shoulder-length, dark brown hair, umber-colored eyes, and unkempt facial scruff.

His attire consisted of golden armor and a pure-white cape with the same symbol that Angelique wore.

"You're not Aaron," Lucian said, wheezing.

"You're right. I'm not Aaron!" the man exclaimed, a hearty laugh rising from his gut.

"Who?" Lucian asked, the clarity of his words dwindling with each consecutive cough.

"The name's Darius," the man answered, "Darius Grindenwald."

20

THE MISSION

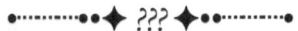

Darkness shrouded the skies. No stars, no moonlight, blessed him that night. Creeping shadows littered his path, revealing and receding on a whim. But the darkness of the night wasn't as frightening as the indiscriminate light scathing him with its sharp rays.

Like the shadows, Lucian wanted to sink into the inky puddles. Unseen and unnoticed by the day walkers, who threatened his solitude and peace. His steps were slow, the path winding into circles and straightening into a long lane.

Near him, distorted figures wandered: some tall, some

small, and some figments of his imagination. He didn't know what was real and what was not, but he didn't seem to mind the absurdity of the scenery. It was like his life: disorganized yet desolate.

When the pathway abruptly rounded a corner, one of the buildings was close enough for him to see inside. His heart sunk in his chest.

Albeit its wooden foundation rotting, this ungodly structure was his house. The sound of frightful screams and rageful shouts slipped through the house's cracks, resurfacing terrors that he thought he had smothered and buried. He needed them to be buried deeper to forget the ones he left behind...deeper and deeper...

With a satisfying *swoop* and *crunch*, the shadows devoured the house.

Moving on, the surrounding buildings revealed painful memories. The Holy Chapel was to his left; The Sanctuary of Gaia was to his right.

"Go away!"

Like his house, everything fell before him.

Beyond the buildings, the world was hazy, a gray mist submerging dark secrets. The shadows snickered as he walked; they snickered as he stopped. Their laughter tried to drown him, their voices becoming distinct. He knew *them*.

Among the chorus of voices, Lucian specifically recognized two of them: Elias Daye's and The Var's. They were distinct, as he remembered their tones well. Elias's laughter was as cruel as a devil's and The Var's as slippery as a snake's. He would never forget their malicious and sadistic words, seeking to plunge him into darkness.

Hearing their voices was like poison to him, but he couldn't find the words to rebuke them. He was strangely calm—the calm before the storm.

As he continued to walk, in the dead of the night, he started to feel a connection to the desolation and the silence. The darkness didn't scare him since his own darkness was far deadlier. Its shadows paled in comparison to the demons that he subdued daily.

"I'll protect you!" his sister's sweet voice exclaimed, which then warped into a vile cackle. Like a witch's. "Who would ever love you?"

Nothing. He felt nothing. Her words didn't register with him. He simply sighed, wondering when his anguish would end. He continued to walk without a destination. His path finally straightened, a fuzzy light spreading out in the distance.

Is this the end? Lucian asked himself.

"No," a wisp of a voice answered. "It's only the beginning."

What is?

The distant light lingering far away, a seemingly unattainable thing, swooshed toward and past him. Now, everything was as clear as day in the dark of night. An unnatural light, it was. He was blinded by it.

When he regained his sight, two familiar figures stood before him. Swords in hand, they fought, the sound of metal-on-metal ringing.

Blood stained their cloaks.

One of the figures donned a pitch-black cloak, while the other wore a pure-white one. The flaps of their cloaks swished with each strike and block. Their faces were hidden under the fabric of the hood.

They each performed their roles perfectly. While the black-cloaked figure fought recklessly, slashing left and right and relying solely on instinct, the white-cloaked figure made calculated moves. It was like watching a chess game: Black versus White.

They spoke, but their words were garbled. Lucian was an observer, merely watching the match play out before him. Even if he intervened, there was nothing that he could do. It was their fight. It was their battle. He had no right to...

And then, it was over. The black-cloaked figure jumped upward, thrusting the blade into his opponent's gut. The blade broke through skin and bone, sticking out of his opponent's back. The white-cloaked figure refused to be defeated without a final strike. His sword slashed at the black-cloaked figure's face.

The attacker pulled backward, but the blade caught onto his hood and tore the fabric off.

Lucian's mouth widened, and his lips quivered.

The black-cloaked figure's face was exposed. A devilish smirk curled on his lips, as he twisted the blade deeper into his foe's stomach.

The figure released an insane scream, shaking Lucian to his very core.

Retreating and staggering backward, Lucian fell to the floor. The black-cloaked figure looked at him, flashing a wicked smile and beckoning him forward with the flick of a finger.

Lucian shivered.

What he saw was a demon wearing the mask of a human. And what shocked him the most was that the boy beneath the hood was none other than *himself*.

•···········••✦ *Korakk* ✦••···········•

Tzzzst.

Lucian's eyes creaked open, reacting to the strange noise. Wrapping around his body was a thin layer of rose-colored mist. It seeped into his skin, flowing like a tiny stream—a stream that smelled like soap.

Where am I?

Dainty hands hovered over his torso, releasing the mist. His eyes focused on the figure leaning over him. His body jerked, causing the figure to click her tongue.

With her right palm, she returned him to his original position, putting pressure on his shoulder to keep him still.

Why is she here?

"Angelique?" Lucian's voice croaked, puzzled at the girl's peculiar actions.

"Don't speak," she ordered, "and don't move or else the healing will take longer."

Healing? he wondered. *What's she talking about? Why would I need...*

Images of the match flooded into his mind.

Oh, that's why... But why is she healing me?

Appearing out of nowhere, the bulky man from the BOTB said to Angelique, "Good, the healing's working. Looks like you can do it *if* you try."

"I didn't say that I *couldn't* heal him," she said with a sour tone. "I said that I didn't *want* to heal him."

"But you are," the man said, "and I'm thankful. We need him, after all."

"Ahem." She coughed. "Darius, he's awake, you know."

"Oh! Our sleeping beauty finally has awakened from the evil Mage's spell."

Lucian looked at Darius. Instead of the armor worn at the arena, the man had changed into a simple brown tunic with an amber-colored belt.

"Where am I? Why is she healing me?" Lucian asked, frantically. "Where's Barren?"

"Hold your horses, Lucian," Darius said, waving his hands up and down, trying to calm him down. "I'll explain everything, but you must remain still. Angelique's healing magic is extremely effective, but for it to work to its fullest capacity, you can't resist."

Lucian lay still, nodding his head in compliance.

"To recap, I am Darius Grindenwald," Darius pointed at himself and then at Angelique, "and this is my comrade, Angelique Maroon. Not many people know this fact, but she's both an Earth *and* Water Mage with a specialty in healing."

"You still didn't answer any of my questions," Lucian said, impatiently.

"Darius, you're way too slow when explaining things. Let me do it," Angelique interrupted. "First, you're in The

Shed, an eastern inn in Korakk. Second, I'm healing you because we need you. Finally, we told your *friend* that you were in safe hands."

She flipped her hair and infused more healing mist into his body. He felt tingly, and his wounds stung. He ground his teeth together, stiffening his muscles to avoid excessive movements. The healing felt like a thousand needles piercing into his skin all at once.

"Consider this treatment an upfront payment," Darius said. "We need you to do something for us...regarding your *other* friend."

Ah, Aaron...

"Do what?" Lucian asked, suspicious of their intentions. "You said you're Aaron's clients, so why can't you just ask him yourselves?"

Darius ran his fingers through his hair while saying, "We are his *future* clientele. He refused our request. But we need him to do it, no matter what. So, we thought you could help us with a little convincing."

"I'm grateful that you're healing me, but this is blackmail," Lucian said. "If Aaron refused your request, then I'm the last person who could change his mind."

"But he's more familiar with you than he is with me, as I'm pretty much a stranger," Darius responded, seriously. "If he doesn't accept, then Korakk will be in great danger! Don't you care about innocent lives?"

Lucian's tone lowered, and he asked, "Why would anyone be in danger? Just what are you trying to make my friend do?"

Averting his gaze, Darius said, "I can't give you the specifics, but just know that it's vital for Aaron to accept this job. It's an S-class adventurer's mission, and I'm willing to pay double—no—triple the normal amount!"

Angelique, whose hands stopped producing the rosy mist, said, "Don't trouble the poor boy. He's just a tiny shrimp. What could he possibly do?"

What did she just call me?

The vein in his neck bulged, threatening to burst. His eyes flared. "Well, this tiny *shrimp* and *rat* demolished you during the match, so what does that make *you*? A *bug*?"

"I'll squash you," she sneered.

He repeated her words back at her by saying, "I'll exterminate you."

Her face flushed a bloody red color.

Stepping in between them, Darius said, "That's enough, you two. Let's get back on topic. Look, I can't force you to do anything, but if you could at least give him this..."

Darius handed him a tan parchment wrapped up like a scroll. As soon as Angelique finished healing him, Lucian rose from the bed. He surveyed his surroundings, noticing some strange tapestries hanging on the walls.

"I can at least relay the item since you *did* heal me, but I can't promise anything else," Lucian said. "I might not make it out alive if he finds out about the—"

"Don't worry!" Darius exclaimed, a bout of heavy laughter rising from his gut. "Our lips are sealed. We won't tell a soul."

Lucian stuffed the parchment into his cloak's pocket, rising out of the bed with considerable ease. His body felt refreshed, and his muscles no longer ached. His ribs were mended, and he could breathe naturally, without pain.

He felt like a new man—a new person.

What a surprise. She really is a Healing Mage. To think such a rude, brute of a girl could have such a gentle ability.

Lucian stood up. "So, why Aaron? Why do you need *him* to do this job? I don't see why someone else couldn't complete it. You said it was an 'S-class request,' so can't you find another adventurer?"

Darius let out a light chuckle. "You don't seem familiar with how the Adventurer Guild's requests work. S-class is the highest level of difficulty assigned to a request. Only those who have an S-class rank can complete these missions. To put that into perspective for you, there are only about twenty S-class rank Guild members in Avrith, where the highest concentration of guilds and Mages are located. In Korakk, there are only five S-class rank members, who are all out on missions."

"Aaron's an S-class rank adventurer?" Lucian asked in disbelief. "I don't believe you for a second. Besides, you're both members of 'The Royal Guards' or whatever that is, so why can't you just do it?"

"What we need are his skills. He's a high-grade Lightning Mage and Summoner, so this request shouldn't be too taxing. While I'd love to do the mission myself, we aren't accepted by foreign guilds, so we aren't allowed to participate in high-ranked missions outside of our base in Terras."

"What's a Summoner?" Lucian asked, sifting through Darius's words.

"He's fully healed, so we should get going," Angelique interjected with a tinge of frustration laced in her words. "Just do whatever you want and stop asking such obvious questions, you simpleton."

Angelique stormed out of the room, as her patience was running scarily thin. She saucily flicked her hair at Lucian as she exited.

What a witch of a woman...

Darius let out an awkward laugh and then said, "Sorry for her attitude. She's actually a pretty sweet girl when you get to know her. Anyway, take as long as you need. In the meantime, we'll attend to some pressing matters in the neighboring Tribe."

Once Darius had passed through the threshold, Lucian

retrieved the parchment from his pocket and unrolled it. He scanned over the paper, looking for anything interesting.

Two words underlined and embellished with swirls and extra ink caught his attention.

Magnus Serpens, he read.

What's a Magnus Serpens?

21

THE DRAGONIAN CURSE

 *Korakk*

The real demon lay beyond the thin, glossy veneer of the door. He pressed his ear to its wooden frame, trying to ascertain whether his snarky companion was inside or not. Muffled sounds came from within. It was almost like he was speaking to someone.

But who?

Lucian turned the handle of the unlocked door, twisting it ever so slowly. He worried about a loud creak, so he pushed the door open with extreme caution and care. He practically pleaded with the inanimate thing, praying for it to remain silent. He opened the door wide enough for him to see through a small slit.

Who's he talking to?

Lucian's eyes roamed around until he found Aaron's worn-out figure. His companion's body faced the mirror with his shoulders slouched.

The raven-haired boy seemed to be accessing his injuries. The mirror's reflection revealed small, freshly made scratches running along the sides of his face and exposed arms. The blood was still fresh, and he wiped it away using the back of his hand. His eyes were bereft of emotion, and he had a menacing expression. He had a look that could kill...the malicious sneer of a bloodthirsty devil.

Widening his view, Lucian opened the door a few inches more. Just enough to see the full extent of Aaron's figure but not so much as to reveal himself.

Aaron stripped off his dirty, brown cloak along with his loose, beige undershirt, flinging them both onto the nearest bed. Lucian forced down a yelp, the sight of his companion's exposed back causing him to slightly stumble backward from shock.

What is that!?

Lucian heard about Aaron's condition from Barren, but he didn't expect his body to look that gruesome.

Lucian regained his balance, peeking into the crack to see large, black bumps riddling his companion's skin. Barren's words flooded into his brain, as he tried to comprehend the curse, which distorted Aaron's body so ravenously, so disgustingly.

He had *scales*.

Inky, vein-like tendrils were attached to the black blobs, reaching down to his waist. No part of his body was spared. As reflected by the mirror, the flesh of his upper arms, the backside of his neck, and the front of his torso were affected.

Amid the bumps was a strangely colored gemstone wedged into his back where a thin layer of skin had formed over it. From what Barren had shared about Aaron's disposition, this object had to be one of the mysterious, powerful El Stones.

The El Stone glimmered a dark-red hue, its light extending toward the inky blotches. However, the stone didn't seem to be working at full capacity, as there was a dark crack, and the color was muted.

The Dragonian Curse, Lucian frowned. *I had no idea that it was this severe. Maybe the curse is why he...*

Twisting the door handle, Lucian silently shut the door. He backtracked several steps.

Calm down, Lucian. Focus. First things first, I have to figure out why he tried to attack me...

He sucked in a lot of air—*Fwoooh!*—as he suppressed his nervousness. His heart pounded in his ears, making each step more taxing than the one before it. His shoes slightly squeaked on the wooden floorboards.

Here I go!

Standing directly in front of the door, Lucian's right hand wrapped into a tight fist, and he knocked. The sound of scurried movements within the room caused him to panic, and his hands were shaking. His ears picked up several grunts and the screech of an object being dragged across the wooden floorboards.

What is he doing in there!?

The door swung open, and an anxious-looking Aaron appeared. He let out a long sigh.

With the beckoning motion of his hand, Lucian had been herded into the room. His friend shut the entryway the moment they were both completely inside.

Why is he being so finicky today? Does he know that I... No, that's impossible. He didn't show any signs of it. It must just be my imagination. But what if...?

"—Lucian, what happened to you!" Aaron interrupted his thoughts. "You're covered in blood and dust! And what's with that sword?"

He peered down, looking at his clothes that were stained with spots of blood from the aftermath of his match with Angelique. The sword hung low on his hip. His partly opened mouth widened to a gape. How could he have completely overlooked this major detail?

"I-I...M-My..." Lucian stuttered. "Actually...!"

He's going to murder me when he finds out!

However, nothing happened. No interrogation, no suspicions, were directed at him. Instead, a pitiful smile spread across Aaron's face as if he knew what Lucian had done but decided not to say anything.

Lucian had been expecting a punch to his side or a high kick to the gut, so when nothing happened, he felt a tad bit guilty. Since Aaron's reprimands and taunts were his norm, his companion's "nice" side came off as fake and forced.

"I have a spare set of clothes on the nightstand," Aaron said, with a subdued and slightly solemn tone. "Get changed, and then we'll talk. I'll be waiting downstairs."

Before he left, Lucian grabbed Aaron's arm. Retrieving the parchment from his pocket, he handed it to him. "This is for you," Lucian said with an urgent tone. "A man by the name of 'Darius Grindenwald' desperately wanted your help. He told me all of the details are inside here."

"He hasn't given up yet?" Aaron sighed, the lines on his forehead creasing. "I can't believe he got you involved. Wait, don't tell me that he's the one who did this to you!"

"No!" Lucian burst out. "I mean... No, he wasn't the one who... Anyway, he said this mission would save Korakk! Why did you refuse his request?"

Aaron clicked his tongue, a look of displeasure

surfacing on his face. "I don't know what he told you, but he's just messing with me. This isn't a normal S-rank mission! He wants me to fail. It's his sick form of amusement," he scowled while saying. "If he sent you with this paper, he must have a better deal to offer."

"H-He said that he would raise the reward to 250 mana crystals," Lucian stuttered, taken aback by Aaron's blatant hostility toward Darius. "Do you know him?—Darius?"

"Know him, I—" Aaron's face lowered while his fists clenched. "Let's just say, we have an unfortunate habit of meeting at the worst times and places."

"He also said that you, well, really needed the crystals for your...health."

"It's just like him saying something like that," Aaron said, bitterly, shaking his head. "His request is one thing, but the blabbing about my personal affairs is another..."

Diffusing the tension, Lucian said, "Don't worry, I'll forget about it. I wasn't trying to pry into your personal life. They saved me, so I wanted to repay the favor, that's all. I didn't mean to put you in a bad spot."

"You're something else, you know that?" Aaron lightly laughed. "Okay, that's enough chit chat. Go change, and then we'll head to Barren's and ask him about the request."

"You're not mad at me, are you?" Lucian asked, his eyes staring at the floor. "After all, I disobeyed—"

A pat on his shoulder communicated a full conversation's worth of words. It seemed like Aaron was trying to tell him—*"It's fine"*—at least, that was how Lucian chose to interpret it.

"Ah, before I leave, I have one more thing to tell you," Aaron said, stopping in his tracks. "I know I'm not the most personable, but I wanted to thank you for accompanying me. And well, I wanted to apologize to you. I'm sorry for the way I treated you the other day."

Rather awkwardly, Aaron slipped out of the room.

It took some time for Lucian to process Aaron's apology. If Aaron was talking about the attack the other night, this delivery was rather shallow. However, if it was about Aaron's behavior when they arrived at Korakk, his apology was more than enough.

Now, it was his turn to change his clothes. Standing in front of the mirror, Lucian tore off the ragged, brown garments and slipped into the spare clothes, which had been neatly folded on the nightstand. Albeit not a perfect fit, he felt grateful for the clean clothes.

Since the light brown pants were a little loose, he bunched the extra fabric into a ball and tied it with a spare rubber band. He checked the pants out in the mirror, wondering if he could get it stitched or patched in the future. Next was his shirt. Right after slipping it on, he realized he had accidentally put it on inside-out. Laughing at himself, he flipped the shirt so that it was in the correct orientation.

Before he put his shirt back on, he glanced over to his chest, surveying his scars and wounds. Amidst them, there was something else—a small dot. He blinked several times, wondering if his vision had been skewed. But the tiny dot was still there, no matter how many times he rubbed his eyes or blinked.

What is that?

Getting closer to the mirror's surface, Lucian found a tiny, dark-blue spot on his upper chest. The spot had root-like lines extending out from it. He rolled the pads of his fingers over the spot, but there was no external bump or skin rupture.

It was like a blotch of smeared, blue paint.

"Get yourself together," Lucian rebuked himself. "Just forget about it! It should go away in a day or two, right? Leave it alone. Don't touch it anymore. Let's go!"

Slipping the brown shirt on, he went to leave the room, but he stopped in his tracks. Out of the corner of his eye, he saw the dirty, dark green cloak, which made him shudder in morbid remembrance. After retrieving the cloak, he hurried out of the room and descended the stairs. He suppressed his anxious thoughts about the spot into the depths of his subconscious.

Reaching Aaron at the bar, the raven-haired boy

repeated what they were going to do for the rest of the day: First, they would meet with Barren. Second, if the request was authentic, they would set off to fulfill it. With each passing second, Aaron seemed more and more willing to take on the ridiculous request.

However, the more Lucian thought about The Magnus Serpens and the mission itself, he had a creeping suspicion something was awry...

ALTHOUGH THE SHOP'S SIGN SAID "CLOSED," Aaron brazenly walked in, acting like he owned the place. Lucian, on the other hand, double-checked to make sure he could enter. Beholding the old Aaron made him feel like all of his worries had been for naught.

Walking inside the shop, Lucian noticed Barren's attention was captivated by a pitch-black sword, which he held in his hands with extra care. It looked brand new—the blade of the sword reflecting in the light.

Ah, that must be the Dragonite sword that he was talking about! Lucian thought. *My new sword!*

His spirits lifted higher.

Clutching onto the sword, which he had borrowed,

Lucian approached Barren and handed it to him. "Here it is." He winked. "Look, it's all in one piece, right?"

Barren examined the irregular sword. He turned the blade in his hand, examining every angle.

Lucian noticed the man's gaze rested on the different gem wedged into the holder. "Well, you see..." Lucian said, scratching the back of his head. "I didn't mean to—"

"Well done!" Barren belted. "It looks like you used it to its fullest potential!"

"He did *what*?" Aaron scarily smiled. "Mind explaining what you two are talking about?"

"Ahaha." Barren nervously laughed. "It's nothing you should worry yourself over. I asked him to test it out on one of the forest trees, and it worked perfectly!"

Placing the borrowed sword on the table, Barren beckoned Lucian closer, handing him the Dragonite sword. Lucian was prompted to hold the expensive treasure with two hands, as he was clumsy by nature. He was even given a separate sheath, so he wouldn't accidentally scratch or chip it.

This sword costs more than my life, Lucian lamented. *If anything happens to it, two people will try to kill me.*

"Are you planning to give Lucian that sword for free?" Aaron inquired, his expression darkening. "You better have a good explanation for your generosity. I don't like being indebted to anyone, let alone from a fellow like you."

"A deal's a deal," Barren said. "I made a bet with Lucian and lost. That's why this isn't so much 'generosity' as it is the fulfillment of a promise. Got it?"

Grumpily, Aaron asked, "Why would he even need a sword like that? You know I hate anything and everything to do with dragons. Do you like antagonizing me?"

"I'm not antagonizing you." Barren retorted. "Do you really think a normal sword will fit your friend's current state? Any normal sword would break if he tried to use it. He has too much mana. Even with those things around his wrists and ankles, there's no telling when his output will eclipse its suppression capabilities. Besides, your client's request entailed defeating The Magnus Serpens, right? Without that sword, Lucian wouldn't stand a chance."

Huh? How does Barren know about the request? Lucian wondered.

Lucian's confused face was so obvious that Barren was forced to respond. "Look, Lucian, there's only one outstanding S-rank mission in Korakk...and that's defeating the big snake. The Adventurer's Guild verified the request as an official mission, so it's legit."

Barren turned back to Aaron and continued explaining, "Unless you want your one-and-only friend to become a nasty serpent's meal, then I suggest you overlook my *generosity*."

"Tch." Aaron's mouth twitched. "Fine, I'll let him

have that wretched sword. In exchange, Lucian, don't you dare use that sword without my permission, understand? I'll be the one to defeat The Magnus Serpens, so your sword will stay in the sheath. Do you still want it?"

Lucian quickly nodded.

"So, does this mean you're taking the job?" Lucian asked, cocking his head to the side.

"I decided to do it a few minutes ago." Aaron's voice wavered. "Don't start complaining now. Isn't this what you wanted?"

He's gone back to being difficult.

"Then, it's decided!" Barren exclaimed. "Grab your belongings and have fun!"

Fun? Is dying fun? At least I'll have Aaron. Without him, I'd be The Magnus Serpens's next meal...

Barren escaped to the back room, reappearing with a woolen poncho in his hand. He threw it at Lucian, which he caught easily.

"Why are you giving this to me?"

"Because you need it for where we're going," Aaron answered, matter-of-factly.

"Going? Where are we going?"

Although Aaron's patience seemed to already be running thin, his companion calmly said, "Didn't Darius brief you on the request?"

Lucian shook his head, communicating an emphatic

"no." Even what little he remembered of Darius's explanation, he kept to himself. He didn't want to contradict himself or Aaron, for that matter.

"I'll only say this once, so you better listen carefully," Aaron warned. "We're going to fight the legendary, colossal creature known as 'The Magnus Serpens.' She lives in the depths of the desert, and she primarily stays dormant during most of the year beneath the sand, only coming to the surface to feed. The Tribal Nations usually come together and prepare offerings for The Magnus Serpens to quench her thirst and hunger; however, she has resurfaced early due to pesky treasure hunters digging deep into the sand and disturbing her sleep. Countless villages surrounding her nest have been destroyed, as a result."

"Why do The Tribal Nations prepare offerings for her? I thought she was supposed to be a ferocious beast?"

"Because The Magnus Serpens is said to be their patron deity, the cursed incarnation of the goddess of nature, Flora."

"Aren't you afraid?" Lucian asked. "This creature is still a *goddess*, you know."

Aaron lifted his lips into a sly smile, as he said, "Not really."

"Why not?"

"Because I've always wanted to defeat a deity."

22

MAGNUS SERPENS

•·········•◆ *The Wastelands* ◆•·········•

"Hey, Sleeping Beauty, we're almost there!" Aaron announced. Lucian whined, his head resting on the Venari's back.

"Five more minutes."

"You've been sleeping for over an hour," Aaron scorned. "And, if you haven't noticed, it's late afternoon!"

"It's not my fault that I tripped over some random garbage and sprained my ankle." He puffed out his lips and pouted. "You're the one who wanted to keep going, knowing I was injured."

Aaron abruptly stopped his Venari, forcing Lucian's ride to halt as well. Lucian fell off the Venari's back and plopped onto the sand.

"Hey, what was that for!" he cried out. "Be more careful with me. I'm injured!"

"Pfft!" Aaron spurted. "You're weak."

"Wimp!" Eteria chimed in.

"Eteria, when did you—"

"You're going to fight The Magnus Serpens, right?" she asked. "I don't want to miss out on the entertainment!"

Lucian let out a sigh. "This isn't a game, Eteria. I don't even stand a chance against The Magnus Serpens. Thank goodness Aaron's doing the brunt of the fighting. All I have to do is sit back and watch. I can barely wield a sword, to begin with, so I would just be a burden."

"Ehhhh!" Eteria shouted with a shrill voice. "That's no fun! Even though I know you would be eaten right away, I still want to see it with my own two eyes!"

"Sadist."

"Worrywart."

"Hey, Lucian, are you alright?" Aaron asked.

Ah, that's right, Lucian thought. *He can't hear her voice... He must think I'm going crazy. I need to be more careful next time.*

"Just tired," Lucian deflected. "What about you? You haven't been sleeping well lately, have you?"

"Late nights won't kill me," Aaron softly said, as he dismounted his Venari. "If you have enough time and energy to worry about me, then you should be training more. There's always something to learn and to experience."

"Ah, uh huh." Lucian nodded in agreement for formality's sake, thinking back to the BOTB match. *I think I got a month's worth of training out of that battle, but if I tell Aaron, he'll surely skewer me alive.*

The clear, blue skies transformed into an ominous gray, storm clouds forming above them. There were no signs of rain, thunder, or lightning, but Lucian couldn't shake a feeling of impending doom.

His muscles tensed, the hairs on the back of his neck sticking straight up like a cat sensing danger. A chilly wind swooshed through the sand, lifting it and other objects skyward.

Once the sand started to rise and fall like ocean waves, the Venaris took flight, leaving them behind. Something was heading Lucian and Aaron's way.

But what?

"Aaron, what should we do?" Lucian asked with a trembling voice. "I don't want to become serpent fodder!"

Lucian started panicking, forcibly shaking Aaron.

With a stern voice, Aaron said, "Get your grubby hands off me."

Lucian retracted his hands.

A shift in the sand snapped both of their attention to the forefront. The small ripples formed by the wind evolved into giant waves, rising, falling, and crashing at a scary speed. Everything happened so quickly.

The entity's emergence from the depths was swift. The creature's stocky, scaly form broke through the surface, strong winds spinning and spiraling around them. It was nothing short of a miracle that Aaron and Lucian were able to maintain their footholds.

Broad, yellow mass of scales and flesh made an appearance, the serpent's hissing amplified by the rough winds. Her black, cruel eyes pierced into Lucian's. An aura of certain death surrounded the beast, her fork-like tongue flicking back and forth as if taunting him.

"Aaron, what's the plan?" Lucian quavered, as he took a few steps backward.

"Can you run?"

"Run? I can barely walk with this ankle!"

"Can you make a run for it?" Aaron asked again, with a more dire tone. "Do you see those dunes over there? If you can at least run and hide behind them, I can draw the beast's attention away from you. This is the best I can do for you."

"I can try."

"There's no trying," Aaron warned. "You have to do it, or else you'll be that serpent's meal. Just remember what I taught you about your feet."

My feet? Lucian wondered. *What about my—of course, all I need to do is infuse the mana in my feet!*

"Okay, you need to go on the count of three."

"Got it!"

"*One...*"

"*Two...*"

Lucian's feet assumed a runner's starting position on the sand. He forced the circulating mana into his legs and feet, feeling a resurgence of energy.

I can do this, he repeated in his head. *All I have to do is get to that dune.*

"*Three...*"

Lucian sprinted toward the tall dunes. The Magnus Serpens's gaze initially followed him, but she soon became distracted by Aaron's taunts. Reaching the dunes was no facile endeavor. They were farther than he had estimated, and his injured ankle was an issue. Pain shot up his leg whenever he put his weight on it.

Come on, Lucian! Run faster! Don't let Aaron's sacrifice go to waste!

He raced to the side that was out of the serpent's field of vision. He crawled up the dune, surveying the scene that played out before him: Aaron versus The Magnus Serpens. Even he couldn't predict what was to come—after all, he had never seen Aaron fight at full force, let alone challenge a creature of legend, no, a Fallen goddess, to a fight to the death.

He held his breath as he watched Aaron.

The Magnus Serpens, at her full height, towered over the boy with an overwhelming size. Her height was comparable to two Holy Chapels stacked on top of each other. As the largest building in Caelum, this comparison couldn't be dismissed.

The Magnus Serpens truly was a monster.

Aaron, however, seemed strangely calm and unnaturally silent. Apart from the size difference, it was impossible to tell who the *hunter* was and who the *hunted* was.

He's like a different person, Lucian discerned. *I've never seen him like this.*

Aaron drew his sword, wielding his blade dexterously and aptly. No motion was wasted. He surged into the serpent's domain, openly challenging the beast to a fight. Since Lucian was a good distance away from his friend, he couldn't be certain. But his friend's expression reminded him of something that he had seen in a dream.

Whether intentional or not, Lucian sensed Aaron's hungry, bloodthirsty aura. It radiated off him like the scathing heat produced by flames. What tragedy in his life caused the creation of such a tortured soul?

Strike after strike, the serpent bared her fangs at the boy, striking at the sand like a bird digging for worms.

Swing after swing, Aaron didn't waver in focus or show any signs of weakness. Instead, it seemed like he was diving deeper into himself. His movements sharpened, the blade of his sword clashing against the beast's scales.

But to no avail.

Aaron retreated, putting some distance between him and the serpent. He was up to something. He lifted the Phantom sword above his head with both hands. The sword plunged into the sand beneath him. The effects were instantaneous. Bolts of lightning shot out from his sword, gliding across the surface toward the serpent. That was when Lucian remembered... Aaron was a Lightning Mage.

The shots of lightning, which streamed close to the surface, hit The Magnus Serpens with a *Tzzatzz!* and *Tzchhh!* However, the beast was barely fazed. In a single shake, the serpent ridded her skin of the stinging and burning bolts. Aaron, in turn, wasn't deterred by the beast's apathetic reaction. Instead, it seemed to further fuel his motivation.

Unfortunately, all of his successive attacks failed.

What are you doing, Aaron? Lucian internally shouted. *I thought you were supposed to be an S-class adventurer! Come on, Aaron!*

The end came swiftly.

The swish of the serpent's tail sent Aaron flying sideways. He violently smacked against a small outcropping of rock. Lucian expected Aaron to rise back to his feet and shout at the serpent or torment the thing to death. However, his friend's fallen figure squashed his naive hope.

Aaron didn't even budge.

"Aaron!" Lucian screamed.

Still no reaction.

"Aaron, get up!"

The Magnus Serpens slithered toward Aaron's unconscious body.

What should I do? What am I going to do? If I move, I'll be dead! If I don't move, Aaron will be dead!

It was now or never.

In the midst of scrambling off the dune, Lucian assessed the serpent's mana flow. He overcame his nervousness with intense concentration and an unyielding determination to save his friend. The closer he went to the serpent, the more he analyzed her mana.

Wait... What is this!?

Not one but two mana cores existed within The Magnus Serpens. The first core was a yellowish-orange color embedded in the serpent's chest; whereas, the second core was a deep, red color located somewhere in her stomach. Or what Lucian assumed to be her stomach since her body was just one long string of scaly flesh.

Running at full force was his only option.

He thanked Barren as he ran and drew the Dragonite

sword out of the sheath, gripping the hilt tightly in his hands.

A nasal cry escaped his lips.

Close enough to attack, Lucian slashed the sword across the serpent's scales.

The sword's impact with the scales made a *Kirik!* sound. The blade snapped in half. The bottom half of it fell and sunk into the sand. The remaining half had a jagged appearance.

Lucian scurried away but not fast enough. The serpent struck, thrashing his thigh. He stumbled but forced himself to continue the retreat. Sweat drizzled down his face, and his heart beat out of his chest. A wave of fear overtook him.

Darkness consumed him.

"Fear is an honest foe. Its power depends upon what you have to lose. Darkness, however, has no such boundary."

Why were those the words that surfaced from his memories? Master Felix's words had been certainly powerful, but what could mere words do in the face of a monster that had led so many men to their demise?

The Magnus Serpens was no normal fiend. She was a malicious devil covered in sharp scales and even sharper fangs. Legendary or not, this was neither the fight that he had foreseen nor the outcome he had wanted. After all, what human could defeat a goddess?

With his comrade unconscious, his sword broken in two, and his will to fight overcome by fear, what could he do?

To face a foe so powerful, Lucian needed much more than shallow resolve to defeat her. The Magnus Serpens's scales were impenetrable shields meant to dismay even the sharpest of weapons. What he needed most was something outrageous enough to be unexpected and create a chance.

It was neither pride nor confidence that pushed him past his limit. It was desperation.

But what was this other feeling welling within him? Deep down, further than he cared to wander, was an all-consuming darkness. A darkness that threatened to extinguish the light that he had so desperately nurtured.

Neither fear nor joy lingered there. In that space of creeping shadows, only a pair of crimson eyes glowed, staring into the blueness of his own.

Revenge, the eyes conveyed. *Merciless, unrelenting revenge on those who betrayed me. Kill them. Burn them all.*

The disconcerting voice, which he had heard so many times in the depths of his dreams, mocked him. "*Weak,*" the voice said. "*You are far too weak. Let me take control, then you shall seize victory with your own two hands. Don't fear the darkness. Embrace it. Embrace me.*"

Another strong emotion—or will, if you could call it that—arose as a response to the mocking voice, saying,

"You are nothing but an apparition that haunts my dreams. You will never have full control over me. Your revenge ends here. You will rot in your darkness for as long as you reside in me. Know this, I will become the light to vanquish you. Just wait and see, you monster, I will defeat you."

"*Defeat me?*" the voice snickered while saying. "*I am you, and you are me. Never forget that the grave you dig for me, you'll soon be buried in yourself. A mere vessel shouldn't seek to rid itself of its godly soul.*"

"Begone!" Lucian commanded.

"*As you wish, my successor,*" the voice cackled while saying. "*As you wish...*"

Black, beady eyes replaced the crimson ones, the obscure atmosphere shifting back to the sandy expanse of The Wastelands. The moment of truth was upon him. The beast's tail rhythmically slapped against the sand, dredging skyward clumps left and right, up and down.

Lucian's eyes locked onto the serpent.

An unnerving calmness assumed him. What towered over him was no longer a predator preparing to kill but rather a contender ready to be challenged.

"Here goes nothing!"

Heroism wasn't his forte. It was not bravery that allowed him to conquer his fears. No, his reaction was the consequence of plain stubbornness. Desperation drove his unflinching determination, and an unthinkable plan formed.

There he was, fighting an unwinnable fight, staking blood and bone on this crazy strategy. This was it. His legs propelled him skyward. Manipulating the broken sword, he plunged the blade into the serpent's eye. Her squinty, slit eye twitched, the serpent jolting her mouth wide open.

And then, he did it.

He jumped right in.

Straight into the mouth of The Magnus Serpens.

23

SLAYER OF GODS

 *The Wastelands*

Sliding down the innards of The Magnus Serpens, Lucian gagged at the putrid stench of digestive fluids and rotting corpses. Due to the huge drop, he almost vomited.

As he fell, his fingers wedged into the inner walls, tearing into and scraping to slow his fall. However, nothing he did was enough to stop his descent into the dark abyss.

The walls secreted layers of goopy mucus, the texture feeling slimy and sticky to the touch. Repulsive as it was, blood and pus spewing out of both sides, Lucian bit back the urge to vomit. Jolted left and right, up and down, he was tossed and turned like a fish in a frying pan.

I'm going to die! I'm going to—

Splash!

Lucian landed in a steep pond, the murky liquids sloshing around him. He struggled to stand, the liquid reaching his knees and the serpent's external motion affecting his internal equilibrium. Slowly but surely, the yellow and green liquids seeped into his clothing and stung his skin.

Lucian retreated to the side of the stomach wall where he could keep his feet dry and out of the gastric juices. He hastily ripped off the bits of his pant legs that were soaked in the acid, and he threw them into the pond, watching as they sunk to the bottom. They wouldn't last long.

Instinctively, his hands smoothed over the affected areas of skin that had direct contact with the acidic juices. There was a slight burn here and there but nothing to warrant any panic.

This is nothing compared with when my father used to pour his drink on my open wounds, Lucian sorely recalled.

"Stay focused," Eteria stated. "At this rate, you'll suffocate before you're digested."

What is she babbling about?

Out of the acidic pool, a neon-green mist emerged. It hovered relatively low, clinging to the pond's surface, but the presence of a possible meal released it upward and outward.

"Don't breathe it in!" Eteria cried. "It's toxic!"

Lucian pulled the poncho over his nose and mouth, wrapping the extra fabric around the back of his head. He tied a knot to secure its position. But this was only a temporary measure. Sooner or later, the mist would seep through the fabric and invade his lungs.

He distanced himself as much as possible, his back pushing against the pink flesh of the serpent's insides. His toes pressed into the bumps and grooves of its flesh, avoiding an accidental slip into the pond. Along with the proliferating mist, the liquids in the acidic pond rose higher and higher, until the toxic liquids burned through the tips of his shoes.

"Eteria, instead of bossing me around," Lucian coughed out, "why don't you tell me something useful? Like how to defeat this stupid snake! Aren't you a goddess? Do something...anything!"

"Lucian, watch out!" Eteria shrieked, as the serpent jerked again, causing a wagon's wheel to fly at Lucian.

Attempting to dodge, Lucian jumped out of the way. Right as he landed back down, his heels slipped out from beneath him. With his arms flailing and his hands grasping at the air, he fell onto his butt in the swampy liquids.

Sitting in it, his skin sizzled and burned. The pond's acidity seeped through his skin, his muscles locking and refusing to cooperate. He slowly sunk into the obscure waters, while his stiffening legs thrashed about. "Why can't I move!"

"Lucian, get out now!" Eteria commanded. "It's releasing a demobilizing toxin! If you don't move, then you won't be able to escape!"

"Stop telling me what to do and help me, Eteria!"

His legs, which had been struggling to stand, seized and stopped. His arms were becoming numb, and his body started tilting, as he couldn't maintain his balance sitting upright. His shoulder sank into the pool. At this rate, even with the poncho covering his face, he would eventually succumb to the toxin.

"Lucian!" Eteria shouted. Her sniffles and screams fell on deaf ears, as he helplessly was being swallowed by the blackness.

As he sunk, his mind went straight to cursing the creators of his misfortunes: the ancient gods. *You sick and twisted gods! Are you having fun trying to kill me? Is it that entertaining to make my life miserable?*

"Be still," a low but firm voice ordered, disrupting his curses. "As long as I am with you, your body shall never break, and your soul shall never shatter. I am your everlasting shield, the one known as 'The Aegis.' Call me by my true name, Master."

Lucian's mouth moved to form the words, air bubbles spilling from his parted lips.

"Aerus!" Lucian cried.

Instantly, his body began to radiate heat, warmth welling within him. The same blue light that Aerus had produced during the Succession Ceremony surrounded and acted like a protective shield. Lucian's muscles relaxed. He slowly managed to regain control of himself, his arms and legs moving at will.

"Breathe," Aerus said. "You cannot die from such weak toxins, now."

Lucian's first breath was a test. He sipped in a small stream of air, which he found devoid of the acidic mist. It was a satisfying discovery as he slurped in ample air, drinking it down in speedy spurts.

Standing up was within his current capabilities, but the shiny glint of an object lying at the bottom of the acidic pond captured his curiosity. Since the acid wasn't burning his body anymore, he stayed longer, moving through the pond to reach a deeper area.

The obscurity of the liquids was only applied to the surface. He bent down on his hands and knees. He was close enough to the surface to see what lay on the pond's lowest level. Aside from slowly decomposing bones and arrows, all else had been destroyed by the serpent's digestive fluids. The arrows were dull, their metal corroding and rusting.

"What do you seek?" Aerus inquired. "If it is within my knowledge, I can assist you."

Lucian's eyes scanned the sunken items.

Not this one. Not that one either. Where is it?

He spotted a red glint.

Ah, there it is!

With its blade sticking straight upward and its hilt wedged into the serpent's flesh, a shining sword was stuck. He reached toward it, his arms pushing through the repulsive juices. Like a moth drawn to a flame, Lucian was unable to resist the urge to investigate. With his right hand outstretched, he reached for the alluring sword, his fingers wrapped around its blade.

Unlike Aerus's faint blue light, the sword emitted a bright, red glow. And unlike the Dragonite sword's coldness, this sword emitted warmth.

Lucian grabbed the sword, pulling it out of the serpent's flesh. Upon closer inspection, this sword was unlike any weapon Lucian had ever seen. Albeit supposedly protected by Aerus's shield, the blade managed to cut his skin, blood running down the edge.

Something strange, however, happened when the blood met with the blade. Almost like a living creature, the blade absorbed the blood. After a few seconds, the intricately engraved markings on the sword produced a brilliant red light, nearly blinding him. Without assistance, the hilt ascended, pulling him up to his feet.

It was like the sword had a will of its own. A sudden voice broke through the sound barrier exactly when they exited the waters.

"I never thought I'd meet your sorry self again, Aerus!" a voice like a foghorn exclaimed. "If you're here, you must've found *him*—our true master."

Aerus refused to respond.

"Who are you?" Lucian asked, looking directly at the talking sword. "How do you know Aerus? How are you able to talk?"

"What a cheeky brat you've brought along, Aerus," the sword said. "Hey, kid, I'm not much of a talker, and you don't seem to be much of a listener. That's why I'd like to keep this exchange short."

"Where have I heard that before?" Lucian irreverently mumbled.

"You want to leave this godsawful place, don't you? This stinky, death-ridden stomach isn't that comfortable for even a magical entity like me," the sword stated. "If you want to leave, there's only one thing you have to do."

"And what's that?"

"Call my name."

"I don't know your name."

The glowing sword floated closer to his face.

"I'm not too keen to let a scrawny fellow like you be my new master, but it seems like I have no choice," the sword said. "We're cursed, both this serpent and me, and I have no chance to leave her innards if I don't have a wielder to use me. You'll have to do, for now."

"What do you mean 'I'll do, for now?' Who *are* you?"

Sliding through the shield and into his palm, the sword sat snuggly. "If you don't hurry up, then your friend, Aaron, won't live to see tomorrow," the sword warned. "Call my name and slash through Flora's stomach."

"W-Wait, do I really have to kill her?"

"Death is different for us," the sword stated. "Besides, Aerus's shield can only cover you for so long. Don't get cocky. It's not your power that's keeping you safe. It's *his*. Now, do as I say and call my name. *Ignis*. Just say 'Ignis.'"

"Ignis," Lucian grumbled while saying.

"I guess that'll have to do, for now." Ignis sighed. "You're just like he was in his youth... Just like him."

Red flames encased the blade.

Heading to the thinnest side of the serpent's stomach, Lucian raised Ignis above his head, his blade readying for a blow. A moment's hesitation passed over him and disappeared as fast as it appeared. *Deep breaths*, Lucian recited internally. *Deep breaths.*

Slashing the sword against the serpent's flesh, the blade easily sliced through her skin. Ignis's flames enveloped the opening, destroying everything in their path. The Magnus Serpens violently shook and squirmed, slamming her body against the ground. The only thing that kept Lucian from being tossed around was the blade stuck in the serpent's pierced flesh.

Once the flames burned through the serpent's inner stomach and outer skin, he hurled himself outward. Dropping to the sand, which lessened the impact of his fall, he rolled several times before stopping.

With Ignis in his right hand and Aerus's shield protecting him, he had nothing left to fear.

The Magnus Serpens squirmed about, as Ignis's red and orange flames engulfed the entire entity. After the serpent's final attempt to struggle against the fire, she fell. Her fall dredged up chunks of dirt, sending buried junk flying every which way. Her scaly skin flaked off and turned to ashes, the beastly eyes of the serpent losing their malevolent glare and color. Her eyes turned ghastly-white, as she withered away.

With what little strength Lucian had left, he crawled on his hands and knees toward his unconscious friend. His ankle, now completely black and blue, was useless as he inched his way toward his comrade.

Lucian was running on nothing but fumes. He saw his friend let out some coughs and groans, but his breathing seemed irregular.

He reached Aaron, trying to pick himself up and then his friend. It took many hopeless attempts, but Lucian finally managed to stand up. Dragging Aaron by his collar across the sand, Lucian felt like he was holding onto a sack of potatoes, as he trudged along in the suffocating heat. He wondered why he was so adamant about saving someone to the point of self-destruction and why the pain didn't immediately incapacitate him.

Then, he remembered.

Years of enduring countless beatings and bludgeons forced his mind to disconnect from his body. It was like a survival switch. When the extremities of physical torture racked his body, his mind tuned it out. It usually only lasted a few minutes at most, but it was enough to get through the desert, one step at a time.

He knew that he could do it.

For once, I have something to thank you for, you worthless father.

A mixture of sweat and blood drizzled down his scalp, dripping onto his lips. His extreme concentration on every consecutive movement caused the world around him to swirl.

Extraneous sounds were silenced, so he had no clue

what the three higher powers had to say to him. Eteria, Ignis, and Aerus were muted in his mind.

As Lucian was about to black out from fatigue and the heat, there were two figures in the distance racing toward them.

Thank the gods.

Lucian recognized them, even with his wavering consciousness.

Better late than never, he thought, heaving and huffing as his focus dwindled. *Stay awake, Lucian. One of us has to be awake.*

Right as the two figures reached them, Lucian hoisted Aaron onto one of the Venari's backs and then climbed atop the other one. With the last of his strength, he tugged them in the right direction. And then... Lucian rested.

••••••••••◆ *Korakk* ◆••••••••••

NIGHT FELL.

Upon arriving at the inn, his knees threatened to buckle. His body was exhausted. Before entering, Lucian released the Venaris so that they could find food and water.

Once inside, Lucian quickly surveyed the area. Wearily, he noticed that neither the innkeeper nor the normal customers were at the bar.

They're probably sleeping sweet and sound in their nice comfy beds.

He dragged Aaron upstairs one step at a time, the stairs creaking the whole way. Once he had ascended the stairs, he headed to their room. His legs shook like a newborn fawn's.

Room 4, he remembered.

Reaching their room, flashes of his past resurfaced. The moonlight trickled inside from the entrance, revealing a broken door, a ransacked room, and a bloody mess on the floorboards.

But there were no dead bodies. Not this time.

"Not...again," Aaron groaned, regaining consciousness. His words fell heftily as they sunk into Lucian's brain. "*They* found us..."

"Aaron, you're awake!" Lucian exclaimed, letting out a sigh of relief. "You said, 'they.' Who are *they*? You also should've said something if you were awake."

"Stop shouting in my ear," Aaron said, sharply. "And I *did* wake up multiple times on the way back. It was when *you* were knocked out on your Venari."

Lucian shifted his eyes to the side, avoiding further confrontation.

Aaron continued explaining, a grimace flashing on his face and his voice as fragile as glass. "They're the ones who cloak themselves in shadows and darkness, whose eyes are like hollow, darkened orbs, and whose skin is as pale as death... They're the *Soulless*."

24

IN THE SHADOWS

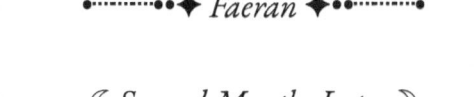

·············•✦ *Faeran* ✦•·············•

·——·❨ *Several Months Later* ❩·——·

For the past few months, Aaron had been working Lucian to the bone. Traveling from town to town, training until sundown, and listening to tedious lectures, he knew no rest.

Aaron, his trainer, taught him the ways of the sword and magic. His sword-wielding lessons ranged from simple swings to advanced attacks, while his magic lessons mainly focused on improving his elemental fire magic and optimizing his mana output.

If there were any gains to the intense training sessions,

they were Lucian's ability to produce flames from his fingertips and to wield his sword steadily and efficiently.

However, every passing day had been a struggle, for his friend often disregarded formalities such as regular sleeping schedules and consistent eating regimens. Thus, they both consistently had dark circles lining the bottoms of their eyes and starving stomachs that grumbled and screamed for sustenance.

What made matters worse was that Aaron demanded constant movement. Every day or two, they would travel to a new territory, whether an established town or a damp cave. If it fit his strange standards, there was nothing that could change his mind, not even a piping-hot meal or a pleasantly warm shower.

From Ferris's note to Eva's prophecy, they were supposed to travel to The Talis Mountains to find the "tree that alters life's time." Although that was their ultimate goal, Aaron had shown no visible interest in it. Only after bugging the boy to death, Lucian finally forced him to concede, so that their travels would lead them closer to their destination.

Their next destination was Faeran, the town closest to The Talis Mountains. It was rumored to be a magical settlement established by a tribe of ancient fairies centuries ago. He also learned that the townspeople, the Faeranians, were the only ones permitted safe travels through the mountains due to a long-standing pact between the fairies, dragons, and humans.

Aside from the pact, there was another reason no one dared traverse the mountain range...its dangerous terrain.

Lucian knew why Aaron was adamant about avoiding this village adjacent to The Talis Mountains. However, they had neither the time nor the leniency to ignore Eva's dying wish. As a bonus, Lucian wondered if he could find a way to reverse Aaron's Dragonian curse in the region, as dragons were rumored to inhabit the mountains.

Additionally, within Faeran, an Adventurer's Guild with whom Aaron had connections was located. If they stayed out of trouble and completed some side missions, their room and board would be free of charge.

Sitting inside that very Adventurer's Guild, height-wise standing a little lower than The Holy Chapel in Caelum by comparison, the two of them were at a wooden table in what looked to be the main dining hall.

Although devoid of customers or Guild members, the intensity of the building and the atmosphere seemed to suffocate him. Its aura screamed, "scary," "danger," and "death."

Aaron, as always, was comfortable even in this situation—in all situations—which wreaked of death and destruction. It seemed fitting for him.

"Oh, there you are," Aaron greeted, speaking to

someone who wasn't in Lucian's line of sight. "Lucian, meet the current Guild Master, Master Thaddeus."

Lucian's eyes trailed to where Aaron was facing, but nobody was there. To see whatever or whoever his friend was talking to, he resorted to kneeling in his seat. His body bent over the table, trying to get a glimpse of the mysterious fellow.

Aaron guided his sight to the ground, specifying the space nearest to the table.

Yep, Lucian ascertained. *He's insane.*

Looking over the table to the floor, Lucian's eyes linked with "Guild Master Thaddeus." His eye twitched. He didn't know whether to laugh or to cry.

Master Thaddeus was a *pig*.

Oink! went the creature with its pink, rubbery flesh, rounded snout, and pudgy neck.

He blinked.

He blinked again.

He looked at Aaron.

"Is this some sort of sick joke?" Lucian fumed. "Your Master is a *pig*."

"He prefers the term 'War Hog,'" Aaron stated, nonchalantly.

Pointing at the porky pig, he exclaimed, "How is that thing a War Hog? It's more likely to be my next meal than a valiant and powerful War Hog!"

Oink!

"Look, you've already offended him!" Aaron repri-manded, slapping Lucian's hand. "Apologize to the Guild Master right now!"

Lowering his head, Lucian said through gritted teeth, "I'm sorry, Master Thaddeus."

Aaron broke out into a fit of laughter.

Lucian growled.

"Y-You're too gullible!" the boy proclaimed, tossing and turning in his chair. "I-I didn't think you would actually—"

Glaring at the piece of raw pork, Lucian snarled. "That's it! He's my next meal."

Reaching for its neck, the pig went for another *Oink!* that never came. Instead, out of its mouth arose an angelic voice. "I'd rather you not eat my Familiar, if that's alright with you."

"It can talk!"

"No, you dolt." Aaron swiveled in his seat, facing the voice's real owner. "If it isn't the she-devil herself, Rena Croft."

Lucian turned to find a young woman with a strange allure and a sense of refined grace. Approaching the table, the woman possessed lavender irises that glistened in the iridescent lights. She had long, silky hair, the color of midnight, and olive-covered skin that accentuated her full, plump red lips. Her hips swayed side to side, wearing a vibrantly colored dress, swooshing back and forth.

Like the time Lucian had encountered Sal, the words refused to come. He was like a broken machine, and his words haplessly spilled out of him.

Aaron and the mysterious woman conversed for a while, but Lucian couldn't focus. His mind wouldn't compute. She seemed amused by his reactions, the slight lift of her lips proving his suspicions correct.

Burying his raven-hued head in his hands, Aaron scolded, "That's why I keep saying you're too gullible, Lucian. Stop falling for every woman that you meet. She's an Enchantress, for Gaia's sake! Don't fall for her charms!"

With a light chuckle, she asked, "So, you're finally recognizing my charm, Aaron?"

"It's nice to meet you," Lucian said, fidgeting. "I'm Lucian Roux, Aaron's companion."

Bemusedly, Rena stated, "You didn't tell me you brought *him*, the hero of legends... I didn't, however, think he would be so young and naive."

"Beggars can't be choosers," Aaron replied. "If you don't believe me, ascertain his credentials for yourself. You'll see what I mean when you look at his mana. He's like a treasure trove. Why do you think it took me this long to bring him here? If I took him through normal means, *they* would have something to say."

"*They* can say all they want." She crossed her arms, a fiery look rising in her eyes. "It doesn't matter what *they* say, because what I say is more important than their rules and regulations. I'm the most renowned Guild Master in all of Gaia, not *them*. I can surpass *their* measly status any day."

She's the Guild Master? Lucian questioned. *I thought the Guild Master was a man...*

"I'll let you have him for the day, Master Croft," Aaron stated.

Rena's face lit up.

"...on one condition," the boy slyly added.

"Name your price."

"Make sure the brat doesn't roam around the town unsupervised," Aaron stated. "You know how dangerous the city can be after dark. Deal?"

"Barren was right." Rena snickered. "You've become soft."

"Do we have a deal?"

"Yes, we have a deal," she stated. "Alas, I didn't raise you to become such a swindler."

"You didn't raise me," he sneered. "I raised myself, thank you very much."

"That doesn't make sense," Lucian interrupted. "I thought Ferris and Eva raised you?"

"Hah!" Rena cried. "Did you really tell him that those

two raised you? What a joke!"

Rolling his eyes, Aaron stated, "I don't have time for this foolishness. I have more important things to do."

"Shoo, shoo!" Rena waved her hand. "Go and play."

From Aaron's fingers, a spark of lightning flickered in the air.

"Don't test me," Rena warned, lowering her tone. "You're a kid, but I won't hold back."

"Tch."

In that short exchange, an unseen battle took place. Lucian couldn't fathom their abrupt actions or aggressive words. He sat still, refusing to move even as Aaron left the Guild in a huff. Rena's frown disappeared the moment the boy had departed.

"You seem to be a smart boy," she warmly smiled while saying. "Let's talk upstairs. I bet your knowledge of Faeran and magic are limited, seeing as Aaron isn't the most traditional teacher by any means."

Entering Rena's office, Lucian's jaw dropped. Like Master Felix's observatory, there were tons of shelves filled with ancient textbooks and tan-colored scrolls. It was like a dream come true. He walked along the walls, brushing his fingers over the pristine books.

Scanning the long line of titles, he stopped at a strange scroll covered in silver strokes. He lightly tapped it, the scroll unraveling before him. The text on the scroll was indecipherable to him, as it wasn't written in a language that he had studied under Master Felix.

Too bad... he thought, unpleasantly.

A pair of eyes burned into his back but not with rage or hatred; instead, they conveyed an unbridled curiosity. He whipped himself around, deeply apologizing for his intrusion into her book collection. She waved off his apology, stating that a curious mind was always welcome in her presence. She was just like Master Felix.

"Aaron hasn't spoken much about you," Lucian prefaced, slightly disheartened. "Actually, I don't know a lot about my companion, to begin with. I can't call him my friend, if I don't know about him. Like about Barren, Caspar, or you."

Rena ruffled his hair, stroking him like a mother would her child. "You're closer to him than I've ever been. He's never shown concern for anyone, so I think he's just a tad bit awkward. I wouldn't mind him too much. He seems to cherish you. I mean, he went as far as to threaten me with his magic to keep you safe. That's a pretty clear sign that he cares about you."

"I suppose..." Lucian responded, sheepishly.

Nearing her mouth to his ear, she whispered, "Let me tell you a little secret about that boy. He's deathly afraid of...*snakes*."

"How afraid?"

"He shakes at the sight of them."

Cocking his head to the side and pulling his face away from hers, Lucian retorted by saying, "I highly doubt that. We recently fought The Magnus Serpens, and he seemed fine. Well, not fine, but he did fight it with all his might."

"Did he win?"

"No, but—"

"See, that's what I'm saying," she said, lightly laughing. "If Aaron fought at full force, something like a silly snake wouldn't have stood a chance. He was probably shaking in his boots and couldn't move! He was useless, wasn't he?"

"He was knocked unconscious by the serpent," Lucian defended him. "I had to transport him back to the inn using the Venaris."

"Did you see his wounds?"

"No, but—"

Her voice rose in pitch, and she exclaimed, "That's hilarious! I can't believe that he deceived you and played dead! What a coward!"

"Don't speak badly about him!"

"I'm sorry. I'm sorry," she apologized, wiping the tears

from her eyelashes. "I've never seen him act so vulnerable in front of anyone. He was probably too embarrassed to tell you of his fear. He didn't want you to think less of him. I still can't believe that child cared so much about his image."

"I feel terrible," he lamented. "If I had known about his fear, I wouldn't have taken advantage of his kindness."

"Kindness?" she questioned. "What kindness? I bet Aaron wanted to show off his strength in front of you and then failed miserably."

"Why would he want to impress me?"

Scratching her head, she said, "I think that boy was simply happy making a new friend. He never really got along with any of the local kids, since they were too "immature" for him. He was such a picky little bugger and the friends that he did manage to make, well, you know how that went. Still, to think that a skilled Summoner like Aaron would back down in a fight, especially against a Fallen god!"

"Summoner?" Lucian asked. "What even is a Summoner or a Familiar, for that matter? Everyone keeps throwing out terms but not explaining them."

"Oh, sorry about that." Rena walked over to one of the shelves, retrieving a picture packet. She opened it, showing him a drawing of a harmless-looking creature and then a malicious-looking one. "See this creature on the left?" She pointed at the small, feeble animal. "That's an example of a Familiar. A Familiar is amiable to humans, and it forms simple contracts with its users. It doesn't take as much mana to control and doesn't require constant feeding. Its main jobs are protection and information gathering."

"What about that one?" he asked, pointing to the scary beast to the right. "Is that one a Familiar too? It looks intimidating."

"No." She shook her head. "That's a Summons. Specifically, it's a beast from The Fallen Realm. Since it's a creature that has higher-level mana, it takes a user with comparable mana to form a contract. Although it can protect the user, its main job is offensive attacks and undercover infiltration. It's a nastier kind, using the user's mana as compensation for its services."

"Is that why you have a pig as your Familiar?" he asked. "It sounds too dangerous to form a contract with a Summoned creature, so can I form a contract with a Familiar instead?"

"Thaddeus is a surefire War Hog," she corrected. "He's just a little smaller than his siblings... And, to form a contract with a Familiar is fairly simple, but the Familiar itself has to initiate it. That's why, while the contractual process is easy, finding a Familiar that matches your magical affinity is not."

"But Aaron's a Summoner, right? How's he able to have a Summons, when his condition is...?"

"He's an exception," she said. "His contract is more complex than a top Summoner's, and I'm not too keen to pry into his personal affairs. One thing I can say for sure is that he's beloved by the beasts and spirits that inhabit The Fallen Realm. I assume there must've been a loophole that he found to retain control over his contracted Summons."

"How do you become a Summoner?"

"Ah, that's a different story," she stated. "You'll have to ask Aaron about that when you get a chance. I'm not a Summoner, so I'm not sure of the precise process. It's pretty secretive even amongst the higher-ups in The Academy. The selection of Summons is exceptionally convoluted, and it's not widely known to the populace. Sorry, there's not much else that I can say."

"So many secrets," Lucian mumbled.

"Oh, look at the time," Rena stated, her eyes trailing over to a ticking clock on the wall. "I've got a meeting with some of my Guild members, but you're free to do anything you want as long as you come back within the next hour or so."

"Even outside?" he asked, expectingly.

"What Aaron doesn't know won't hurt him," Rena winked, speaking in a playful tone. "You're old enough to make your own choices. Just make sure that if you see a swaddle of black-clothed hooligans, you run away and return to the Guild, understand?"

"Yes, ma'am."

"They're everywhere these days," she muttered, "those vile fiends."

Before the "who" could escape Lucian's lips, Rena had already left the room.

People love using senseless pronouns, he thought. *I wish they could just tell me who they're talking about.*

AFTER FREELY ROAMING THE TOWN SQUARE, Lucian decided it was time to return. The sun had set, and his eyes were threatening to shut. Sleepy and sore, he walked along the sides of the streets, following the straight sewer gutters back to the Guild.

The shifting shadows seen in the dark alleyways brought him to a halt.

What's that?

Lucian's feet followed the shadowy figure, twisting and turning at each corner. At one point, he had lost his target, wondering where to go next. Another glimpse of it sent him back into motion. *Stop moving already!*

The figure seemed to reach its destination and abruptly stopped. It felt almost as if the shadow was waiting for someone.

Lucian hid behind a corner and watched. Two more figures emerged from the darkness of intersecting alleyways. They stood in the middle of an opening, the moonlight revealing their fully black attire.

I shouldn't be here. But it won't hurt to listen for a few minutes. It might even be beneficial somehow...

Only garbles could be heard from his position. Whether they were speaking in an entirely different language or not, he didn't know. All he could hear was mere echoes, bouncing off the concrete buildings.

The wind whooshed through the alleyways, converging on the three figures. One of the figures took the brunt of its force. The black hood sat loosely on the figure's head fell off, and a familiar face was revealed.

He gasped.

Aaron?

25

THE TALIS MOUNTAINS

 *Faeran*

The whistles of the wind died down. With the curiosity of a cat and an inkling of doubt festering, Lucian suppressed his initial shock. His fingers clawed into the corner, clinging so tightly that his nails chipped. He listened closely, desperation inundating him.

Had the darkness of night deceived him?

The moonlight's revelation was no lie.

It truly was Aaron.

The three nightly-cloaked figures abruptly switched to speaking in the universal language. With the wind picking up, the echoes grew louder, more pronounced, and easier to follow with the switch.

Lucian crept closer to hear the content of the conversation, masking himself in the shadows provided by the protruding buildings. His footsteps were light as a feather. His breath was short and silent. His face was twisted, appearing intrigued yet suspicious.

Picking a discreet position, he vigilantly watched and listened. Heart thumping, blood rising, he couldn't fully control himself. He had no proof of anything yet, but he had a creeping suspicion that Aaron hadn't been completely transparent with him. All of those late-night outings were dubious from the very start.

And now, he had proof.

"Our Master isn't pleased with you, Aaron," one of the forms hissed. "He is growing impatient with your antics. The Harvesting is near. Give the child to us. We will deliver the chosen vessel to the Master ourselves."

"He's not ready," Aaron argued. "The seeds have yet to be sown. I need more time to prepare the boy's body for the Master. You know that one mistake can affect the success of our Master's rebirth. The boy himself has yet to realize his full potential. Let me continue to cultivate his powers for our Master's prosperity. All for the glory of our Master."

"All for the glory of our Master," the two forms replied. "May he prosper forever. May The Harvesting bear everlasting fruit. May he live forever."

Hearing those words, Lucian shivered. The strong winds turned into a light breeze. What he felt wasn't the wind but the chilly tendrils of fear creeping up his spine.

"Recite the Oath," the shorter figure stated.

"Remember the Risen, for they will Fall again," Aaron responded.

It's the exact opposite of the phrase at the cells in Caelum... What's going on?

"What is the status of those pesky gods?" the shorter one inquired. "You know the dangers of keeping them close to the child. They could defile him. We can't let them tarnish him as they did with you."

"That's none of your concern," Aaron said, firmly. "They're caged birds anyway. What bird can fly with clipped wings?"

Shifting in the shadows, the *clank!* of a broken bottle clipped by Lucian's foot alerted the cloaked figures. The wind picked back up and shot through the alleyways, blowing the other two hoods off the figures' heads. Their awkward motions as they tried to cling onto their cloaks gave Lucian time to slip to a safer spot.

Aaron seemed to scan the shadows with steady focus. If anyone were to find Lucian, it would be his hypervigilant companion. Not many could easily escape his gaze.

Lucian finally seized a chance to observe the two figures, whose identities were revealed with the wind. Their grotesque, ivory-white skin was riddled with nasty cracks, shining in the moonlight. With inky-black sclera and chalky-white irises, the glow of their eyes pierced the darkness. An aura of death assumed them.

While one was shorter than the other, their colossal frames far exceeded even the tallest of men. With hunched backs and spindly appendages, they were like a living nightmare. They were as thin as sticks. It was a surprise that the wind hadn't snapped them into two.

The words were on the tip of his tongue.

"The Soulless," Lucian unintentionally let out, the words traveling with the wind.

The taller of the two Soulless pointed its finger in his direction. Opening its mouth, the figure revealed razor-sharp teeth that sat within its scarily thin cheeks. "He's here."

Lucian's position had been compromised.

As soon as he had been spotted, Lucian sprinted in the opposite direction, tearing through the alleyway at lightning speed.

All he could think about was his impending doom.

Arriving at the inn, he took a moment to breathe, sweat drizzling down his forehead. He then ran toward his room, rushing through the main dining hall. In passing, he saw several adventurers passed out with their faces smooshed onto the wooden tables. Glasses of wine, whiskey, and gin sat loosely in their rough hands.

He made sure that Rena wasn't present before he fully retreated. Doubts swirled in his head. Who could he trust? What if Rena was in on the whole thing this entire time?

"Eteria, say something!"

Without hearing a response, Lucian reached his room. Slamming the door open, he raced inside to safety. He quickly sealed the door behind him, securing it with chains and locks.

Out of breath and out of time, he buried himself in the bed sheets.

He wanted to wake up.

He wanted to escape this nightmare.

He wanted to trust Aaron.

He couldn't do any of them.

The creaking wood of the inn made him sink further into the sheets.

Although fear gripped him, his exhaustion took hold of him...

A KNOCK AT THE DOORWAY STARTLED HIM awake. Several sunrays streamed into his window, alerting him that another day had dawned.

Lucian stood dumbfounded in the doorway. He expected you-know-who to show up, or at least another human. Instead, a familiar small and round pink sausage looked up at him: Master Thaddeus. He scratched his head and let out a prolonged sigh. The tension welling within him subsided. His fears were almost laughable in the face of his current situation.

But he couldn't laugh, and he couldn't erase the sinking feeling of despair.

The pig's mouth widened, and its teeth clomped onto Lucian's cloak. Inch by inch, Master Thaddeus managed to pull Lucian out of the room and down the hallway. Lucian was perplexed by the pig's determination, but he allowed himself to be dragged along.

As they approached the entrance, however, Lucian resisted, not knowing what awaited him outside. Master Thaddeus, on the other hand, was excited. He ran circles around Lucian, while holding the cloak in his teeth. Lucian was so tangled up in his cloak that it only took a small shove from the pig to knock him over. His face hit the concrete with a *thud!* He almost cursed in response.

"Come over here, so I can cook you!" Lucian seethed. "I'll turn you into bacon!"

Master Thaddeus squinted his beady black eyes and proudly huffed. It sounded like the pig was content with his work—his work being to force Lucian into harm's way. After several seconds, he heard the pig's hooves clopping away back into the safety of the inn.

As Lucian stood up and dusted himself off, he felt a tiny weight pulling down on his cloak. Reaching his hand into the cloak, he rummaged around to find a heavy object with a papery texture at the bottom.

The pig had put something in his pocket.

Carefully, he wrapped his fingers around the item and took it out. He unfolded the paper that had been crumpled and molded around the weighty object.

What he uncovered was a rock.

A crumbly, bumpy rock. Instead of smashing the rock on the ground like he wanted to, he stuffed it into his pocket. Most items that he had received, in one way or another, happened to be useful... Maybe this rock would be the same. Taking several seconds to calm down, he noticed the piece of paper had something written on it.

The words were just legible enough to read: "*Climb The Talis Mountains. There, you shall find me.*"

"Another stupid riddle," Lucian grunted in dismay. Other than avoiding the creepy creatures, there nothing else on Lucian's agenda for the day. So, he decided that he might as well follow the note's instructions. He knew that it was dangerous, but he had to take whatever opportunity he was provided with.

From where Lucian stood, he had a clear view of the towering mountains—an intimidating climb for even the most trained adventurers. "I really do have a death wish, don't I?" Lucian sighed, staring at the arduous hike.

After gathering some provisions, Lucian headed to The Talis Mountains. Each step to the foot of the mountain was grueling and painstaking. It wasn't the climb itself that proved arduous but rather the weight on his heart. He had been betrayed by the person closest to him. Whether Aaron was the one who sent the letter and was awaiting him at the mountain's peak or not, Lucian's mind swarmed with suspicions, and his heart swelled with sorrows.

What is the worth of finding the truth if it breaks the searcher's soul in the process?

Unknowingly, Lucian's hand gripped the pendant around his neck tightly. He breathed deeply, allowing the air to fill his lungs to their maximum capacity. Turning his eyes skyward, he let the majestic mountains calm his nerves. The beauty and radiance of The Talis Mountains momentarily diminished the murky feelings of his heart. With one last look, he started his trek up the mountains, ascending the side with a gentler slope.

The path was barely visible and not well traveled, so the

terrain was harsh on Lucian's legs. Luckily, the map of The Talis Mountains was still ingrained into his memory. Along with strengthening his sword and magic skills, Aaron taught him strategy and survival tactics. Among those skills, he knew how to navigate an area's terrain, no matter how harsh.

Thanks to that training, Lucian followed the path to the smaller summit, even when the route became indiscernible by conflicting human and animal trails.

Several hours passed as Lucian steadily climbed up the rocky path. Upon reaching the section of the mountain where the terrain leveled out, his legs collapsed under him. Although his strength training helped him, he couldn't continue without some rest. He let himself take a break. His legs stretched to their full length, and his arms propped himself up from behind.

Lucian observed the vast expanse of fluffy clouds that sat almost level with his sight. Noon arrived, and the sun reached its highest point. He yawned quite loudly. The lack of proper sleep and the physical fatigue clouded his senses. Even with sleep tempting him, he kept it at bay by focusing on the unique surroundings.

He was nearly above the clouds, but the air neither thinned nor the greenery diminished. Life abounded. Thick, green vines with oddly colored flowers lined the rocky walls. Layers of grass covered the flat platform, comforting his aching glutes and cramping thighs. A sweet scent swam in the breeze, filling his nostrils with pleasant fragrances and lulling him into a delightful daydream. Deep inside him, however, something was trying to warn him.

No! he thought, resisting the temptation.

Just as he had snapped back into full consciousness, he saw several vines slithering toward him. He reached for his sword, swinging it out and cutting the tendrils that sprung and attacked him with a fearsome force.

"Rule number two: Never let your guard down, especially with people or in areas overflowing with mana," Lucian said, quoting Aaron's advice. "The most alluring people and places are often the deadliest ones."

Flinging his body to the right, he dodged a jab from one of the vine's spear-like thorns. Back and forth, right and left, he dodged and counterattacked. He was so focused on killing the monstrous vines that he didn't notice the silhouette skulking behind him.

The *swoosh!* of a sleek object against a stray vine caused him to lurch forward, escaping the possible attack on him. He made a full one-eighty turn, pointing his sword at the unknown entity. Whether friend or foe, he wouldn't go down without a fight.

The wily vines shockingly calmed down after the

stranger's attack, slinking back into their original positions on the walls.

"I thought I heard your wimpy cries," a familiar voice said. Brandishing a sword, the stranger wedged the blade into the tufts of grass beneath him. "You really can't do anything without me, can you, Lucian?"

A playful smirk lingered on the figure's lips.

"I got your note," Lucian said.

"What note?" the raven-haired boy asked, playing dumb. "Well, whatever. We need to talk regardless."

"About what?" Lucian caustically asked. "About the Soulless or your 'Master?'"

"Neither one. Let's talk about us. You know what we've been through together. You know I would never..."

"Betray me? Hah! Funny coming from the person who's pledged his allegiance and blood to a devil and his demons." Lucian's facial expressions darkened, and his eyes were filling with fury.

"Just listen to me, Lucian," Aaron stated, with a solemn facial expression. "You don't know what you're up against. I can promise your safety."

"Save your excuses," Lucian retorted. "Even if I wanted to believe you, I know what I saw. How could I trust you?"

"I haven't betrayed you!" Aaron yelled. "When will you grow up?"

Lucian lifted Ignis and pointed his blade at his former companion. "If your version of a grown-up is to lie and betray your friends, then I think I'll pass. I may not be a master swordsman, but I at least know that my mana is stronger than yours. I'm certain that I won't lose to a traitor like you."

The contrite and guilty expression that Aaron wore tore off like a mask. Instead, a coldness assumed him. His body relaxed, and his eyes were empty of emotion.

"Fine, have it your way," Aaron said with a bone-chilling tone. "I've had enough of an ignorant brat like you ruining my plans. If you won't believe me, there's nothing else to say."

Aaron didn't move toward his sword stuck in the grass; instead, he mumbled something under his breath. When Lucian finally realized that Aaron was chanting an incantation, the attack had started. Aaron's fingertips sparked with lightning, but Lucian wasn't shot with bolts. Rather than a magical attack, Aaron's Summons sprung forth from the lightning, lunging at Lucian.

A devilish smile crossed Aaron's face, and he mocked him while saying, "I wonder if you can kill two of them when you almost died to one."

It took a while for Lucian to process Aaron's comment, but the appearance of the Summons said more than words could. The Summons were woefully familiar sights.

"So, that beast at Eva's was yours?"

"Sadly, not. The same species, though."

The two creatures that materialized had pitch-black fur with lightning racing along their backs. They bared their razor-sharp teeth at Lucian, licking their black lips as they stalked. A quick flick of the wrist by their Summoner put them into motion. Picking up speed, the beasts jumped at Lucian. Each attack was swifter and more accurate than the beast he fought in the woods; each strike drew blood. They seemed to be stronger and faster than their kindred.

Or, worse yet, they already knew his movements.

"Don't come crying to me when you lose," Aaron stated. "I warned you."

A wave of attacks followed. Lucian's sword couldn't keep up with their blows. Each scrape, each bite, battered his body. His muscles were seizing, becoming rigid like stone. He fought against it, but he could only slow down the process. He couldn't stop it. He was bleeding profusely, causing his consciousness to falter. The creatures kept attacking.

Strike by strike, bite by bite, they tore through his skin and resolve to fight. Their speed rendered his mana useless. He couldn't even recite a single incantation in defense.

After the worst of the attacks, Lucian fell to his knees. Only then did the Summons stop attacking, circling him and waiting to finish him off. Their flaming azure eyes followed his every move, flitting back and forth. Lucian glared at Aaron, who stood completely still. Aaron hadn't been actively orchestrating the attacks, but it didn't lessen the chance that the next order would mark Lucian's demise.

"Why?" Lucian cried out with rage. "Why did you betray me!?"

The raven-haired boy replied with words as cold as ice, "Rule number one: Don't trust anyone, not even me. Don't you remember what I said in the desert?"

Aaron casually approached him. His Summons momentarily stopped their circling to allow their Summoner inside. After, they continued their repetitious motion. He grabbed Lucian's cloak, lifting him midair and holding him by his collar.

Lucian struggled, wildly kicking and punching at the space between them. Nothing landed—no punch, no kick, and no words reached *him*. The darkness seemed to consume Aaron. An ominous black mist hovered above him.

"Can't you see what you're becoming!" Lucian futilely argued through bared teeth.

"And what would that be?" Aaron asked, a malicious smile surfacing.

"A *monster*."

The grip around his collar tightened.

Lucian was losing his vision, as the void started to claim him.

"Ignis!" he cried.

No response.

Why is no one responding? Eteria, Ignis, Aerus, have you all betrayed me too?

Just as the light had almost faded from his eyes, a screeching voice emerged and said, "Aaron, where is the boy? We will report your failure to the Master. Hand him over to us, and you will be forgiven for acting out of turn!"

Aaron's body froze, and his grip loosened ever so slightly. Lucian took advantage of his hesitation and latched onto Aaron's shirt, forcing them to the ground. Lucian struggled to escape, kicking violently in Aaron's stomach and chest, landing multiple hits to his sides.

Lucian kicked Aaron in the stomach, using it as a platform to propel himself backward, away from him.

But Aaron didn't let him recover, hurling himself at Lucian and latching onto his bruised and torn legs. Lucian cried out in pain, as the boy tightened his hold. To escape the locked position, Lucian threw his body to the side, rolling and rolling until they both landed near the cliff's edge.

Lucian caught a glimpse of the mountain's base and gulped down an unmanly squeal. They had been separated during the squirming and rolling, but the struggle wasn't over yet.

"Get over here, you worm!" Aaron yelled in frustration, crazily clawing at the air.

The voices of the Soulless grew louder, placing even greater pressure on the two. Aaron would indefinitely have an advantage when his frightening-looking friends arrived. Lucian had to act soon, or he would become demon fodder.

It's now or never.

"Rule number five: Believe in the impossible!" Lucian shouted.

The edge of the cliff was merely feet away. Lucian made a last-ditch effort and dove at it. Even Aaron couldn't stop his initial momentum. Lucian felt his body slam against the spiky edge of the mountain and flipped over the side. He forcibly closed his eyes, awaiting the impact to crush his body...

...Awaiting death to come.

"Is this what you wanted, Aaron!" Lucian screamed, as he fell.

Opening his eyes for the last time, he realized something even worse happened than a splat at the mountain's base. He was alive and staring straight into Aaron's eyes, whose face was scrunched up in a scowl. Both of his hands had latched onto Lucian's cloak with incredible force. The only thing keeping Lucian from his death was the fabric of the cloak and the string of the pendant interlaced between Aaron's fingers.

In the background, he could see the ghastly-white figures approaching them. "Let go!" Lucian gritted his teeth, fighting to break free. "Let go, you traitor!"

A painful expression crossed Aaron's face for a split second, as he said, "If you die…"

Lucian's last string of consciousness snapped. Emerging from his subconscious, another voice cried at the heavens, "*Adonis, why hath you forsaken me?*"

Why do you only come out when I'm about to die?

His former companion's face was fading into darkness. Lucian's eyes deceived him, showing him what seemed to be a single tear falling down Aaron's cheek. He convinced himself that it was only his imagination, showing him something good at the end, as Aaron let his life slide through his fingertips. Everything happened so quickly. The break of the fabric holding him in midair and the snap of the pendant rang mockingly in his ears.

A blue mist escaped the pendant, forcibly wrapping itself around him.

However, without the support, he dropped, falling faster and faster to the mountain's base. His body felt light, extremely light. His eyelids closed with fatigue, and his body released its tension.

Three...

Two...

One...

He sunk deeper and deeper into his subconscious. His eyes remained shut. His body went numb. He could hear someone shouting his name from far away. None of it mattered. He felt as light as a bird. He felt his body warming up. He felt his breathing slow.

He felt *free...*

TO BE CONTINUED IN...

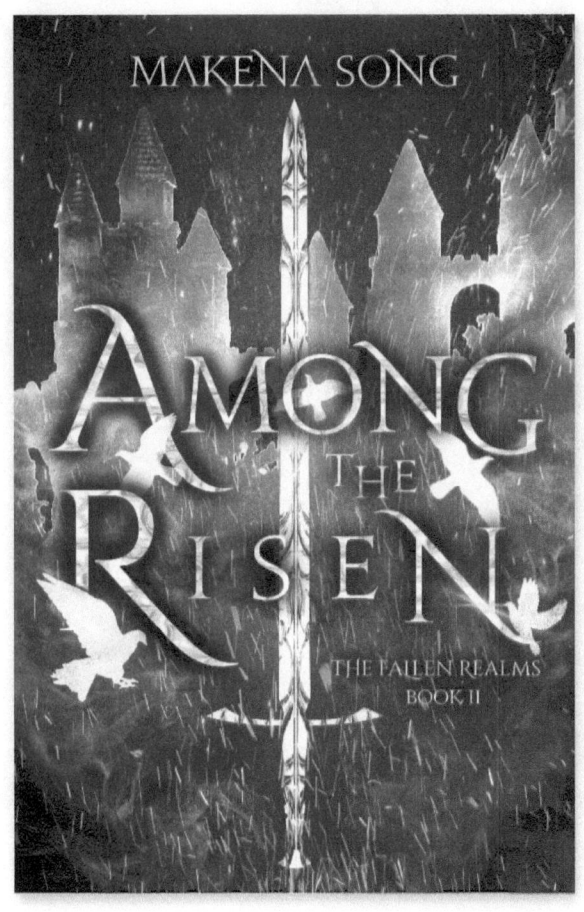

AUTHOR'S NOTE

From start to finish, *Among the Fallen* took more than eight years to complete! To be completely transparent, I created the core concept of the novel when I was in high school. The novel was inspired by numerous sources, including world history, Naruto Shippuden, Christian themes, and Studio Ghibli films. While these themes may seem random, they merged in my mind and formulated everything from the characters that I wrote to the world that I crafted.

Regarding the novel's writing timeline, I rewrote the starting sections at least three to four times before I settled on a specific plot. As many of my friends and family are aware, I am a "pantser" type of writer, not a "planner," so my inspiration and motivation to write varies depending on my environment, emotions, etc.

Additionally, this novel was written from high school to post-college. As my main character, Lucian Roux, was experiencing character growth, I was undergoing personal growth!

I truly believe that this novel has been a blessing in my life, connecting me to countless online and offline friends, who share a passion for writing and reading. At the end of the day, I hope that *Among the Fallen* has impressed upon your heart in some way or another. If you're interested in the rest of Lucian's story, please consider purchasing the second book in the series, *Among the Risen*!

Until next time,

Makena Song

ABOUT THE AUTHOR

Makena Song was adopted from Seoul, South Korea, and was raised in Longwood, Florida. From an early age, Makena's mother, Tina Song, read countless books to her, including: *The Tale of Despereaux*, *The Shadow Children Series*, and *The Missing Series*. Reading allowed Makena to let her imagination run free, as these magical scenes played out in her head.

When she was introduced to Wattpad in middle school, she gained a creative outlet to express her countless story ideas. By the time she was in high school, this vault of random ideas turned into a set of fantasy novels. After she graduated Summa Cum Laude from Furman University, Makena pursued not only a full-time writing career as a marketing copywriter but also a dream to publish *Among the Fallen* and *Among the Risen*.

Website: www.makenasong.com
Instagram: @makenasong